JAMIE DIBS

Red Fidelity

First published by Dark & Stormy 2026

This novel is entirely a work of fiction. The names, characters, and incidents portrayed in it are the work of the author's imagination. Any resemblance to actual persons, living or dead, events, or localities is entirely coincidental.

Jamie Dibs asserts the moral right to be identified as the author of this work.

First edition

ISBN: 979-8-9888236-7-4

Cover art by Gem Butcher

This book was professionally typeset on Reedsy.
Find out more at reedsy.com

Contents

III The Red

I

The Auction

Chapter 1

Segreti was crossing under the bridge, wheeling his suitcase and thumbing through emails, when a navy-blue sedan screeched into his path. He recognized the vehicle: Dodge Charger, nimble for its size, government issued and freshly washed. The passenger window lowered. Belmont, keeping his hands on the wheel, leaned across to show his face. Two cars behind, irate drivers honked their horns.

"Pop the trunk." Segreti threw his luggage inside, ignoring the chorus of honks and indifferent to the protests from the people waiting in the taxi line.

He got in the passenger seat, his shoes leaving grimy prints on the vacuumed floorboard of Belmont's neat interior. Malcolm Belmont, thirty-eight, African-American—his mind and his style just as tidy as his ride; even his suit didn't allow for a single crease. As a linguist, he spoke everything invented by white people, and particularly relished the reveal when some German fraudster or Russian gangbanger realized Belmont had understood every word.

They cruised towards Newark Liberty's exit.

"You got through quickly, sir. Thought I was early."

"I hate airports." Segreti regarded the concrete layer cake through the dimness of his sunglasses. "They slow me down."

He checked his phone.

"Office?"

"Nah, Bronx. East side, make for Hunts Point." He tapped his smartphone. Being in motion is what passed for joy in Segreti's life these days. "That auction? It's confirmed. And it's tonight. I want to see this place."

* * *

Segreti and Belmont approached the waterfront at the edge of a lifeless parking lot. A barbed-wire fence guarded stacks of rusted shipping containers. Behind them, the cement factory's chimneys emitted a chalky smoke. Most of the harbor view was blocked by a giant cargo ship at berth.

"That might be it," Belmont said, pointing at an island partly visible beyond the ship's hull, a not-too-distant patch of dark green on the sun-speckled river.

"That's it." Segreti had a feeling that this was where he was going to continue his winning streak, be the Bureau's indispensable man. He stuffed one earphone in and rang Chlebek at her desk downtown. "How do we get there?"

He heard her working her keyboard. "You don't," Chlebek said. "Off limits to the public since the eighties." *Clack clack clack.* "You can apply to the parks department and charter a boat. But there's no dock."

"What's there?"

"Used to be a quarantine asylum. Hm."

"What?"

"Typhoid Mary lived there."

"Let's skip the history lessons."

"Nothing but ruins. A hospital, a nurse's home, that's about

4

all that's recognizable."

Segreti had a moment's doubt about the intel. But what he had heard this morning in DC overwhelmed any second guesses. "Where's Ram?" he asked.

She didn't have to answer. They heard Ram's car before it rounded the wall of cargo containers. Chevy Impala, giving off a cloud of dust, windshield too covered with dirt to reflect the sun. The Impala parked at a crazy angle beside Belmont's Charger.

"About time."

The door flung open, and Ram started to run over.

"Drone!" Segreti shouted. "The drone!"

Ram heard him and waved, pivoted to his car trunk. When he hustled back towards Segreti and Belmont, he was carrying the drone and a control. He unfolded the quadcopter and blew on its main camera.

Segreti pointed to the distant island. "There."

Ram toggled the control and snuggled his iPhone into its rack. The camera's view of their shoes popped onto the screen. Ram's thumbs massaged the panel and the drone shot up with a plastic whiff.

Bhavin Ram, thirty-eight, was born in West Texas and wore the accent like a sheriff's badge. Got sued by Microsoft when he was twelve for hacking Windows and telling them what he had found. Sometimes wore a ten-gallon hat and told people he liked playing cowboys and Indians because he could never lose.

Ram should be trimmer, Segreti thought. *The whisky's softening his edges.* But no one did this job without needing an antidote, something.

The white drone disappeared from eyesight over the East

River.

Segreti leaned over Ram's shoulder, watching the drone's feed on the iPhone screen. A smudge of blue turned to a blur of greens and browns as the drone followed the island's coast. It hovered over what looked like a crumbling pier and a blackened gantry.

Segreti called Chlebek. "You getting this?"

"Yes," she said into his ear. "That's an old factory. The hospital's to the south."

"Roger that," Ram said, clicking his controls.

The image showed an industrial brick chimney and some sagging remains, and then the drone was headed over a patchwork of grassland and dense foliage.

"Sir," Chlebek said, "what if there's nothing there?"

Just this morning, sitting beside the US Deputy Attorney General in a windowless office shielded from every spectrum of wave, Segreti had been told that a source had died for this tip—an asset of BND, the Bureau's German counterpart.

"Focus on the job," he snapped.

The drone revealed a big square structure.

"The hospital," Chlebek said.

"Lower down," Segreti told Ram. "I want a good look."

The building seemed to rise up the screen, its bricks ripped askew by relentless vines, its windows black negatives.

"Wait. Go up. That."

"There's a light on," Belmont said, peering over Ram's other shoulder.

"Go in."

The building's wall filled the screen, and the window devoured them. After a moment the interior faded into view. A large hall with clean lines of modern folding chairs.

"Doesn't look abandoned to me," Segreti said, ignoring a triumphant impulse.

Chlebek's voice said, "The infrared is running hot. Someone was sitting there."

"Do we take a look?" Ram asked.

Segreti was eager to see as much as possible. But it was foolish to stay. "Pull out."

The drone retreated from the room. The screen jolted.

"What happened?"

Ram's thumbs worked furiously. "Hit the edge of the window."

Segreti bit his tongue, letting Ram figure how to back out.

"How much noise that thing make?" Belmont asked.

"Just get clear of there," Segreti told Ram, calmly.

Ram flew the drone outside. His shoulders relaxed.

"Stay high but let's see what they've done with the place."

The ground retreated. They saw the old hospital and a clearing and more ruins, and then a big clearing.

"Go down."

The green-yellow grass filled the screen, slashed by parallel lines.

"Chlebek, are those helicopter prints?" Segreti asked.

"Looks it, sir."

"Bring it back," he told Ram.

The view rotated. On the ground, a different kind of movement. A white man in a black T-shirt, long blond hair, running, cradling a long black object, like a rifle without a barrel.

"Time to go."

The screen showed descending treetops, froze, scrambled, and went blank.

"What just happened?" Belmont asked.

Ram's hands danced on the console. "The signal's dead."

Chlebek said, "That was a radio frequency jammer."

"Where's the drone?" Segreti asked.

"Probably in that guy's hands," Ram said.

"We're blown," Belmont said. "They know they're being watched."

"But not by who," Segreti said. "There's supposed to be a big event on that island. Tonight. Lots of buyers and sellers. Heavy players only."

"I removed the memory card," Ram said. "Scratched out the serial code."

Segreti turned to Belmont. "The POI still in play?" Their Person of Interest.

"Tremain...yes, sir."

"We're going to catch ourselves a traitor." Segreti gazed at the corner of the island. "Security's going to be tight. We need to get ourselves a boat."

"What kind of boat?" Belmont asked.

Segreti smiled. "A fast one."

Chapter 2

Justine was... well, it was like she was floating—no, flying—towards a door. A magical mystery door. And she gripped the reins and willed herself towards the portal, because the tunnel was constricting and tensing and she needed to break through, the scents igniting her cravings, lifeforce coursing through her, and if she could just, only, open that door...

Steve grunted and pulled out. His hands maneuvered her to lie beside him.

The hunger rocked Justine, but the door was closed. Slammed shut.

They laid in their sweat, panting.

She noticed he was still erect. He had brought her so close. They had been writing a poem reminiscent of one of their early epics. He had discarded the lines unfinished, the rhyme botched.

"What's up, hon?" She made it sound sympathetic instead of irritated.

He sat over the edge of the bed. "Just not able to, uh..."

It wasn't too late to go back and open that door. She kissed his shoulder and ran her hands on his chest. "I could help you with that. You were doing so good."

"Believe me, I want to." He stood up and looked helplessly

at his hard-on.

Justine realized he must have taken Viagra. It came as a shock because Steve had never mentioned it. That would explain why he had seemed so unstoppable today. And maybe why he couldn't finish? She didn't know. Durability had not been his problem of late.

"Well," she purred, "I'm not finished either. What do you say, rock star?"

His glance was like a punch to the gut. His stiffie might say one thing, but the rest of his body broadcast a loss of appetite. He scratched his beard. "I'm pretty tired, babe. Aren't you?"

Lazy, selfish bastard. That's what she should have said, instead of: "Fine. I've got to get going."

"Okay, I'm going to take a shower."

She jumped out of bed. "You made me late. Get in line."

He had that hangdog look that suggested he realized he was doing this wrong. "We could go together."

"I don't have time." Justine cut him off and slammed the bathroom door behind her.

As she showered, Justine's resentment reduced to a simmer. Work had never been more tense. Dangerous, she had been warned. Steve had started fooling around with her at her desk—both of them working at home today—and she had gotten into it with gusto, enjoying the physicality and craving the release. She thought about finishing matters, just her and the showerhead, but anxiety about tonight's meeting intruded. She really was out of time.

He banged on the door. "You almost done in there, babe?"

Justine could have made him wait, tortured him a little, but she was now strictly business. "All yours."

She stood at her closet. What does a girl wear to an

invitation-only criminal convention? She had lost sleep mulling this, finally opting for Armani corporate. Neutral, businesslike, minimize the kind of attention she could attract in a room full of ethically challenged males.

Now she fingered the gray suit and blue button-up blouse. No.

By the time Steve came out with a towel around his waist, she had squeezed into the kind of thing she hadn't worn for three years because that's how long it had been since she'd gone clubbing. Call it thirty-six, call it Covid—call it being in a relationship.

He stopped. "This is for work?"

She looked at how the black leather pants gripped her hips and ass. Not bad. She fisted her blond hair into a ponytail, then pulled it back for a sleeker look. Yeah.

"Yes, it's for work."

"You, uh, you look amazing."

She smiled. He had gotten that much right.

"Where you going again tonight?"

"I'm still working undercover, you know."

"Yeah, you told me about that."

"What do you think undercover means, Steve?"

"From the looks of things, Justine, I'd say it means picking up guys."

She put gel in her hair. "You don't trust me?"

"Of course I trust you. But this is, uh, well..." He watched her slip on a tight-fitting, sleeveless black top. It was cut high to show a little midriff. "I know you said it's a big story and all, but, hey, Justine, listen to me, babe, okay?"

She turned to let him say what he was going to say.

He looked sincere. "I love you, you know that, right?"

"I love you too."

"Do I need to worry about you? About whatever you're getting into? This thing of yours. You had said it'd be a week or two. It's been months, the weird hours, the, you know, the way you're so careful with your phone."

"I'm fine, Steve. Really." She put on a white shirt jacket. New York's early summer had hit a cool spell.

"I deserve to know what's going on in your life, Justine."

"Can we discuss this tomorrow? I don't have time." She picked her shoes, ignoring the sensible flats.

"You're not coming back tonight?"

"It'll be late. Probably crash at mine."

She kissed his cheek and headed downstairs barefoot, high heels dangling from a finger. Steve's cell rang and he said hello. Good, she could make a clean exit.

The late afternoon sun never lingered in his Gramercy duplex. It filled the lower floor with a momentary gold that would soon turn to gloom. It was, however, a beautiful apartment, if spare: white walls and floors, gray furniture, a milky Cy Twombly knockoff framed above the dining table. Orange pendant lamps painted the only color. Justine had initially ascribed this cohesive look to Steve's being an architect, but his ex-wife was an interior designer for unimaginative Manhattanites. They had split ten years ago, back when minimalism was still the rage, and the apartment had remained stuck in her amber.

She heard a soft thud from the kitchen.

Like the rest of the place, the kitchen was mostly monochrome, brightened by copper pots that neither Steve nor Justine ever cooked with, the ex being the culinary whiz. Now a bulging backpack occupied the center of the floor, its owner leaning into the fridge.

"You're home early," she said.

Zach bolted straight. "Oh, hi, Justine."

"Hi yourself. Shouldn't you still be in school?"

He had Steve's russet hair, only a mountain of it, piled in curls, and a cleanshaven face that was only as pimply as the next teenager's. "I thought you guys wouldn't be here." He opened a can of soda.

At least lying wasn't his default mode. "We've been working from home today. And you didn't answer my question."

He was checking out her outfit, and she hoped his hormones wouldn't blow a gasket. "You look dressed for success."

Justine smiled. "Thanks. Want to talk about why you're home early?"

"No." He looked around, waiting for Steve to appear.

"Okay then. You can tell it to your dad."

He slumped as he thought it over. She was late, but she didn't want to leave Zach stranded. He was moody and tense, but a good kid. He rewarded her by digging into his backpack and handing her a crumpled notice.

"What's this?" She looked at the school form. "Suspended? Zach?"

"Just for three days," he mumbled.

She heard Steve come hustling down the stairs.

"For what?"

Steve was flushed. "Zach! I just got off the phone with the school."

Zach looked as though he wanted to disappear into himself. He picked up his backpack.

"Where do you think you're going?" Steve demanded.

"My room. For, like, forever."

Justine threw her hands up. "Is one of you going to tell me what's going on?"

"He got caught with drugs, that's what."

Zach turned angry. "It was just a joint like this big," fingers barely touching. "And it wasn't even mine. The whole thing's total bullshit."

"Stay here and you talk to me," Steve demanded, but Zach brushed past him. "Don't walk away from me, Zach. I said—"

Zach's bedroom door slammed shut. Justine caught Steve's arm before he hurled himself against it.

"Look at this," she said, showing him the school's form. "It says they're investigating. Not that he was caught for sure."

"What difference does that make?"

She took a breath and made herself tall and calm. "He might need a lawyer. Do you understand?"

"A lawyer. Jesus. You sure?"

"No, but you know what his school's like."

"I know what they charge me."

She nodded. "Why don't you go back upstairs and ask a law firm?" He regained control and nodded. She embraced him. "It'll be okay."

"That kid..."

"I know. Make the call."

He pulled her close and then retreated upstairs. Justine checked her watch, thought about traffic time, but then knocked on Zach's door. "It's just me. Can I come in?"

He opened the door a crack, eyed her for a long moment, and then retreated with the door ajar. She followed him to his bed where he picked up his gaming console. Tinny explosions burst from the headphones beside him as he resumed shooting bad guys on *Counter-Strike*. She sat beside him and rubbed his back. He flinched but kept playing.

Justine didn't know what to say. She had no children of her own. Sometimes acting the cool adult got Zach to open up to her, but it didn't mean she was qualified to give advice. This was supposed to be Steve's department. Or the ex's, who last year had forgotten Zach's birthday. "When you want to talk about it, your dad will listen," she finally said. "Me too."

"What difference does it make?"

"All the difference in the world. You'll see." She hugged him. He let her, which she took as a minor victory. "See you soon."

Zach put on his headphones.

Justine went to the foyer and wiggled into her heels. Three of her smartphones waited on the console table by the door. She selected the one in a Faraday sleeve to ward off Bluetooth or other intrusions and slipped it inside the white shirt coat's interior pocket.

Zach might get the drug charge removed from his record. He had a chance for a do-over. For Justine, for whatever awaited tonight, there was no going back.

Chapter 3

Tremain didn't need the menu. He told the waiter, "Grapefruit juice, egg white frittata, the berries, the seven-grain toast. Decaf." He smiled at the man sitting opposite. "And for my guest?"

The guest—Black, cleanshaven with wide cheekbones, compact hair, late thirties, suit creaseless but off the rack, Macy's striped tie—was doing a good job of pretending to not be shocked by the prices. He handed the menu to the waiter. "I'll have the Caesar and a Perrier."

Tremain said, "You still dress like a fed."

The guest, who called himself Braun, smiled. "That obvious?"

"You're a contractor now. If you deliver what you say, you can wear a T-shirt and flipflops."

"I think I prefer your style."

Tremain adjusted his silk tie, revealing his sapphire cufflinks. "I'm not a contractor."

"No. And me and my team, we appreciate that. We appreciate what you've put into building your network, Mister Tremain."

Tremain withdrew a Montblanc pen from his jacket pocket. "And your team. I've heard some things about you."

"I would expect you to have made a few calls."

"More than a few." Tremain twirled the pen. "I still have friends at various agencies. They said interesting things."

"I think I should be glad to hear that."

"Six months in Riyadh. Listening to whom?"

Braun made a helpless gesture.

"Client confidentiality," Tremain said. "I get it. But here's the thing, Braun. If I make an introduction, I need specifics."

Braun looked around.

"Yes, I know, it's public here. But you and I know, my friend, that if someone wants to hack our phone or our watch or the hotel's security cameras, they can listen to anything you've got to tell me." Tremain reached into his other pocket and pulled out a small notepad. He pushed it and the Montblanc across the table. "Be as specific as possible."

Tremain observed Braun pause. He had heard a similar story from two people he had queried, about Braun working in a tightknit team hustling a zero-exploit to the ruler of Saudi Arabia. The State Department had known about it but looked the other way. The team was led by a man who was ex-NSA, just like Tremain. Tremain had never heard of this man, Verdi, but that was not unusual for an organization so compartmentalized. What mattered was correlation. Besides, "Braun" and "Verdi" weren't anybody's real names.

The guest named Braun wrote with his hand guarding the pad. He closed the notepad's cover and handed it over the table with the pen.

The waiter returned with their food on a silver platter. The two diners waited for him to pour Tremain's coffee and Braun's Perrier. Below the fizz of sparkling water, the hotel lobby murmured with investment bankers and real-estate moguls cutting deals; Manhattan soared behind the floor-to-ceiling windows, towers blocking the midday sun, cutting the view into grids of chiaroscuro.

Tremain opened the notebook.

EMERALD TRUST TO MBS. (Initials Tremain assumed were those of the client.)

IRANIANS.

JOURNALISTS.

CLIENT'S FAMILY.

POTUS VISIT.

Tremain flipped the page over and tapped 'Emerald Trust'. "That's the name of the tool?"

Braun nodded. "And those are the people we used it against."

"You thought you were still on government service?"

Braun nodded. "We were. But the client took things too far. We weren't allowed to leave the hotel. I'm talking gunpoint here."

Tremain grunted.

"And then we were ordered to expand our net."

POTUS visit. 'MBS' had taken liberties with his surveillance. Tsk-tsk.

"Which you managed to do," Tremain said.

"And then we got fired. First by the client and then by our own government."

"And went freelance, to address your financial straits." At which point they went from being called a team to being called a crew. "I understand."

"You? What's your story, Mister Tremain?"

Tremain cut his frittata. "My departure from public service was more deliberately motivated by financial incentives." His cutlery froze. "Do you think that makes you better than me?"

"No, no it does not."

"Because I think it just makes me smarter. Look at these people." He gestured to the fancy restaurant, the five-star view. "You think these are the Boy Scouts? Sure, they all recited the Pledge of Allegiance in school, said their prayers every night, and now they tweet about climate change. But how do you think they got to a point in life where they can drop a hundred and seventy bucks—without blinking—on fucking *brunch*?"

"I think my crew is pretty settled on the benefits of capitalism."

"Damn straight." Tremain resumed eating. "And you need my help getting you into the game."

Braun tried to appear relaxed. He spooned his yogurt. "It would speed things up for us."

"You don't have access to product anymore."

"But we have access to buyers. And we can handle operations. We know our business. That's why we came to you."

"That's why you came to me," Tremain said. "But for what I've got, special distribution is required."

"Okay."

"For this exploit to work, it has to run via very specific cloud networks."

Braun thought it over. "We can get that."

"We'll see. Anyway, your story is a match."

Braun took that as permission to swallow a bite. "I'm glad you're satisfied."

"Satisfied is not in my vocab. But if it's my representation you want at the auction, then it's yours for a ten-thousand-dollar fee and fifteen percent of any deal value."

Braun set down his spoon. "We agreed on the performance fee. Not money up front."

Tremain said, "Consider it my version of due diligence."

"The auction's tonight."

Tremain flipped the notepad open and wrote a long hash on the page. "As my guest, you're welcome to enjoy brunch. Eat at your leisure. If you feel pressed for time and need to leave now, I won't be offended." He tore the page free and handed it to the man called Braun. "I accept Monero, Dash and Zcash. No Bitcoin, too easy to trace. Be sure the transfer is made before six p.m., and I'll message you where to pick me up. If there's no transfer, we will never see each other again."

Braun folded the paper. "Oh, we'll see each other."

Chapter 4

Segreti cut the throttle to neutral. He guided the Ferretti speedboat towards the sunset blazing through Manhattan's towers. The long wood-finished bow cut through the glimmering East River. A pair of white yachts were already berthed at the private club, sprawling along the slip like fattened whales.

"I see them," Ram said, his cowboy hat shielding his eyes from the slash of sunlight. He looked like an oil mogul, hat and white leather boots and a big brass buckle to go with his pinstripe suit.

Chlebek, sitting in the wraparound seats behind, and wearing big wraparound shades, checked her watch. "We're right on the dot, sir."

"No more *sirs* tonight," Segreti said, nudging the boat between the yachts. "It's showtime."

Two figures waited on a pier extended between the yachts. Belmont, preppy sleek in a fitted blazer with a bright knife of pocket square, plaid slacks, suede shoes. Beside him the POI, a broad-shouldered white man with a casual flop of blond hair that he drew back from falling over his aviators. He wore a purple polo shirt, floppy collar up, with black jeans and indigo sneakers. Money masquerading as something sloppy.

Segreti pulled alongside. Chlebek was ready with a stay line. She had practically begged Segreti to come, paranoid the boys weren't going to let her leave her desk, fenced in among a tower of computers and screens. The bumpy ride had made her queasy, but Segreti hadn't heard her utter a complaint. Miriam Chlebek, the oldest of the team, forty-seven going on thirty, determined to be in the action while she was still nimble, her big Polish curves belying a dancer's fluidity. Her linen jacket and pants were an ode to red, daring anyone to ignore her, but her Puma sneakers were white and her cropped hair wasn't naturally black.

"You must be the man I've heard so much about," said the blond POI.

"You must be the guy I just messaged ten grand to," Segreti said.

The blond swiped his phone and smiled at what he saw. "Yes, yes I am." As Chlebek steadied the boat, he extended an open hand. "Robert Tremain. Bobby."

Segreti shook his hand. "Verdi. Come aboard."

"Tight fit," Tremain said, Belmont following him on.

"This is built for speed," Segreti said. He and Chlebek had leveraged the joint task force with NYPD to get the cops to unlock their toys taken off the hands of a busted cocaine lord. It had cost Segreti political capital and Chlebek the indignity of agreeing to dinner out with a precinct captain.

"Better hold on to something," Segreti added as Chlebek wound in the lines. Before she had quite finished, he wheeled the nose around and gunned it.

The speedboat gathered speed as lower Manhattan receded to the left and Brooklyn awaited them far to the right. The mirrors atop the Chrysler building blazed red behind the dark, brooding façade of the United Nations. By the time they reached the narrow blade of Roosevelt Island he was hitting sixty knots, bouncing hard and turning the calm river waters into a punching bag.

Segreti wasn't a happy man, but, at this moment, he felt rapturous. He was with his team and an unsuspecting perp, headed for a breakthrough, the city lights winking on, transforming it into something heady and dangerous—a city that felt like his. All with pounding water, cold spray, and the pulsing resistance of the powerboat's wheel in his hands.

The river forked and he kept to the east, seventy knots along Randalls Island, rounding the tip of Queens. Rikers Island appeared around the corner, a depressing hulk in the twilight, but Segreti kept his aim straight. The lower Bronx sprawled ahead, but he couldn't see the two little islands, always overlooked in this corner of the river and now hidden in dusk. North Brother Island and South Brother Island, closing in on South, the smaller. Once a city dump, now a nature conservatory. The notorious of the pair was North Brother, with its quarantine hospital history. Smallpox, typhoid, tuberculosis; after the war, junkies—a city dump of another kind. Since the sixties, though, these islets had hosted nothing but herons and egrets.

Until tonight.

He cut speed as the northern isle hove into view. Before them winked overlapping lines of bobbing boat lights.

"That's a lot of company!" Ram shouted, barely audible over the roaring engines.

Beyond the armada, the island's ruins were illuminated in red and yellow spotlights. A rotted gantry served as a demonic gateway. Beyond it rose a brick chimney, part of some long-lost industrial building, aglow.

He slowed the Ferretti to a crawl, the motor easing into a purr. They mixed in with the flotilla, a random selection of skiffs, aluminum fishing boats, jet boats, and a trio of yachts, one oligarch-sized, sitting furthest out. As Segreti approached, they could see a chopper lift off from the superyacht's roof and head for the island.

A white boat bobbed by a shifting puzzle of pontoons. Its marking was clear: NY PARK POLICE.

"These people have a permit?" Ram marveled.

"They even got the cops here to manage traffic," Segreti said, noting the makeshift queue the boats were forming by the pontoon pier. "Bobby, guy like you doesn't need to wait in line, does he?"

"Not likely," Tremain said.

Segreti accelerated toward the police boat. As they closed in, they could hear a policeman on a loudspeaker. "One at a time! One at a time!"

He shot in front of an incoming aluminum boat, his wake nearly toppling it, and hit the police vessel with a wall of spray. The loudspeaker bombarded them with protests.

"We've got a five-million-dollar boat," Segreti said. "Let them shout."

Tremain laughed. "The security on land will be a little different. No electronics, remember?"

Belmont asked, "How do we get back?"

Tremain nodded at the police boat. "One of us waits and they give us a call."

"Svetah stays," Segreti said, meaning Ram, who had adopted the Sanskrit word for 'white'. "Everybody else, out. Now."

Belmont jumped onto the makeshift pier of floating pontoons, the big floating square angling beneath him. Tremain and Chlebek handed Ram their cell phones and followed.

"Check out that yacht," Segreti told Ram, eyeing the giant.

He handed over his phone and jumped onto the pontoon, one of a dozen hollow aluminum cylinders held together by cables that led to the gantry. He and Ram exchanged nods. Behind the Ferretti, he saw the aluminum boat that he had nearly capsized now making its unsteady way to the end of the pontoon pier. Whoever was arriving in that leaky thing, they weren't important.

Segreti followed the others to shore. Men in black T-shirts and baseball caps formed a waiting committee. "No phones, no tablets, no Apple watches, no wearables, no electronics!" None of the men had long blond hair.

There was a gathering line of people waiting to get past the T-shirts, some of whom held lockboxes.

"Put your gear in here! Call your boat driver from the pier!"

T-shirts were frisking everyone.

Segreti joined the line. The T-shirts didn't have the crisp bearing of military, but they didn't look like rent-a-cops either. They waved electromagnetic wands and patted people down with efficiency. One of them held a rifle-like jammer, the kind that had brought down Ram's drone this morning. Mercs?

A T-shirt halted Chlebek, his wand squealing. He said something and she unbuttoned her jacket. "You want to see my boobs or my Glock?"

The T-shirt thumbed her to go ahead with a grin.

She wasn't the only one.

"Looks like everybody's packing," Segreti said.

"That bother you?" Tremain asked.

A Glock 19M was holstered under Segreti's left arm beneath his black leather jacket, and a Sig P365 was tethered to his ankle.

Behind the T-shirts was another welcoming committee, this one composed of young women holding trays laden with cocktails and open bottles of beer. People were here to do business, and to party, but it would take only one fragile ego fueled by Dutch courage to turn the island into an instant bloodbath.

"It's a free country," Segreti said. "Let's get a drink."

Chapter 5

Justine clung to the crossbar for life. The big speedboat kept going, its wake sending the fishing boat tipping at the water. For a screaming moment she thought they were all going in.

As the boat rocked back to stability she said, "Everyone okay?"

Bert's ogre body was bent over. The retching sound came from him. Patty placed a bony hand on his back and gave Justine one of her withering looks, like this was all her fault. Which it was.

"That was close," Josh said, unable to hide the thrill from his young voice. He might as well have said, *That was awesome.*

Justine watched the speedboat claim its place beside the floating pier. Despite her anger she couldn't help but admire it—a long, sexy wood-paneled craft that maneuvered as agilely as her outboard motor rental was clumsy.

"Josh, get behind that boat."

"On it." Josh—in the front row, hair a gathering mass of black locks looming above his big frame glasses, white skin bright against the dusk—gave the tiller a nudge and everybody nearly fell into the river.

"Jesus, be careful," Patty said.

"I'm trying!"

"I swear, J.J., if I have to swim because of an intern, I'm quitting."

Justine wasn't interested in Patty's complaint. "Get closer," she told Josh. "I want the name of that boat."

Josh somehow negotiated their rust bucket behind the beautiful speedboat as it settled neatly alongside the bobbing pontoons. Above loomed the ruined gantry, lit up a baleful scarlet. The loudspeaker from the Park Police boat told everybody to go one at a time, but the other boats, big and small, seemed to find their own way towards the pier.

"Cut the engine, Justine," Josh said.

Justine and Patty were in the back row. Justine turned and hit the fat red button. The motor began a long sputtering sigh. As they bobbed a few feet behind the luxury speedboat, she counted four of its crew walking among the pontoons toward shore. A fifth, too dark to make out except for his big white cowboy hat, was at the wheel. He gave his engines a nudge and the speedboat headed out. Justine caught the cursive lettering.

"What's that say?" she asked Patty.

Patty squinted. "Something miso?"

"Tiramisu," Justine read. "Hey Josh, what kind of boat is that?"

"Uh, kinda busy here, Justine." But he already knew. "It's a Ferretti. Super luxury brand. Italian. Looks like a forty-footer. Sweet ride." The skiff banged against a pontoon, shaking them all.

"You little shit," Patty barked.

"Sorry," Josh said. "But we're here."

Bert put his head up. For a Mexican, burly and mustachioed and brown, he looked greener than Kermit the Frog. Bert Gomez had been her cameraman for eight years and his presence always calmed Justine. He had been with her when she cornered a mafia boss in a basement for illegal boxing. He had kept her from falling when she found the corrupt Senator paragliding in the High Sierras. He'd saved her from a bullet in Tijuana. But she had never been on a boat before with Bert Gomez.

"You okay?" she asked.

The plan had been he'd be the one to stay on the boat. No cameras where they were headed, so he might as well remain on the water.

"Come on," she said. "You're coming with me. Patty, you'll be on your own."

"I can't drive this thing."

Justine gave Josh an apologetic look. He was wearing a light-blue blazer, skinny tie over a dark gingham shirt. She'd seen him wear this outfit twice: once when he interviewed for the job, and last month when he skipped out of Friday drinks, smelling of cheap cologne that was intended for a date. This was Maximum Dress Up Josh.

"I'll stay," he said.

"You'll get your shot," she said.

Justine made the jump onto the pontoon holding onto her heels. Male planning at it again.

The gang from the Ferretti were almost at the gantry. They walked like they drove their boat, with an arrogance that piqued her curiosity. She wanted to know who they were.

"Bert?"

He jumped from the lip of the boat, nearly capsizing it and the pontoon when he landed. He grabbed Justine's arm before she fell into the water.

"You big oaf!" Patty shouted from the rocking boat.

Bert took a deep breath and straightened himself.

"Ready?" Justine asked.

He nodded. He dressed the same wherever he went: zip-up windbreaker over a rumpled polo, jeans, sturdy shoes, and a gold chain leading to a cross tucked beneath. No matter the occasion Bert Gomez always looked like a bouncer. Justine put aside her thoughts about appearances and was glad to have him along.

"Hey, wait for me," Patty called.

"I thought you were going to stay on the boat," Justine said, not hiding her irritation.

"When you said 'pleasure boat' I thought you meant one of those," Patty snapped. "The kind with wine coolers and seat cushions."

Patty—never "Patricia", got it?—Yamagata jumped onto the pontoon. Whippet thin beneath her unbuttoned plaid shirt and Ramones T-shirt, basketball hightops, black hair with unwelcome silver streaks mostly hidden beneath a Rangers cap, Patty looked ready to murder them all.

"Besides, I'd rather get shot by a criminal than get drowned by an intern."

"Okay, boomer," Josh retorted from the skiff.

"I'm a fucking Gen Xer, you little snowflake," Patty shouted.

"Enough," Justine said, looking at Patty's attire with a mix of snobbery and jealousy. Her bare feet felt slippery and gross against the pontoon's surface.

"What?" Patty asked.

"Nothing," Justine said. "Let's go."

Josh pulled the outboard motor's starter rope and it hacked to life.

"Do I embarrass you, J.J.?"

"No, Patty. It's fine."

"Because I'm the one who fits in here. You just look desperate."

"Thanks," Justine said, marching forward. She knew fear lay behind Patty's rudeness. If any of them had reason to be scared, the fault was hers. Besides, she was right, Patty did fit in. Most of the men here were in jeans and hoodies—except for the glamorous visitors from the Ferretti.

"Ease up, will you?" Bert said.

"This place better have booze," Patty snapped.

Justine crossed the seesawing pontoons. The speedboat's crew was being checked for electronics. A curvy white woman in red, a Black man who looked like something out of a 1960s country club, and between them the two white guys who carried themselves like Bros In Charge. First was Blond Ambition, corn-fed cheeks, purple polo and jeans and pricy sneakers, shades slung from the V in his shirt. He didn't look casual; he looked privileged. Of course, no one on this island was poor. Then there was Bomber. Tall and lean build, wiry black hair turning to steel. He wore a brown, bomber-style leather jacket—plain, no zippers or patches—over a white, button-down shirt and dark slacks. His tapping leather sneakers radiated impatience.

She wanted to get a look at his face.

The men in T-shirts ran a wand up and down the bros. One of them opened Bomber's jacket to look at what was inside, then waved him through.

"Did you see that?" she said out of the corner of her mouth.

"Hunh?" Patty asked.

"Yeah," Bert said. "Those guys are armed."

Terra firma, finally. Justine leaned on Bert to wiggle her

feet into her heels while he looked the place over. She knew he would be thinking camera angles and lighting. Within the confines of his way of looking at the world, Bert was a good observer.

Patty, who spent most of her waking life in front of computer screens, said, "No way I'm handing over my phone."

"Then Josh'll pick you up," Justine said, placing her phones into an open steel box. The young man in the T-shirt closed it and handed her the key. He told her it would be waiting right here. The key had a number: sixty-two.

Bert handed over his phone, and then Patty followed suit with a dramatic sigh. "Security fail one-oh-one."

Justine pressed through the welcoming line of cocktail-bearing cutie-pies. She needed to keep Patty safe but out of the way. "Patty, why don't you get a drink, and keep an eye on those phones. Bert, you're with me."

She walked towards the rising hulk of the old hospital, its surface half-covered in vines, its upper windows gaping black but the ground floor interior aglow with colors that shifted with thumping electronica. The ground was treacherous with shrubs and wild grass, although the organizers had thrown down wooden planks and crates that served as islands. She wondered how many times tonight she was going to regret her choice of footwear. The word from her sources had been party. They had left out the part about rollicking pontoons and being abandoned to nature.

It was a party, though. This little clearing of the island was filling up. Small groups of people wandered in no direction, in twos and threes, drinking and smoking and talking in voices lost beneath the music. She floated past one and then another, catching bits of words she couldn't recognize.

"Those guys are speaking Spanish," Bert said. Another group strolled by. "I don't know what language that is."

"Doesn't matter. These guys all speak money."

Justine checked out the scene. No sign of Bomber or Blond Ambition.

She had worked parties before, conferences and meetups where she didn't belong. It had been three years since she had managed to crash one of these conventions through the official channel, as a reporter for *Vice*.

The cybersecurity conferences tolerated reporters because they were supposed to be fostering legit business. People from Google and Microsoft and the Pentagon went to those things. She had wanted to talk to them, sure, but she had really wanted to talk to the other people in attendance, the ones who were there to do a different kind of business. They always ran for cover as soon as they saw her media badge.

She hadn't come through the official channel tonight. No journalists were welcome at this event.

"Let's go inside."

She made for the ruined hospital. The music seemed to carry her. The organizers had built wooden steps inside and filled a large room with a makeshift platform. The room had been a theater, and through the cracks of the freshly laid planks she could see rotted chairs from a bygone era. At the end of the newly planked floor, someone had built a little stage, complete with an auctioneer's stand.

A few people were gathering now. All men, but otherwise diverse, everyone a different hue of shady.

Why had she dressed up like this? Steve had been right. Not that she had any intention of using her appearance to get anything more than information. But that's what she had told herself three years ago.

She joined a trio, counting on their maleness to let her in. From their body language, they were happy to oblige. "Well, hello," said one. "What's your Telegram handle?"

"Any word on what's being sold?" she asked. "For someone to go to all this trouble, you know?"

"I've heard expect the bids to be seven figures minimum."

"The NSA lose some more weapons? Because those prices..."

A second man asked, "And you? What do you hear?"

Here we go. Justine said, "Bitcoin's become so traceable that the Shadow Brokers decided to turn a virtual auction into a real one."

The first man chuckled. "The Shadow Brokers? Stolen cyberweapons? My oh my."

"You have some wild theories," the second man said.

"Sorry, I don't know you," said the third, uncomfortable with the conversation. He headed for the exit.

"Gee, somebody's jumpy," Justine said. Bert stood nearby, hands folded in front, and although he wouldn't hurt a fly, she was glad for the way he hulked.

The room was filling up and the departing man shuffled around some newcomers...

Bomber.

He had a serious face, an intensity that made him interest-ing and a little intimidating. Good looking—great looking, actually, with eyes that seemed to canvas the room in one go, pausing on her because she was unusual, nothing more, but he unleashed a spark whose heat only Justine felt. His coolness was palpable, and his gaze resumed its scan.

"Nice to meet you guys," she said and walked towards Bomber, readying her smile for launch. People intervened, the music amped up a few decibels, and then they were face to face. His eyes were chestnut, a light contrast to his swarthy features, and they took her in with professional interest.

"Hel—" she began, but booms replaced the music, making everyone wince. Over her shoulder, a man in a black T-shirt had walked onto the stage and was tapping a mic with his fingers, filling the room with thudding waves.

She turned back to Bomber, who said, "Excuse me," as he pushed past her into the gathering crowd.

Chapter 6

Segreti paused by the foot of the stage, shaking the image of the blonde from his head. A man in the ubiquitous black T-shirt was up there. Older, heavyset, whitening beard, and a ridiculous black top hat that looked pinched from a Monopoly board.

"Welcome one and all to the greatest market event on Earth!" The loud mic and the music sent ripples of sound through Segreti's chest.

The room cheered, and he thought of the woman, knowing she was packed in somewhere behind him. He had only caught a glimpse but that had been enough to register the details of the Valkyrie with cheekbones that could sharpen a knife and a smile that was cute as—

"House doesn't care what currency you negotiate in—rupees, renminbi or rubles, air miles or Apple shares—we clear only US dollars for our fifteen percent. We've got three oh-days guaranteed to be of interest to clients, friends, and foes. House doesn't stand by any provenance, we're strictly a facilitator. Do your own research."

Segreti saw Tremain in the nearby corner gesturing for him to come, and he jettisoned any more thoughts of the woman as he waded through the people pressing to the stage and met

Tremain, who was flanked by two T-shirted men with rippling muscles. One was short and brown; the other was tall, white, and had long, feathery blond hair. Up close, Segreti saw the bodyguard had beady eyes and a buttery soul patch beneath wide lips.

The man who had zapped Ram's drone.

Belmont and Chlebek angled towards them.

Tremain held up a palm, then raised his finger. Admission was for one only.

Segreti's people looked upset. Belmont subtly shook his head in warning, but they had known it was likely to go down this way. Segreti gave Tremain a single nod: *let's go.*

He followed Tremain and the bodyguards, bending beneath a doorway that had been partly obstructed from below by the makeshift wooden stage. He jumped after them onto the concrete floor of the original hospital, the swirling lights from the auction room casting the space in a dark parody of color. They were in a hallway that led to a large, circular chamber, windows lining its curving exterior, all of them covered in cage mesh. A white-tiled hearth dominated the center. A portable lamp lit up the hearth's tiles with a harsh glare. To one side, a mobile kitchenette of steel, complete with washing basins and counters, still standing after so many decades, waiting for one last round of KP duty.

A silhouette stood just beyond the border of the lamp's light. Medium height and build, probably male.

"This is Verdi, the guy I told you about," Tremain said to the Shadow. He closed the door behind him, muffling the auction's din.

Segreti waited as the Shadow took his measure.

"Verdi," the Shadow said, baritone barely audible, the

accent thick. "Mister Braun. Miss Rouge. And in the boat circling my yacht, Mister White."

"Yeah, they play cute," Tremain said.

Segreti slow clapped. "Wow. You really figured us out. Congratulations. But you know what we are."

"Emilio Verdi, Lieutenant Commander, Twenty-Fourth Air Force, US Cyber Command, San Antonio. Joined National Security Agency cryptologic center in Colorado." The voice was thick; over the din, he couldn't make it out—Belmont would've known—but Segreti would guess Slavic. "Divorced, one child. Seventeen thousand four hundred dollars in a deposit account at SunWest Credit Union. Paying eighteen hundred dollars a month in alimony. Hearings last year regarding a sexual harassment charge resulted in dismissal. Over this, you decided to steal files of zero-day exploits developed by NSA to compromise steam turbines used in nuclear power plants, which you sold to buyers in Buenos Aires."

Segreti had no idea if the man was buying the cover story, or just enunciating it. "Don't tell my ex," he said. "She'll think she's entitled to forty percent."

Tremain said, "Verdi here's looking to make markets. But for some products, a public auction just won't do."

"Why the big show then?" Segreti asked. "This is your show, right pal?"

Tremain answered for the Shadow. "It's what people will be looking at."

An illicit auction of zero-day cyber exploits to cover up the real dealmaking.

"You know me," Segreti said. "You want to show me your face, my friend?"

"And after?" the Shadow mocked him. "We go to NBA game and eat hotdogs together?"

"Sure, we can do that. Or we can just cut to the chase. Bobby said it, I'm here to buy. You here to sell or you just want to watch Durant shoot field goals?"

The Shadow removed a hand from his jacket pocket—a gesture. One of the bodyguards plucked a USB drive from the Shadow's palm and handed it to Segreti.

"What the hell is this?"

"Code."

Tremain added, "It's half the code of Red Fidelity."

"Red Fidelity."

Tremain grinned. "Straight outta Kunia." Kunia Field Station, an NSA hive on Oahu. Tremain's old stomping ground.

The Shadow said, "It's a million dollars to get a preview, another ten for the full code."

"You serious?" Segreti snapped. "You want a million dollars up front just to show me half a product?"

Tremain said, "Red Fidelity isn't just another cyber-weapon that we buried inside an Iranian nuke lab."

"You said it has to be set off on some kind of network."

"You'll see from the code."

"Eleven million. To make my margin, I'd need to sell this thing for..." But Segreti wasn't thinking math. He was thinking, what's an ex-NSA spook turned crook doing peddling a cyber-weapon being offered by a Russian?

"For a lot," Tremain finished his sentence. "Hey, you wanted to become a broker of the biggest toys. Well, that's the toy."

"How'd this guy get his hands on it? You sell it to the

Russians first?"

"No," Tremain said. "My friend here is a kindred spirit. They stole it, and he can either send it up the chain and go back to his desk and a lousy pension and a shitty retirement in a dacha in the woods. Or he can make this deal happen and retire to a lifetime of blowjobs on the French Riviera."

Segreti took the USB. "How do I check what's on this thing?"

Tremain snapped his fingers and the bodyguard with the hair and the soul patch approached with an open laptop, which he placed on the steel kitchen counter. That's when Segreti knew that the setup—the island, the auction, the party—was Tremain's doing, either solo or with the Shadow. The man wasn't just a go-between.

He'd underestimated Bobby Tremain.

"I need Rouge," Segreti said. "She's the one who can verify what you're showing me."

"Get the woman," Tremain told the smaller, dark-haired bodyguard. The blond one hovered near the Shadow but kept his eyes on Segreti.

The bodyguard returned a few minutes later with Chlebek. She looked nervous.

"Tell me what this is," Segreti said, handing her the USB.

"How safe is that computer?" she asked.

"It's brand new, offline, and air-gapped," Tremain assured her.

"Okay," Chlebek said, inserting the thumb drive. "Wouldn't want to blow up the world just yet." She typed commands, summoning lines of code on the screen.

"You wouldn't anyway," Tremain said. "Like I told your associate, Braun, this needs special care to activate. At least, that's what my client tells me."

The Shadow didn't comment on this. He said, "You have ten minutes."

Segreti added, "That means, Rouge, ten minutes to tell me if we're giving this guy a million dollars to take that home for further study."

Segreti stood and waited. Above and around them the auctioneer's monotone chants cast a spell. *A tool to get right to the metal—the circuitry—of Google Cloud, suck up all the data flowing by.* And if someone had figured out Google's flaw by themselves, selling that knowledge was legal. To make a bust depended on the buyer, but with this crowd, spotting bad guys should be easy.

A huge potential bust in the making, and he was standing around this ruin of a hospital waiting for Chlebek to tell him, what exactly? Tremain had the ability to stand with arms folded for long minutes. The Shadow was equally stoic. Segreti shifted foot to foot, eyed the bodyguards, looked for weapons, tried to keep his heart calm and his head clear. But dammit this felt wrong.

"You have one minute," the Shadow said.

"Bobby, come on."

Tremain looked apologetic. "I don't make the rules."

Segreti doubted that.

Chlebek stood straight. Maybe it was the glow of the screen, but her face seemed drained of color.

"It's got the Doublepulsar implant," she said. "It's either NSA code or someone wants us to think it is."

"Code to do what?"

"There's programming language here I don't know," she said. "Some kind of communication decryption protocol. I need more time."

"Tell me: am I giving this guy a million bucks to take that home? It's only half the code. We have to pay him ten more if we want the rest."

She nodded. A bodyguard closed the laptop and handed the USB to Tremain.

The Shadow stepped into the light. He had a gray, gaunt face, like a permanent mark of melancholy, and his colorless hair could use a trim. "Agreement depends on your execution methods," he said to Segreti. "If she can't see that, we have no deal."

"It's written in Python," Chlebek said, "but some version that I haven't seen before." To the Shadow, she said, "But I'm a quick learner."

Tremain made a 'well?' gesture to the Shadow, whose frown made him look even sadder, and he relented with a nod.

"We have a deal," Tremain said. "You can pay me the deposit and I'll take my cut. Same channel as this afternoon."

Segreti said, "How about we all go back to my boat? I've got a suitcase full of twenties."

Tremain chuckled. "I don't think so. But we can go back and get your phone, and we can do the deal at the pier."

The Shadow receded into darkness.

"What about him?" Segreti demanded.

"I'm the only representation on this deal now," Tremain said.

"Nah," Segreti said, "I think we should all go together. Since we're going to be business partners. Assuming this code doesn't turn out to be worth a mil."

"I'm your counterparty," Tremain said firmly. "And you won't find me if I don't want you to. You've reviewed the code. We either complete this deal or my men escort you back and put you on that nice boat of yours."

The Shadow was climbing over debris at the far end of the kitchen, headed outside.

"How about this," Segreti said, pulling his Glock, "I'm FBI and you're under arrest."

Tremain moved fast. The two bodyguards hurled themselves at Segreti and Chlebek. She was drawing. The Shadow disappeared into the night.

"Stop or I shoot!"

Tremain kept going. Gun—bodyguard, with the blond locks. Segreti didn't hesitate. *Bam.* Bodyguard down, gun skittering.

Above, the auctioneer's staccato stopped, the music kept going, but the sound had shifted. The crowd began to murmur.

Chlebek had her gun trained on the other bodyguard, who had frozen. "On your knees!" she shouted. "Hands above your head!"

Tremain broke in a different direction, around the hearth. Segreti found him clambering through a loose opening in wire mesh through a broken window. He grabbed his pants and pulled Tremain back in.

"Resisting arrest," Segreti said before he punched Tremain in the gut. Resistance quelled. "Hands on the wall." He pushed Tremain against the wall and began to frisk him.

"Sir?"

Belmont, gun clasped in his hands.

"This man is under arrest," Segreti said, pocketing the USB. "Read him his rights and take him to the pier." He ran back to the doorway leading outside. Trees filled the landscape. He paused to look; his ears pricked. The Shadow had a good minute's start, and he might have a destination in mind. Segreti trotted towards the clearing facing the water.

There were still people drifting around, drinking and haggling. In the distance the bay bobbed with the lights of tonight's armada.

He looked this way and that. The music was still thumping, the lights playing on the clearing and in the treetops. Segreti kept going and banged his shin. He grunted. A half-decayed metal trashcan from some lost decade poked from beneath the tall grass.

A slash of white, bright against the night, caught his eye. The blonde—the one who had tried to chat him up, big bright white shirt over a black leather ensemble. She had left the hospital and was looking around, confused. He had an impulse to go to her—any pretext would do—but she wasn't part of the game. Just a beautiful spectator.

Segreti thought he heard the auctioneer start up again, with his flat repetitive chant, until he realized the sound was coming from behind him and that it wasn't human at all. Then the chant turned into a heavy *whump*. The helicopter lifted above the treetops, aimed its nose at faraway lights, lights that swayed because they were on the river. It buzzed over his head, low enough for him to get caught in the zephyr of its draft, and he could only watch it whisk the Shadow back to his yacht.

Chapter 7

Justine couldn't believe her ears. The auctioneer wasn't trying to hide anything. He had just sold what he claimed to be an exploit of something called Facet. She didn't know what that was—a software program, yes, but to what?

The brazenness stunned her. The market for cyber-weapons was always murky and semi-legal. Programmers made a living finding bugs in all kinds of code. The honest ones tried to get the software developers to pay them for revealing the flaws—quietly. In the old days, the buyers had been the companies with the buggy software, paying up to hide their own mistakes. Now the biggest buyers were governments. The Pentagon was the biggest buyer of all, but so too were the Russians, the Chinese, the Saudis. In truth, most governments were in the game, looking for a quick way to get their hands on a hack.

Such deals were always in the dark. She had spent the past several years of her career trying to work out who the players were, what they were after—and how much they'd pay.

She'd never seen anyone *publicly auction* exploits.

The crowd around her seemed juiced by the novelty. High on their own audacity.

That's when she learned what Facet was: The Future Air

Traffic Management Concepts Evaluation Tool. The software developed by NASA to help the government operate air-traffic control.

An anonymous hacker had found a flaw. NASA, for whatever reason, hadn't bought it off them. The hack had just been put up for bidding, here.

Her sources had been right about tonight. More right than they had probably known. It had been just wild rumors pinging around in the ether. Some of the people in this game, the ones haunted by what they had witnessed and what they had done, had come to trust her enough to tell her about an auction of the hottest gray-market exploits.

The hack was to a sub-system of Facet that predicted airplane trajectories. A pair of dark, bearded men in jeans and flannel shirts purchased it for two hundred and fifty thousand dollars. The auctioneer called them Mister Eighteen and Mister Nineteen. They could have been from anywhere—Mexico, Saudi Arabia, Iran, or just from your local friendly family of Mafiosi.

Everyone clapped as the two men approached the stage wiggling their keys. The keys they had been handed upon arrival on the island. Justine fished hers out of her pocket. Number Sixty-Two.

Justine joined in the applause, one eye on Bert, who was keeping watch over her from the nearest wall, the other eye roaming for Bomber and Blond Ambition. Something about those two made them stand out of this crowd—the way they dressed but more how they carried themselves with haughty aloofness. Their disappearance made her even more curious.

She leaned into the men standing beside her, young Latin-looking hotshots who hadn't hidden their interest in her. "So, who's running this thing?" she shouted over the music. "Two hundred fifty... the house must get a nice cut of that, right?"

"Whoever it is, he crazy," one said. "This transparency... I mean, why?"

"New business model," said another. "Mamacita, you need a refill."

She handed him her empty plastic cup. "Sure do. You guys know what else they're dealing?"

"The Google thing, that's big."

"Yeah," Justine said, her ears buzzing. *Google thing?* "But I mean, after that."

"There's something after?" said the man with her cup.

"That's what I heard," she lied.

"The quantum cloud thing," the first man said.

"The what?"

"Hombre, de que estas hablano?" the cupholder added.

The first guy looked sheepish. "Just a thing some of those people were talking about." He gestured vaguely at the crowd.

"An exploit of a code written for a quantum computer?" Justine asked. "That's a thing?"

The auctioneer was back. The music volume moderated.

"And now, ladies and gentlemen, if you thought that was insane, wait till you hear about our next item for sale. This is an oh-day exploit of an infrastructure-as-a-service computing software for Google Cloud. We have road-tested this puppy, and it is the legit shit, designed specifically for J.P. Morgan and all those other big banks where you reprobates deposit your hard-earned fiat. We do not endorse illegality, but..." The auctioneer cocked his top hat at a saucy angle. "This exploit is down to the metal. I'm talking it crawls inside data centers with a digital ear right against the beating heart of data flows. And, people, someone could learn some seriously private stuff if they knew what to do with this thing. Of course, we know all of you out there are really just going to do the right thing. Bidding begins at five hundred thousand dollars. Five hundred… five hundred… five hundred—do I hear six? Six to you, sir. Six hundred… six hundred—a million? Thank you, sir, one million dollars…"

Justine was standing right there with no way to prove any of it was happening. She was going to need to identify either the seller or the buyer—or the person in the middle. The crowd was taking the auction on trust, because so far, no names had been revealed. Only the product, and the price.

That's when she understood. The auction house was assuming the risk of identity. That was how it justified its fees. A clearinghouse for danger. Instead of these people shuffling around in shadowy corners, trying to figure out what something was worth, who could they deal with, who could they trust—they had decided to use this old-fashioned, digital dead zone to make deals.

Doing it in New York City was just a way to thumb their noses at Uncle Sam. Giant middle finger to the powers that be.

The bidding hit two million.

She edged her way to Bert. "When this is done, I'm following whoever wins. There has to be some kind of exchange, money for code."

"They'll need their phones."

"You're right. Can you go back to Patty? Keep a watch on everyone collecting their cells."

"You okay here?"

She nodded and he waded through the throng to the exit.

The bidding was at two and a half when she heard a single

loud cough that pierced the music. The auctioneer heard it too and for a moment faltered. Looks of worry rippled through the crowd.

Gunshot.

She saw a commotion off to the side. She hadn't noticed it before, but the hastily made stage cut across a darkened doorway, and that doorway was now the scene of a scrum.

Justine tried to go there but a swarm of black T-shirts filled the space.

The auctioneer said, "Folks the bid stands at two-point-seven-million dollars. Do I hear three? Who's gonna give me three for this unique exploit?"

The spell was broken, though. Some of the guests were revealing firearms, faces glinting with sweat, eyes looking jumpy. Time to get out of there.

She made for the main exit, thinking she could walk a perimeter around the hospital until she found someone who looked like they needed finding.

Bomber, Blond Ambition. They hadn't attended any of the auction.

She fought her way out of there. People weren't panicking, but they were in a sour mood. The party had been spoiled. Gulping fresh air outside the crumbling hospital, she looked around, looking for a direction.

A helicopter burst from behind the hospital, picking up altitude. She watched it head over the East River. Something told her she was too late.

There were people wandering all over. Justine decided creeping around in the shadows of the hospital wasn't going to help. She made for the pier.

Mob scene. Everyone demanding phones back, calling their

boats in. No sign of the Park Police vessel. The cops were off duty.

"What the absolute fuck, Justine?" Patty demanded.

"Get Josh," she said.

"Already did. We're going to get stampeded on those pontoons."

"Where's Bert?"

Patty used her chin. "He's got that look."

"What look?"

"That thinking look, like he's constipated."

Bert was keeping a birddog's eye on the people collecting phones.

Justine made her way to him. "Anything?"

He shook his head.

Justine jostled her way in front of the T-shirt with the lockboxes and retrieved her cell.

Josh had gotten their little fishing boat close to the end of the pier. The pontoons bobbed vertiginously beneath many shifting feet. Justine removed her heels again. Patty was too freaked out to make another smart comment. Justine held Patty's arm as they crossed. The final pontoon angled out of sync with the boat. When Josh extended a hand, Patty took it and nearly ended up in the river when Bert jumped too quickly behind her.

"Get us out of here," Justine said as Bert helped her land inside the boat.

Just as Josh pushed the throttle, she saw the Ferretti cruise by. The driver was a dark-skinned man in a gaudy pinstripe suit with a white ten-gallon hat.

"Wait," she said.

Blond Ambition was shuffling down the pontoons, head

low, flanked by the Lady in Red and the Black preppy/country-clubber. They seemed to move in an awkward tandem, Lady in Red and Preppy looking around as if expecting trouble, their hands on Blond Ambition's arms.

Bomber was a few steps behind. From her position it was impossible to know for sure, but Justine swore that was swagger in Bomber's step.

Chapter 8

Segreti tossed another empty coffee cup. He'd lost track of how many he'd guzzled and had no desire to check the garbage can to count. The computer screen presented a maze of boxes to be filled: the 'Disposition File Maintenance Submission'. Third report of the night. It was one in the morning and the fluorescent lights were making him see double.

Even at this hour, the New York Field Office was busy, but in a quiet, serious way. Every fourth desk was occupied by agents putting in the hours, sleeves rolled up and ties askew, if they still wore ties. Segreti, in his leather jacket, looked more like the agents working street gangs than the business-casual guys in the cybercrime division.

Chlebek, still in her reds, approached like a bouncing ruby. "ADIC's come in."

Segreti stopped typing. "She's here now?" He should be pleased if the Assistant Director in Charge of the field office had taken a personal interest in his case. But she could have expressed interest at nine a.m. "Stupid question. Get out of here, Miriam. Tomorrow's going to be a long day."

He made for ADIC's office. Before his knuckles wrapped the door, he heard her say, "Come in."

Deborah Church put the phone down. Short, curvy African-

American with a honey-flecked Mariah Carey hairdo. Off duty she was renowned for martinis as dirty as her jokes. On duty she was feared for the by-the-book diligence that had helped make her the first Black woman to run a field office, and New York at that. She sat beneath an American flag and a photo of her shaking hands with the President—Segreti didn't like the guy's Democratic politics, but at least he was a Catholic, a better one than Segreti.

In the photo she was all smiles, but in the flesh, on-duty ADIC Church speared Segreti with a mirthless stare.

He shut the door, figuring offense was the best defense. "You sign my NSL request, ma'am?"

"Your incident report is sloppy, Ed."

The boss didn't want to talk about his National Security Letter request. Segreti assumed she was upset about the shooting. "The guy interfered in an arrest."

"It's a he-said/she-said bullshit collar."

"So, we're not talking about the guy I popped?"

"We're talking about the whole thing. You're supposed to collect evidence."

"Reasonable grounds, ma'am. I busted Tremain committing a felony. Conspiring with a suspect with a Russian accent and a chopper ride to a yacht. Agent Chlebek corroborated—"

"Conjecture." She looked at an open file on her desk. "Robert Tremain. I've heard an earful about him from our friends at Fort Meade."

"The NSA should give us a big wet kiss for busting him."

"Did they accept payment? Can you prove possession of stolen property or government secrets?"

"It's being analyzed."

"The evidence is supposed to come before the arrest. We're

charging Tremain for computer fraud and abuse, but this is thinner than a silicon wafer." She changed punches. "Have we learned anything more about who's behind these hacker auctions? The Attorney General wants to know."

Segreti wiped his face. It had been about thirty hours since he had sat beside the A.G.'s deputy in that sealed room in Washington. It felt like thirty weeks. He noticed Church's landline had a light winking. Someone was on hold. Segreti guessed someone burning the midnight oil in DC.

"Tremain's cooling his heels in solitary over at the MCC," he said. "Let him sit for a day or two. He'll get chatty."

"No dice, Ed. Tremain's about to walk."

"What?"

"His lawyer was there before you even booked him."

"How..." Segreti squinched his eyes. Someone who knew the system had made a call while he had still been crossing the river with Tremain in custody.

The Shadow.

"He's ours until he appears in court," Segreti protested.

"It's a Fourth Amendment issue now."

"Bullsh—sorry, ma'am. But it's nonsense."

"You want to tell the Deputy A.G. yourself?" She pointed at the winking light on her landline.

"He's the one telling you to let Tremain walk." Segreti put his hands on his hips, thinking. "That's one heck of a lawyer Bobby's got."

"Senior partner at Coburn Bergman."

"Wall Street firm." Not mob lawyers or ambulance chasers. The kind of elite whose Telegram chat groups included governors of the Federal Reserve, secretaries of the treasury—and attorneys general.

This was the second time tonight Segreti had underestimated Tremain. The firepower that Tremain, or one of his friends, had brought down upon him. And so fast.

"Ed, listen," Church said, softening her tone. "Everybody wants the same result here. They're going to sue the Bureau, try to drag your name in the mud, but we can handle that. What I need is for you to go back through your reports. There's no wiggle room on this one."

He nodded, brain turning somersaults. "That Russian..."

"Focus on Tremain." She pushed paper across her desk. His NSL request with her signature. "I'll handle the A.G."

Segreti took the paperwork. "Miriam said the oh-day contained confusing computer language. Like old NSA code had been augmented into something we haven't seen before."

"So it says in your report."

"Any idea about that?"

"You're the Special Agent in Charge. Figure it out."

Segreti retreated to his desk, too stunned to really understand it... Tremain sprung, somebody pulling levers in Washington, scoring bonus points by making a fool out of him. He checked online: it was a little past eight a.m. in Moscow. That's how he knew the Shadow would still be awake. Calling it in.

II

The Fidelity

Chapter 9

At three-thirty a.m., Segreti poured himself two fingers of scotch. He slumped on the sofa in his apartment and looked at the towers of lower Manhattan looming darkly around him. His gun and badge, on the otherwise empty coffee table, stared back at him. He drank and tried to allow the booze to unknot his shoulders. He was too exhausted to sleep. Tremain's escape wasn't going to let him find sleep easily. Tomorrow would be hell, but he'd just power through it.

Segreti had rushed to the MCC, the Metropolitan Correctional Center—a prison hellhole right on Foley Square, just across from the FBI field office in Jacob Javits. The MCC looked like an innocent office building in the middle of the downtown Federal district. Inside, however, was innocence's absence. The place was an abattoir of the soul, open sore more fit for disease and rats than humans. Nobody did anything about it because the MCC was useful, a waystation for terrorists, money launderers, drug lords and rapists en route to long-term facilities. A little time in its 10-South wing could get people to reconsider their refusal to cooperate.

Tremain had been booked, fingerprinted, photographed, escorted to a cell, and out of there before the bars had clanged shut. Segreti had had run across the street in time to see him and his lawyer—three-piece suit, silk tie, shiny shoes, the whole nine yards—duck into a waiting limo.

Probably best he hadn't arrived earlier to intercept them. He might have made the kind of remark that would get him suspended. But as the limousine pulled into the night, he saw Tremain looking back at him through the window. That blow-dried smirk...

Segreti wanted another lick of scotch. He got up and crossed the big one-bedroom, the main room cold with floor-to-ceiling windows that backed against a kitchen he didn't use. Except to warehouse one carton of milk, two boxes of cereal, and three bottles of booze.

The apartment was Spartan by neglect more than design because it was never going to be home. But home had become something best kept at a distance. Segreti did *stints*; he told colleagues he liked the variety of postings, and skipped the part about how he could no longer last more than a few weeks at his official home. He had done spells across the country, and when those didn't feel distant enough, the world. His most recent assignment had been to Korea, which had ended with a bullet in his shoulder and the embrace of a woman who wasn't his wife.

He poured another shot and wandered to the bookshelf. He always migrated here to ponder the framed family picture. A marriage that, the racy encounter in Asia the exception proving the rule, he had honored. Living by stint had served to maintain his fidelity, shielding him from the temptation to settle down with someone new. Because he always had to be somewhere else. Duty called him to anywhere but the detached suburban house just outside Washington, DC in Chevy Chase that he pledged one day to return to, the day he got that big administrative job at Bureau headquarters.

He picked up the photo. Katie and their boy, Jake, with Fluff-Fluff the cat. All-American white-people smiles-in-the-suburbs family. Segreti's arms wrapped around them all, like a guardian. They were still his family. He refused to accept that he had abandoned them. Katie was wrong about that.

He drank his whisky and put the photo back on the shelf. He would try to remember to arrange a call next week. See how Jake was doing at school.

Four a.m. He was finally ready to crash. Segreti left the empty glass beside the gun and badge.

* * *

Bhavin Ram thought he wanted to sleep but what he really wanted to do was fight.

The afternoon had been promising. Segreti had told them to dress to impress, and to meet him at the pier at Thirty-Sixth Street. Showing up with Chlebek in that incredible speedboat, once paid for with cartel money and now property of NYPD. Stepping in, wearing his oil baron getup, made him feel for a moment like he was the king of New York. Then picking up Belmont and the POI: Tremain. Ex-NSA pretty white boy, entitled up to his blue eyeballs, traitor. Scumbag times ten.

Ram liked money, sure. He had two kids, two schools to pay, and a tiny pool in the back of his ranch house that ate water bills for breakfast. Bills bills bills. More money out than money in. Money money money. You dealt with it. Your life, your call. You didn't sell your country down the river.

Ram didn't mind staying on the boat while the others went to the auction. He was a tech guy. Liked gadgets, a little drone photography in his non-existent free time. Getting dirty in the swamp, nah—that was Belmont or Segreti's thing.

Still, the stress. They all felt it. When they were working a case, it was a 24/7 thing. And this case had been long. Unending.

He had taken the boat out, making a long circle that would bring him close to the yachts. One of his drones ready to go. Plenty of distance from the jammers on the island.

There were three big boats, but only one had the scale he'd associate with billionaires partying off Miami. Rare sight in New York. He idled a safe distance and swept it with binoculars. Nothing. He sent up the drone. Someone noticed it, didn't like it. Two powerful spotlights burst to life atop the yacht, and they were both crisscrossing straight for him.

Ram stuck it out long enough to read the hull identification number off the stern. He called the drone back but didn't wait once the spotlights found the Ferretti. He careened back to the island as the lights tailed him, then corkscrewed back to retrieve the drone before someone else could. Followed by the long trip around the tip of Manhattan to the Hudson River marina at Twenty-Fifth Street, Tremain sitting in the back with Belmont keeping a gun on him, Chlebek looking wasted, and Segreti... well, Segreti couldn't resist grinning the whole way. That made Ram feel good.

A detachment of NYPD was waiting for them. Put Tremain in an armored truck, bye-bye scumbag. Segreti told Ram to go home. Which meant shouldering his gear and hopping on the subway all the way downtown to Whitehall Terminal to catch the two-a.m. ferry. He was too wired to sleep on the boat, instead he bought a beer and stared at the drunk twentysomething girls headed home from a party.

Alternating between revulsion at their sweary slurriness, a clinical analysis of exactly how he'd like to fuck them, and guilt because Sissy was just a few years away from ending up like that.

He bought a second beer shortly before they arrived at St. George, keeping it in his backpack until he got clear of the cops at the station, and then finished it while walking home. The beer made him brood, and when he reached his house, the lights were on. Now what?

Ram threw open the door and saw Blessy and Sissy—wife in her bathrobe, daughter in a slutty outfit that made him want to smack sense into her. Both with red eyes and tears, standing in the living room. He set down his pack and nudged up his cowboy hat brim. "What the hell is this?"

"Oh no you don't," Blessy snapped. She had never lost the accent from her homeland in Kerala state, India's lush tropical south. Clung to it like he did with his Texas drawl, emphasizing it when she got angry, like now. A house of exaggerated tones and timbres, globalization gone mad. "You don't come in here drinking at two-thirty in the bloody morning and decide now you're going to be the man of the house."

"I'll drink whenever the hell I feel like it." He walked to the kitchen. Beer was fine but he was now in the mood for something stronger. "I'm up because we had to bust a bad guy. And now I'm home thinking everyone should be fast asleep, but my daughter is here looking...like a...like a..."

"Like a WHAT, Daddy?" Sissy one hundred percent New Yawk.

He poured bourbon. "Like something too old for her."

"I'm like sixteen!"

"Don't you shout at your father."

"You always take his side!"

"I'm not taking his side. Your father doesn't have a side. He's like a ghost who sometimes likes to haunt this family."

He joined them, tumbler full, a little booze sloshing onto his fingers. *It isn't the job that makes me want to drink*, he was thinking.

"Sissy," he said, "whether or not your father is a ghost, you have no business being up this late. Especially not wearing that."

"Mom!"

"That's right," Blessy said.

"It's so unfair!"

"Go to bed," Ram said. "We'll discuss this in the morning."

"No, we won't," Sissy said. "You'll still be passed out. Again."

Swear to God, that was the closest he ever came to striking his daughter. Ram caught his anger, reeled it in. He collapsed on his recliner. "Go to bed or you're grounded for a week."

Sissy let out a frustrated moan and stomped upstairs.

Blessy turned on him. "I've been worried sick, waiting up for her. She got home half an hour before you did."

"She's a teenager." He tossed his hat on the coffee table.

"I never tried sneaking home at two in the morning when I was her age."

"You grew up in India. Different."

"I grew up with both my parents looking after me. The entire family. I don't get off work till almost six. She's practically abandoned."

"What do you want me to do about it, Blessy?"

They had met at Rutgers, both pre-law—he, criminal justice, she, psychology. He'd been accepted to the FBI Academy at Quantico; she'd enrolled in law school, but put it off to have their first baby. She didn't quit working when she bore their second, Sammy, now presumably snug in bed upstairs. Bills bills bills.

She looked worn out. "For your daughter, Bhav, maybe it's too late. She's already grown up. But you still have an eleven-year-old who could use a father. Be there for him."

He downed the bourbon. "Okay. I will." He got up and headed back to the kitchen. Opened the cabinet.

"Haven't you already had too much?"

"Nope." Glug glug.

You'll still be passed out. Again. His daughter's words.

Wait till you really grow up, kiddo. Then regretting the thought, and thinking of Sissy put an ache in his heart. Both of them, Sissy and Sammy. Jesus, grown up just like that.

Blessy was climbing the stairs, uninterested in investing more energy in his bullshit.

Ram put the glass down, still mostly full. He checked the locks, pulled off his boots and wondered how he was going to fix this mess.

Chapter 10

The sun set her curtains aglow. No matter what time she went to bed, Justine always woke a few minutes before her six-thirty alarm rang. She felt stiff and her feet ached.

She got up and her phone's alarm chimed. She was in her Upper West Side apartment, top floor of a walkup overlooking Amsterdam Avenue. She put on coffee and showered. Most of her stuff was at Steve's so her wardrobe choice was limited to jeans, slacks, or shorts, with a couple of tops, and the winter clothes jamming up the closet in the hall.

Fridge and kitchen cabinets likewise threadbare. The street below had Starbucks and cafes, and the corner bodega provided the rest. She fingered through email and chat messages on her phone, drank her coffee, and let her stomach grumble.

Nothing from her editor, Paul Chow. They had argued over the story last night, when she and her team had returned to the *Archer's* office to work out what had just happened. Paul's glass-encased office overlooked Ninth Avenue and the byways of Hell's Kitchen. Instead of the *Archer's* and *Archer's Online* posters that peppered the walls on the rest of the two floors, his walls had Matisse prints and black-and-white portraits of old-timey Hollywood. He was twenty years her senior, a holdover from the glory days of print, most of his career with the fashion glossies. Rimless glasses, cropped hair, natty three-piece and French cuffs; it had taken Covid to finally get him to lose the tie.

He had her in there for half an hour, letting her pace as he calmly tore holes in her pitch.

No video. No photos. Nothing on the record. Maybe a gunshot. An auction. Okay, software breach for the Federal Aviation Administration, and one for Google's cloud business—scary stuff, sure, but where are the quotes? How to fact-check this thing?

It was getting on eleven o'clock at night and she had still been in her high heels and leather pants, and she really needed to eat something. But here they were, thrashing out whether she had a story. Not to mention expensing the fishing boat. That would be tomorrow's battle.

"There were these two guys," Justine said at last. she tried to describe Bomber and Blond Ambition. Why she thought they were at the heart of this thing.

Paul removed his glasses and made to wipe them with his tie, before remembering he didn't wear one anymore. "Look, J.J., what you've got is interesting. Don't get me wrong." He fished a cloth from a desk drawer to clean his lenses. "Inside look at the trade in cyberweapons. Everyone will want to know about this. But right now, what you've got is, at best, page forty."

Paul still thought in print terms.

"I could have something up online by tomorrow afternoon."

"Sure you could—eight-hundred-worder tops, just another piece of content. If that's what you want with this story, fine by me. But is that really all you want?"

"No. This should be the cover."

"Feature. Not cover."

Cover not only still a big deal in the world of New York magazines, *Archer's* still had a million-point-one print subscribers, but cover also guaranteed to get a huge online push, an invitation to the podcast, and getting picked up by the dailies. Features were cool, they were cred, but Justine was determined to put investigative journalism back where it belonged.

Paul said, "Cover means quotes on the record, three sources minimum that Cathy's team can fact-check, plus video and photos." He carefully arranged his glasses over his nose, always a hint that he was about to tell you something unpleasant. "Cover means a celebrity."

"There's no celebrity here, Paul."

"Then we're looking at top feature. I've got an opening for the August edition."

"You need June. I heard the Williams sisters backed out."

"One, you don't have enough time to make the July edition; two, I didn't put Bernie Madoff on the cover so I don't see why you think I'd do it for your corporate criminals; and three, we have plenty of A-listers to replace the Williams sisters. Celebrities. You don't even have a single photo."

"I think we're talking high-society people here, Paul. Real wealth. It's not just a business story or a crime story. We could be talking people our readers hang out with at galas."

"One-two-three, J.J. Prove it and then you can pitch me again."

Bomber and Blond Ambition. She had to find out who they were. She had to find a way to confirm what she had witnessed. That the auction had been real, that those oh-days were genuine. That the world of cyber arms dealers had organized a bazaar on an abandoned island in the middle of New York City. And that remark from the men she had been speaking with at the auction—something about an exploit involving a quantum computer. She didn't even know what a quantum computer was.

She left the office utterly drained and demoralized. All that effort, getting so close to the action, only to have nothing but dust slipping through her fingers.

Almost nothing. Two faces. Two men.

She'd figure it out tomorrow.

Justine was glad she had told Steve she'd stay at her place, because she really didn't want to talk to anyone. She needed a break, from everything, including him. She messaged him: *All okay, see you tomorrow.*

So now it was the morning, and she figured she'd better go over to Steve's. Her laptop and work stuff were there, as she liked working part of the time away from the office. Covid-era habit.

Justine took the subway, changing at Times Square, got off at Union Square, and walked north to Gramercy Park. It was a fine morning. Joggers, dog walkers, hoverboarders and roller skates. She resolved to take a break, be like these people who looked like they had that work–life balance thing down. She'd try it, next chance she got.

Justine entered Steve's apartment. Their apartment. That's what he called it, and what she called it when she was with him. *Their apartment.*

"Hello?"

She checked Zach's room, but he was gone. Suspended from school, kid could be anywhere.

"Steve?"

"Up here."

She walked upstairs and there he was at his desk, architectural blueprints on his two big monitors. "Hi," she said.

"Hi yourself." He worked his mouse and keyboard, adjusting the design on the screen.

"So I survived."

"I see that."

"Where's Zach?"

"Zach is out." Steve glanced at her. "Lawyer appointment this afternoon. I'll meet him there."

"Good. I'd go with you but—"

"You can skip that part."

"What's that mean?"

He sighed. "It means we both know there's no way you would stop whatever it is you're doing to go with me and Zach to the lawyer. Let's just drop it."

"Consider it dropped." She sat at the little desk they had snuggled beside his, now littered with her notebooks, laptop, flash drives and an Allen-Bradley hardware security module. She waited for him to ask how the night had gone. In vain. "I didn't pick up any guys."

"Mm-hm."

"It was the weirdest night."

"Justine, I'm working. Just like you, I work long hours. Unlike you, I work normal hours."

"Sorry. I needed to rest." Maybe she'd work in the office after all. She unplugged the laptop. "I won't disturb you."

"Maybe if you got rid of your apartment, you wouldn't have to cross half of Manhattan to come here, and then you'd have more time to sleep."

This again. She was treading delicately, but she was also

starting to grow tired of his complaint. "We talked about that."

"Did we? Did we talk about that, Justine? Because I don't remember how that conversation went. I do remember you storming out of here."

"What do you want?"

"You. Here. In my life. Living with me. I thought the first time I got on one knee would do it. I'll gladly do it again. Right here if you want, right now. But these past two months, Justine, it's like I don't even know who this woman is who comes and goes like, like a poltergeist."

"I'm haunting your house?"

"You're hardly ever here in body, and when you are, you aren't here in soul."

"What do you call last night? I was damn well here. All of me was, Steve."

His expression conceded the point but not the argument. "And that was amazing. It was fantastic. I love you, Justine. But those moments shouldn't be just moments. Shouldn't they be more?"

"More?"

"A way of life?"

She put her laptop in a bag. "I've got to go."

"Sure you do. Justine Jarman, ace reporter, chasing the scoop. Go."

She wanted to find out what part of his career *he'd* give up for more time. What part of the design firm's decisions *he'd* leave to his partners. Which clients *he'd* let down.

But if she asked those things, it would tip over a morning that was already teetering on the edge of shitty.

Taking the stairs, Justine said, "Don't wait up for me."

Chapter 11

Segreti spent Friday on paperwork, a bureaucratic version of jujitsu to avoid the fall of the axe. Feeling very much like his neck was on the chopping block. Ram was chasing the yacht's ID, probably a no-hoper. Belmont was checking out the licensing for North Brother Island. Chlebek was doing the work Segreti knew should be his: liaising with the computer forensics lab, their best lead to find Tremain.

Segreti went to ADIC to ask for more resources. The NSL she'd granted him meant more requests for warrants and court orders. One step forward. And one step back: somebody in NYPD had passed along the tidbit about his borrowing their drug baron's boat all the way to the mayor's office and someone in Gracie Mansion wasn't happy about it. More ways to waste Segreti's time while the Shadow and Tremain schemed their next move.

His direct report was in Washington, but Deborah Church had power over field office assets. Help me out here.

She gave him The Look. Request denied.

Back to his desk. More filling in online forms.

The weekend didn't come soon enough. He'd still work half days, but mornings were downtime. His apartment tower was one of the new builds on Delancey Street, a glass and steel god lording it over the Lower East Side tenements brimming with immigrants from China and Ukraine and Dominica. He considered going for a run, but the pretty weather had surrendered to rainclouds. Decided on the gym on the second floor: early morning on a Saturday, the treadmills and weight machines were his.

Afterwards Segreti stood alone in his silent apartment and decided he was tired of ordering takeout. He had once been a prolific cook. The current bareboned lifestyle was an affectation designed to convince himself that *home*, with its comforts and property, was still in Chevy Chase. It sometimes worked. He had an urge, though, to do something with his hands.

He put on a hooded rain jacket and walked a few blocks to the Essex Market. It was early enough to not be too busy. He'd only been here once before, late last year when he transferred to New York to head up cybercrime. Big, open, post-industrial space, full of boutique stands and kiosks. He got himself a coffee and bagel, and then perused the stalls. Weighed the heirloom tomatoes in his palms, chose carefully his onions by feel and herbs by smell, his senses shaking memories from slumber. Artisanal pastas, handmade sausages, the mozzarella balls freshly drained.

He carried his brown paper bag of goodies to a stall selling wine. Mostly Bordeaux or Napa brands.

"Can I help you?"

The woman behind the counter, wearing a leather apron, had creamy skin, wild dark hair and eyes black as coffee.

"I'm okay, thanks."

"You like the Bordeaux?" Latin accent, although not the Mexican he had once been immersed in—softer. "We've got some Saint Julien, just came in, if you want a look."

"That's all right." He hesitated. Although the market was getting busy, the wine stall was his alone. That explained the woman's attentiveness. But he liked it all the same. "Actually, I'm cooking pasta tonight, so I was thinking Italian."

"They're over here," she said, moving to the other corner. "You're looking for a red, yes? Something light, refined, or earthy and bold?"

"Medium bodied. Medium plus."

"I've got this Barbaresco from 2016 that goes with everything, for seventeen ninety-nine. Or if you want to give yourself a treat, this Barolo is sublime."

"Forty bucks?"

"Take the Barbaresco. It's a good deal."

He was about to say yes—he was just cooking for himself—but a childish instinct made him say, "No, I'll have the Barolo." Telling himself he might not have another chance for a peaceful meal in a while, knowing it was a limp excuse, and not caring.

"You won't be disappointed," she said.

* * *

That evening, Segreti prepared a salad and his pasta, farfalle with sausage and radicchio. A small portable speaker hooked up to his cell via Bluetooth played Mozart's *Così Fan Tutte*. He uncorked the Barolo and toasted his reflection in his big, empty windows.

To the Shadow.

The next morning, he went to St. Mary's over on Grand Street. The priest's mass echoed off the stone interior to the small crowd of mostly elderly Italians and Poles, the ones whose parents had washed ashore and never climbed the ladder.

He listened to the closing prayer and the priest's invitation to communion.

Behold the Lamb of God.

Behold him who takes away the sins of the world.

Blessed are those called to the supper of the Lamb.

"Lord, I am not worthy," he mumbled with the others, "that you should enter under my roof." The congregation continued: *But only say the word, and my soul shall be healed.* But Segreti remained silent. He experienced a sudden urge to leave. The rites drilled into him since childhood didn't feel honest coming out of his mouth. He'd fumbled at his job. He'd just shot a man dead.

He wasn't ready to receive communion. Blessings would have to wait.

Segreti walked home through the rain. A pile of forms awaited him—dispositions and legal filings and internal CYA documents to head off Tremain's white-shoe lawyers. He finished last night's leftovers for lunch and did his best with the paperwork. The rain let up, leaving the city entrenched in a fog that rendered his view a translucent gray. Bored with the drudgery, he hit the gym again and went for a walk, hands stuffed in pockets.

The Remedy was busy for a Sunday. Art deco diner, solid, nothing fancy. Brightly lit, two security guards by the door, Billy Joel a little too loud. The booths were full, so he sat at the bar and ordered steak and eggs and a coffee. The food was indifferent but so was he. Segreti sawed through his meat in dutiful fashion.

"How was the Barolo?"

He looked over. The woman from yesterday at the market. An instinctive suspicion knotted his stomach.

"Good, thanks." He resumed working with his dull knife.

"Ai, I hope the meal was better than this."

"It was."

"...I'm sorry. I'll leave you alone."

"Thanks."

He chewed a piece of meat, thinking Belmont could pinpoint her accent, sense if it was real...

What the hell was wrong with him?

Segreti put down his knife and fork. She had just ordered some quesadillas and was now scrolling on her phone.

"I'm sorry," he said. "I was rude."

"I didn't mean to disturb you." Eyes on her screen, giving him a taste of his own medicine.

He swiveled on his stool to face her. "My name's Edward. Ed. Thank you for your suggestion yesterday. The wine was delicious."

She rested the phone, had a warm smile. "Isabella. I'm glad you liked it."

They shook hands.

"I'm surprised you come here," he said. "You work in such a nice place. All that food."

"This place is cheaper."

"Yeah, it tastes cheaper too," he agreed.

"And besides, you know, people need a break from where they work."

"I guess that's true. My work tends to follow me no matter what."

"What do you do?"

"I work for the government. Bureaucrat. Nothing exciting."

"City, state or federal?"

"Federal."

"My father was a policeman back in Puerto Rico. So I guess we're on the same side."

"Guess so. And you? You're in the wine business?"

She laughed. "The wine business. No. I just work at that stall. Ten hours on my feet. I want to go home but it's far, and I need to eat something before I can face the subway."

"But you know something about wines."

"Enough to upsell you the Barolo."

"Clever lady. And a good memory. You must have a lot of customers."

"We do."

He was getting comfortable with this conversation. He had a flash of the church, the mass. Wife and kid. Fluff–Fluff.

Segreti said, "Is that what you want to do... wine?"

"Heck no. I'm going to be a filmmaker."

"A filmmaker!"

"Yeah. I'm a student at Brooklyn College."

She was obviously younger than Segreti, but that much younger? Could–be–his–daughter younger?

Maybe she saw the question in his face. "Graduate program. I worked in PR before that—that was definitely not me."

"Making movies sounds a lot more fun."

"But in the meantime... Iya gotta sella the wina."

That made him laugh. "I'm Italian, you know."

"I guessed some Mediterranean history."

"Yeah. Roman Legionnaire by way of Baltimore, originally. And you, you're going to be the Latina Scorsese."

"We'll see. There's plenty of talented Latin women where I

study."

"And that's where you live? Brooklyn?"

"Yeah."

"You like it there."

"More than Manhattan. But honestly this whole city is..."

"A pain in the ass?"

"It's very stressful. I never say this to the others, because they're so into being hipster artists in Brooklyn, but I miss San Juan. The warmth of my people."

"Maybe finish your studies, learn the ropes, and go back. Make your own Hollywood on the beach."

"You've never been there, I can tell."

"No, I haven't."

"The optimism of strangers." Her quesadillas arrived. "One day you should visit."

* * *

They kissed in the rain.

He could still feel it, like electricity rippling through his body. Which made it all the more painful thinking about telling her it was a mistake, sorry, can't do this.

I'm married, he had said. But that wasn't why he had said it.

He looked at the photo of his family in his hearty embrace. He gazed at Katie and felt not a twinge. Jake, Jake would be all right, could use a little toughening anyway.

He turned the photo face down on the shelf.

The contours of Isabella in his embrace still warmed his skin, pressed his muscles. A long kiss. In the rain.

Maybe he could save this. Stick a "reserved" sign on it and

go back to it later. Take the Number Two train to Flatbush and surprise her. Remember me, Barolo man?

After he closed the case.

After.

He needed to focus. His mission.

Back in his mute apartment, Segreti stared at his solitary reflection and the Shadow stared back.

Chapter 12

Justine took the Seventh Avenue train up to Hundred and Sixteenth Street and walked to Columbia University, the rain pelting her umbrella. The weather had emptied the Morningside campus save for a troupe of hardcore joggers. She checked her smartphone to confirm she had the right building, trotted up the steps and found her way to the third floor. Sunday-quiet classrooms; the few people she passed were focused on their work and ignored her. Her feet were soaked in her sneakers and left wet squeaky prints on the polished linoleum floor.

She found Doctor Ang's office with the door open. It was a spacious if badly lit corner room, the shades drawn and only a halogen desk lamp illuminating Doctor Ang typing on his keyboard.

"Doctor Ang?"

"You're Justine?"

She entered and extended a hand. "Justine Jarman, from *Archer's*."

Clement Ang was a wiry fifty-something with a sharp jawline that seemed to elevate his head off his stalk of a neck. His outfit was tidy, pressed Oxford tucked into skinny jeans and brown wingtips. He seemed to exist in a fatless existence and his smile revealed the deepest set of dimples she had ever seen. His handshake was confident.

"Please have a seat."

She took the liberty of closing his door behind her and sat opposite his desk. Behind him loomed floor-to-ceiling shelves bulging with books, binders, and great dangling sheets like architectural blueprints. But his desk was bare: computer, a thermos, and a family photo: the Angs backed by a clean cityscape that she guessed was his native Singapore.

"Thanks for seeing me."

"Doctor Suarez is a friend." Another academic, one of her first sources in chasing the cyberweapons trade, advisor to the NSA, frightened by the dangers let loose. She had called him yesterday, flailing for a lifeline, reported what she had overheard at the auction, and he had set her up with Ang.

"I report on cybercrime and digital threats."

"You published a book."

She was glad it was dark because she didn't want him to notice her blush. But flattery—yeah, she was pleased. "Yes. And you won the Fields Medal."

"More than ten years ago. But we're not here to talk about past glories, are we, Ms. Jarman?"

"Justine, please." She put her phone on his desk. "You mind if I record this conversation?"

"Are you going to use my name?"

"May I?"

"Journalists struggle to represent mathematics accurately. I don't blame them, but I'd prefer all the same to review anything you want to attribute to me. To ensure the accuracy. And prevent sensationalism."

"I'd like it if you could help assess the technicalities," she said. "My editor will insist on the sensationalism."

He looked like he'd say no.

"We have a vigorous fact-checking process," she said.

Ang took a sip of tea. "All right."

"Thank you. This is an interview with Doctor Clement Ang of Columbia University—that's you, sir?"

He looked at her over the recorder she had stuck in his face with disdain. "Yes."

She placed the recorder on his desk. "Doctor Ang, I've heard rumors of a quantum computer version of a cyber-weapon. I'm trying to understand what that even means, and how I can track it down."

"I see. That's very strange. I would be very surprised if that were the case."

"Why's that?"

"Quantum computing is at very early stages. We barely have hardware that qualifies as a quantum computer. There are prototypes, and technologies that use classical computers to model quantum-based outcomes."

She said, "I confess I don't know what any of that means."

"Tell me about these cyber-weapons. Maybe if I understand your world a little better, I can see how it intersects with mine."

"Computers have flaws," she said. "Hardware—the microprocessors, servers, data centers—all the pipes that carry information—can be monitored or measured. Most cyber-weapons go after software, though. Software always has gaps, bugs, whatever. Some opening that the original coders didn't realize exists. A hacker can find these flaws. They're called zero-day or oh-day exploits, because the original creator has zero days to patch the hole. Once that exploit is out on the market, it's too late."

Ang nodded. "This is quite common."

"There's tons of them. Most of them are minor, but a few can be serious. They can let someone capture the flow of data, so you can snoop on conversations that are supposed to be encrypted, or you can use that opening to plant your own malware inside a system."

"And launch cyberattacks," Ang said. "Demand ransomware or target a specific process or just unleash chaos. Any bank, or government, or corporation must assume they've been compromised."

"Right. The biggest buyers of zero-days are governments, because they'd rather warehouse these for their own use rather than alert the companies or the public to the dangers. And the most lethal cyberweapons were developed by the National Security Agency."

"I recall they lost track of some."

"Yes. A group called the Shadow Brokers somehow got a hold of zero-days developed by the NSA, mostly Microsoft-related hacks, but very sophisticated. They sold two of these to the Chinese, who probably passed it on to the North Koreans. One was called EternalBlue and was a ransomware attack against Microsoft Windows, and the other was DoublePulsar, which delivers the payload. They were combined to launch the WannaCry and NotPetya attacks that nearly destroyed big companies like Maersk, the shipping line, and the British National Health System. That was my first scoop, but that was also ten years ago. The power of these attacks now could probably wipe out civilization."

"Is that why they haven't been used yet?" Ang asked. "Even with the war in Ukraine."

"That's one theory," she said. "In the first Cold War, America and the Soviet Union had enough nuclear weapons pointed at each other to guarantee the end of the world if someone tried to use them. Mutually assured destruction. With cyber, it's mutually assured disruption. But it's just a theory. Cyber is so opaque, and the rules so unknown, that it's not like nuclear war. We might not know who launched a worm to wreck our electricity grid or sabotage our nuclear power plants."

Ang said, "I can see why it's a difficult subject for a reporter."

"For a while I played it straight," she said. "On the record. Doing things by the book."

"Your profession requires integrity, or else no one should trust you."

"Yes. And these days, when people in the industry are bothered by what they're seeing, or even what they're doing, they sometimes find me. But I'm only known if people bother to ask. I joined *Archer's* three years ago with the idea that I needed to go deeper. I do undercover work now too."

Ang smiled. "That sounds exciting."

"To be honest, the whole thing's been a dud. I haven't gotten any further posing as a buyer than I did as a reporter waving my recorder. But on Thursday night, I got into an auction." She briefly described what she had witnessed on the island.

"Extraordinary."

"Yes. And someone told me there was going to be an auction of an exploit based on quantum computing. I think the gunshot and the turmoil put an end to that. But this means there's something like that floating around."

Ang clasped his hands. "So you come to me."

"That's right."

"You say these exploits are all weapons.   Offensive weapons."

"Yes. The big vendors—Microsoft, Amazon, Google, companies like that—now invest a lot in protecting their code, securing the cloud. But the black market is nothing but tools for attacking. There's no market for defense and there doesn't seem to be any money in it. The NSA and the Russians and the Chinese and the Israelis, everyone... they develop these things to spy, steal, disrupt, destroy. If they don't have the ability to develop these weapons, they buy them. That's the game, and it'll be the game until one day someone unleashes something that brings everything down—and we lose the ability to turn the lights back on."

"Mm."

She waited. *Mm? That was it?*

"Hazarding a guess, Justine, because a guess is all I can make, I'd say quantum computing could provide that defense."

She hadn't thought of that. "How so?"

"One of the use cases of quantum computing is to crack all the encryption used for digital computers. I believe the people running quantum-computing businesses are now trying to sell the idea that all our data should be re-encrypted using their technology."

She tried to wrap her head around that. "Everything would be exposed? Corporate databases, government nuclear secrets?"

"Maybe."

"Can you help me understand how this could work?"

"How familiar are you, Justine, with finite-dimensional vector spaces over complex numbers?"

She laughed.

"That's a no?" His hands made gestures of assurances. "Don't panic. Quantum computing is about computers designed to take advantage of the laws of quantum physics that can allow these computers to manipulate their internal state."

"Their…internal state?"

"Ultimately, the atoms that make up all matter in the universe, including a computer."

She tried to understand. "Quantum computers do something with the nuts and bolts of the computer itself."

"Yes, using the laws of quantum mechanics that govern reality. But these nuts and bolts must be manipulated without any interactions outside of the program that tells the nuts and bolts what to do. In other words, the nuts and bolts must be completely isolated from the rest of the universe if you want to run a quantum program. They can't even touch air."

She shook her head and said, "That sounds… impossible."

"It's difficult but not impossible. This is why building a quantum computer is still experimental. A lot of our lab work is around trying to eliminate those outside influences, which we call decoherence. We do this by reducing the bits to atomic size, at which point they can jump around without other things getting in the way."

Justine tried to follow. "You make the nuts and bolts so tiny that they jump around, or you make them jump one way or another, without anything getting in their way."

"Yes."

"Because…"

"Because quantum computers are far more efficient than

using classical computers. A quantum computer calculates in waves. Not just choose one or zero, go left or go right, like what a semiconductor chip does, but by considering the probability of many points along the way. That flexibility means these computers will be able to make calculations that we can't even imagine today. The use cases being discussed barely scratch the surface of what we will achieve, possibly in our lifetime."

"Those use cases are decryption?"

"Yes, encrypting and decrypting communications is one."

"Okay, but it's really hard now to actually make these things."

"That's right. The knowledge to build such a machine requires advanced skills in mathematics—my field—as well as physics and computer science. But the conceptual theory is now well understood. Quantum physics are very bizarre, very counter-intuitive. I think we'd better save that for another time. Your interest is practical."

"What you're saying, Doctor Ang, is that you don't think anyone actually has a computer that can completely unlock a country's digital secrets."

"You'd need to have, first, incredibly sophisticated code, based on probabilities of identifying these atomic-sized bits. Then you'd need to have the hardware to manipulate those bits and generate an output. These exist in primitive form. IBM has a prototype for a thousand Qbits. The Chinese, I understand, have something even bigger. But to get to the application level you're talking about..." He threw his hands up. "I can't imagine it exists today."

"A thousand cue-what?"

"Qbits. A classical computer uses strings of ones and zeroes to make calculations. Each of those ones or zeros is a bit.

The bits are digital representations of a physical state in the computer: for example, a switch is open or closed, or a magnet is positive or negative. Everything is a binary: go left or go right. In a quantum computer, nothing is binary. Instead, it's a range: not zero or one, but zero to one, with all the fractions in between. Technically we express these as generalizations of complex numbers in commutative superalgebra."

"I'll save that for our next lesson," she said, trying to make it sound like a joke.

Ang smiled with a patience that suggested he had to do this often. "The essence is that you're dealing with probabilities. Einstein hated this idea. 'God doesn't play dice', he said. But it turns out God does. But all of those probabilities mean the computer's operations aren't restricted to binary processes, but a vast number of possibilities, all at the same time. So, as we develop the hardware to manage these atomic qubits, and develop the algorithms to manipulate them, we can process calculations at an exponentially greater rate than even the most powerful supercomputer today."

"You're right, I have a feeling my editor is going to make me stick to the sensational headline."

Ang looked disappointed. "I hope I haven't made a mistake by speaking with you."

"Thank you for helping me try to understand. Given all of that, if I heard someone has a quantum algorithm for sale, what could it mean? In practical terms?"

"Either someone has developed quantum applications that exceed what is known to other researchers, or that someone is full of poppycock."

"Someone lying to make a quick buck?"

"Wouldn't be the first time."

"But it would be that person's last time. Some of these players—they're dangerous. They're not the kind of people you screw over like that."

Ang shrugged. "That's your area of expertise."

"Who has a foot in both our worlds, Doctor Ang?"

"What do you mean?"

"An academic, or a head of research, or someone in your circle who has a background in national security or cryptography."

Ang thought it over.

"There's a man who has fallen...out of repute."

"Who?"

"I'm reluctant to endorse him as an expert. Quantum computing has its own brand of snake-oil salesmen."

Justine's pulse quickened. She pictured Bomber or Blond Ambition. "Okay," she said evenly.

Ang regarded her phone. "I'd rather not be recorded."

She turned it off and put it in her purse.

"Walter Klinger. Data scientist. Rumored to have worked on behalf of the NSA, a spell in Hawaii, I don't know, something about getting fired over an ethical violation. Taught here for a few years, and I sat in on some of his lectures. He's brilliant but seemed to regard his students with nothing but contempt. He lost his tenure over claims of sexually harassing a student; several women spoke out against him, including faculty. Last I heard, he now works at a commercial lab called Q-Vectors. Doing what, again, I don't know. They're one of these VC-funded, secretive outfits. I think they have an office somewhere downtown, but good luck finding it."

"Thank you."

"Please don't tell him I mentioned his name."

"Why?"

Ang made a nervous laugh. "Does this sound like a nice man?"

Chapter 13

Tremain looked down at the roiling sea, which looked like troubles in gray flecked with violent spray. The helicopter ride had been rocky but touching down now looked worse. The yacht materialized as a long white Moby Dick of a vessel. From above it appeared unperturbed by the rainstorm. A burst of wind grabbed the chopper as it descended. Tremain wasn't the kind to panic, but he couldn't do much about his stomach. He gripped his seat and waited as the pilot turned into the rain before trying again.

They touched down and things seemed smoother. The pilot came around to open the door. Tremain got wet, but the yacht was big enough to shrug off the storm. It was just some wind and rain on the open sea.

He hurried down to the topmost deck, noting the men in ponchos, the nubs of machine guns poking from underneath. A crewman in a polo handed him a towel. Tremain rubbed the water from his hair and fingered strands back in place, while winds gusted rain across the broad deck that lay beyond folding glass doors. Handing the towel back, he noticed he had left a trail of wet footprints that divided a coldly appointed living room, all black marble and steel-colored rugs. The only color came from the chandeliers, two hanging clusters of purple glass. Amid this heartless décor was an aroma of warmth: the rich bouquet of a cigar.

White and black sofas faced a giant TV showing Bloomberg News, the sound off but stock prices scrolling beneath a presenter gesturing to a financial chart. A curl of cigar smoke wafted from an ashtray placed on the arm of the black sofa. Tremain saw only the mannish haircut, the edge of a rugged face, a high-collared gray spandex top.

Not Dimitri. Not the person he had hoped to see. The person he would prefer to avoid.

A rough hand raised the cigar to pale lips. The tip's embers pulsed. "Sit."

He rounded the sofas and perched gingerly on a cushion of the white one, aware that he was still dripping wet. Ignoring the discomfort of feeling cold, he put his hands on his knees and waited.

Annika Volkov, age indeterminate. She had the face of a cliffside in the Caucasus, but possessed a magnetism that transcended conventional ugliness; perhaps it was the surprisingly thick eyebrows over flinty eyes and the lush lips amid the weathered skin. She wore no makeup, and her attire was monochrome gym gear and white sneakers.

Tapping cigar ash, her other hand cradled a mobile phone, her thumb darting across its glassy terrain. She eyed the TV and raised the phone to her ear.

Tremain didn't speak Russian, but Volkov soon switched to English. "It's called a fucking margin call, you stupid prick. Fuck what the fucking Bank of England says. Rip their fucking faces off...*Da*." She tossed the phone on the sofa, unperturbed. "English is a language for fucking cunts. You have only the word 'fuck'. In Russian there are so many different versions of this word, it is like poetry, a Tolstoy novel compared to one of your fucking comic books."

Tremain said nothing. Volkov hadn't asked for his opinion. He wondered where Dimitri was, since it was Dimitri who had summoned Tremain to the yacht.

Volkov said, "You were arrested by the FBI."

"Yes."

"You've been compromised."

"They don't know anything or have anything."

"You're a fucking retard. Know what I do with fucking retards?"

Tremain swallowed and glanced at his fingers. They were gripping his knees to remain stock still. "The plan," he said, "was to sell Red Fidelity. That's still the plan."

"To a private buyer. Not the fucking US fucking government. The FBI has the code."

"Half the code."

"They'll link it to you."

"I don't plan to stick around for long."

Volkov took a drag on her cigar. The cloud of smoke did nothing to blunt the sharpness of her gaze. "You'll stick around long enough to fix this."

"I accept that. You have anything in mind?"

"Those agents. Verdi and the other faggots with their fucking colors. You know their true identities?"

"Verdi's real name is Edward Segreti."

"Kill them. Kill them all."

Tremain held back a gasp. "Murder federal agents?"

"I don't repeat myself, ever, you stupid fuck."

"Out of the question. You will bring the entire apparatus of the US government down on your head. The reprisals to your own people—"

"Fuck reprisals. We are at war. Americans are killing Russians. This Segreti killed my—He killed one of us. I am the reprisal."

He slowly showed her his palms. "Annika, if you still want to sell Red Fidelity, you cannot murder FBI agents. If you want to murder FBI agents, that piece of code will never go anywhere."

"Unless you leave your fingerprints. A personal vendetta."

"They won't buy it. Let me help you do this..." He was about to say "smarter" but stopped in time.

"A fucking retard can help me? How?"

"A setback is not a defeat. The entire hacker community will have heard a hundred different rumors by now. Red Fidelity is more valuable than ever. It's got something no amount of money can buy: mystique."

"Big fucking deal."

"Hear me out. Dimitri's idea of the auction was brilliant, but he's the one who put me on to Verdi. He's the one who didn't do his homework." Not quite accurate, so he moved on. "There's no way to hold another sale, so we go back to the old-fashioned way. I will find a buyer, and now I'll get you double the price."

"Twenty million."

"Is that a fair price to let me live?"

She crushed the cigar in the ashtray. "Let's ask Dimitri."

Tremain let out a secret sigh of relief. She hadn't done something rash to Dimitri. This was only the second time Tremain had met Volkov. Maybe it was her being a woman that made her casual brutality more severe. Very little phased him, but Volkov was scary.

They stood up and she led him through a corridor, past a dining room and a cinema room, to downward spiraling stairs. He noted the two deckhands in their polos fall in line behind him, one a muscle-bound blond, the other Asian looking, perhaps from some far-flung Siberian province. They followed Volkov down to the stern of the ship. He felt the feisty winds before he saw it, and he shivered against the cold. They entered a massive hangar occupied by four sets of jet skis, a high-speed motorboat, tanks of gas and shelves of equipment, and a submersible shaped like a torpedo with a round acrylic window instead of a warhead. The equipment was brightly colored in canary yellows and neon green, except the submersible, which lurked in a sinister black.

The rear doors were open, a wedge of floor lowering into the waters. The violent seas frothed white on gray, the wind hurling sheets of rain inside. Instead of a protective mesh guarding the hangar's mouth, there was a thin X of a man, pulled taut by cords binding his wrists and ankles. He was naked and pale, like an off-kilter cross facing a raging chaos. The storm winds and sea had thoroughly drenched him, but Tremain guessed this wasn't why Dimitri Mahalin was sobbing and shivering so violently.

Tremain's instinct was to bolt. He took in a breath of roiling weather and forced himself to follow Volkov through the hangar with its toys of leisure.

Dimitriy had changed overnight. His thin hair had turned white and his skin had shrunken so that his face was nothing more than a terrified sheen on a skull. His colorless skin was marred by long fresh slashes of red and pockmarks like ash.

"Do you think I really need twenty million dollars?" Volkov asked.

Tremain swallowed his horror, tried to remain in a reality in which logic counted for something. "This isn't your yacht. It's registered to Prince Hakim of Abu Dhabi."

"What I mean," she said, turning on him as the deckhands—beefy blond, Siberian gorilla—seized his arms, "is that it is not the money that interests me. It is getting a buyer to execute Red Fidelity."

"I understand," he said, trying not to look like he was squirming in their painful clutches.

"Dimitri," she said, but then she spoke to him in Russian.

Dimitri broke into tremors. Language seemed beyond him now. Tremain knew that Dimitri was going to die like this, and Dimitri probably knew it too. Volkov had simply kept him alive this long to play a final part.

She returned to English. "He doesn't seem impressed by your solution, Tremain."

"I can sell Red Fidelity to someone who will deploy it properly. There's a man, here in New York. Former NSA, Hawaii, like me."

"Fuck off with your useless promises."

The deckhands' arms squeezed like vices. Tremain couldn't stop himself from grunting through his teeth. "Then what more do you want?"

She smiled. It was probably the first time he had witnessed this. Her luscious lips puckered amid her crags, and her thick black eyebrows arched with merriment. She was, in her own way, beautiful—beautiful like an inbound comet.

"I've already told you."

Even Dimitri seemed interested in Tremain's answer, craning his head around and looking at him through exhausted eyes.

She was serious about wanting to waste those Feds. "Will you get me out of the country?" he asked. "If I make it look like I'm the killer?"

She shouted something in Russian to other deckhands, her hands signaling with a spinning motion. Two men wheeled the speedboat towards the hangar doors. The boat was on a wheeled rail that squeaked as it trundled slowly over the depression in the floor. But instead of guiding the speedboat's nose into the choppy sea, they pushed it backwards. Its trio of propellers bristled like blooming steel. A deckhand jumped in the speedboat and started the motor.

The men holding Tremain wouldn't let him move. He was the guest of honor, VIP seating. Volkov could just cap Dimitri in the head and dump his corpse in the ocean. Instead, she had arranged this baroque theater. If her aim was to scare the daylights out of him, Tremain had to admit it was working, He had no choice but to watch, as the deckhands maneuvered the blitz of propellers at Dimitri's spreadeagled ass.

And so, he'd watch. He'd let her know he was watching, indifferent. Sure, this was going to give him nightmares, but when his heart raced in the middle of the night, Volkov wouldn't be there to count the beats.

Chapter 14

Monday morning and the field office was at peak hum: mouths murmuring into phones, fingers pounding keyboards, bodies navigating cubicles and the coffee machine going beep. Segreti was a specimen of inactivity, his desk an office dead zone. He had gotten out of bed too late to work out, had put on a suit and tie as if knowing he would have to muster some image of himself as someone who took his job seriously. He wasn't yet done with bureau paperwork, but it might soon be done with him. He didn't think they'd retire him, but there was no prospect of another field assignment. *No*, he mulled, *they're probably going to put me on a desk job in DC.*

The detached house in Chevy Chase. Half an acre of lawn. Ten-minute walk to the Bethesda Metro Station, twenty-minute ride to work. Katie still driving her Prius to Walter Reed, but now it would be Segreti's turn to deal with Jake's teachers, to take the garbage down for pickup on Tuesdays and Fridays, to do the taxes. Spending every evening doing his best not to get into a fight with his wife.

"We got an ID. Sir?"

Segreti hadn't even noticed Belmont come over, or remembered it was their nine-thirty report. He looked up from the computer screen he hadn't been reading. Belmont, sharp as ever in his checkered blazer, looked pleased as he presented a thin manila folder.

Still a little fuzzy, Segreti said, "What?"

"The Russian guy. We think we've got a name."

Segreti stopped slouching.

"Dimitri Mahalin. Political attaché at the consulate."

"He linked to the yacht?"

"The yacht's registered to Sheikh Hakim bin Saeed al Suwaidi, flies an Emirati flag. Called the *Aizdihar*. Two months ago, it was berthed in Cyprus. CIA had eyes on it." He arranged photos on Segreti's desk. "I got these from my man in Langley."

"That was fast."

"He owed me for that tip we sent down on the Rivera case. Sheikh Hakim was only in Nicosia for three days, but each of those days he had foot traffic board the *Aizdihar* that we traced back to the Russian embassy. They're all accounted for, still in Cyprus, except for this guy." He pointed to a grainy white man in a tan suit. "Dimitri Mahalin, mid-level politico. The Cypriots say he had only been credentialed there in March. I checked all the known Russian diplomats in Cyprus and New York, and Mahalin's name popped up."

Ram arrived, unshaven and bleary-eyed, and Segreti saw Chlebek heading over with a cup of coffee, dressed nerdcore in jeans and a hoodie.

"He only lasted in Cyprus a couple of weeks?"

"Got transferred to New York on May tenth," Belmont said.

"Any sanctions on this guy, or Hakim?"

"No. The UAE lets Russia move all their money through it, it's on Treasury's gray list. But Hakim hasn't done anything out of bounds."

Segreti shuffled through the photos. "We ID anyone else?"

"Mostly people attached to the Russian embassy."

"Mostly? Who else?"

"There's one person we haven't been able to identify." Belmont selected a photo of people on the yacht's deck and tapped at an image. "This guy."

Segreti opened a desk drawer, pulled out a palm-sized magnifying lens and scrutinized the image. "That's a woman."

"Really?" Belmont turned the picture, as if looking at it sideways might reveal a gender.

"Get an AI rendering."

Belmont, not quite listening, said. "Hunh, you might be right."

"Ask our liaison there to look into her."

"Will do, Chief."

"Okay. Ram, what do you got?" He glanced at his email, seeing Ram had just filed his report.

"The North Brother Island license application was made by an LLC out of Cayman. It's a shell."

"Surprise."

"I've gotten through six layers. Delaware, BVI, Cyprus. The beneficial owners are two Greeks. I'm still digging, but I think one of them works as a short-order cook in Athens and the other's his mother in a nursing home."

"Did you put in a request?"

"Yes, sir, I've messaged the Athens liaison."

"I know it's a long shot, but one of them could have a link to these people." His finger tapped Belmont's photos.

"Yes, sir."

"Remember, don't think of them as crumbs..."

"...but as caviar," Chlebek interjected.

"You got it," Segreti said, not quite believing his own morale boosters. "Okay. We know there may be a Russian connection in Cyprus. Maybe there's a law firm or a fund administrator there that signed something. Ram, you got that?"

"On it, sir."

"Anything else?"

"Computer forensics is just waking up," Chlebek said. "Shaun's out sick and they've got this newbie down there fresh out of Quantico."

"So, we don't know if that code was stolen?"

"The NSA's sending someone up today."

"Make sure they don't take it when they leave. That's our evidence."

"Believe me, I spent my Sunday telling them where they could put their pirogis. There's something else."

"Go on."

"I've analyzed the code. I think I know why I can't make sense of a lot of it." Chlebek scowled as she admitted her limits. "I think it's written for a quantum computer."

That stumped him. "I see."

"It's proprietary language, but I cross-checked it against the open-source languages and libraries out there supported by Microsoft and IBM. It's probably compatible."

"What's that even mean?" Ram wondered.

"Someone could probably run this program on a public cloud," Chlebek said.

"And what would it do?" Segreti asked.

She dropped her gaze. "I have no idea, sir. Still working on it."

"Okay. Work on it." Segreti stood. "In the meantime, I've put in a request for a wire on Tremain. We're still just flinging spaghetti at the wall, but something's going to stick." His landline warbled and he picked it up. "Segreti."

"ADIC wants to see you."

"Be right there." He hung up. "The boss."

"She got our back?" Ram asked.

"That's for me to worry about. You all have your assignments." Segreti's phone rang again, a different line. "Segreti."

"We should meet." Male voice, American, white. Sounded like an asshole.

"Tremain?" Segreti motioned and the others scattered. Every call into the Bureau was recorded and traced, but he wanted them to hear this real time. Belmont picked up a secure line and punched into a server.

"You don't know who you're dealing with," Tremain said.

"So why don't you tell me, Bobby?"

"What's in it for me?"

"Oh, I don't know, maybe you don't spend the rest of your life in a security max upstate?"

"That's not going to happen, and we both know it."

"Well, you must be scared, otherwise you wouldn't be calling me. I take it your counselors over at Coburn Bergman did not approve this little chat."

"I'm a free man offering an exchange of information."

"You first."

"In person. If you agree, you come alone."

"Kind of old fashioned for a cyber thief... even one as washed up as you."

"By the time you decipher the signals on this call, you'll be losing to me in a courtroom, and I'll be in a Vegas suite getting fellated by a couple of supermodels."

Segreti didn't mind the scumbag's braggadocio—anything to keep him on the line. "Wow, that's quite the image you've conjured, Bobby. You should move to Hollywood, write for the movies."

"Someday I'll tell my story. Are you interested in the sneak preview?"

"Yeah, sure, why not? I'll meet you."

"I'll SMS you the details when I'm ready."

"You don't have my cell number."

"Don't be too sure, Special Agent Segreti."

The line clicked. Segreti put the phone down. "You get that?"

Belmont nodded. "I'll get on it."

"ADIC, sir," Ram said.

"Yeah yeah, I know." As he headed for the elevator, the phone in his pocket vibrated. A chill descended on him as he fished it out. An SMS from an anonymous number. He opened the message. shook his head and chuckled, trying to mask his fear. He showed them the image.

"A dick pic?" Chlebek chuckled.

"Think it's his?" Ram asked.

Segreti handed Chlebek his phone. "I guess this is evidence now."

He made the journey to ADIC's office. Her assistant told him to go in.

Deborah Church was scrolling on her phone. He stood, waiting permission to sit or do whatever she commanded.

"I got two separate calls this weekend asking me if I was going to disband your taskforce and transfer you to Washington."

He tensed. At least the agony of a looming disaster would

be over. He could start packing his bags. "I see," he said.

"You've got two things keeping you in New York, Segreti. One's that job you did in Asia, rolling up that North Korean spy ring."

But he knew track records didn't mean anything if an agent screwed up.

"The second thing is me, sticking my damn neck out."

"I appreciate that, ma'am."

"But I can get outranked fast. Best I can do is buy you a little extra time—a week, maybe. I understand Fort Meade's sending someone up."

"Yes, ma'am. To assist us with the code—"

"I know why, Segreti. I spoke this morning with our NSA liaison. They're stonewalling. Won't confirm there's a cyber weapon called Red Fidelity. Definitely won't fess up to losing it."

"They tell you it's written for a quantum computer?"

"Say what?"

"Miriam Chlebek says it's some kind of funky code, but she doesn't know what it's for. We need more time to understand what we're dealing with. I've told her to cooperate with the NSA but not to let them have the code."

"I'll back you up, but you know they can go over our heads."

"Ma'am, my team's also got leads on that yacht and a possible ID of the suspect who's the ultimate seller of that code. Russian attaché at the consulate, named Mahalin."

"We can pull that thread, but you know where it'll lead. If he has diplomatic immunity, the best we'd get is a State Department expulsion."

"Mahalin's a diplomat but Tremain's not. He's a traitor. We're going to nail him."

"When you have the evidence, Special Agent…"

"Tremain just called me. He wants to meet me in person to exchange information."

She arched an eyebrow. "He called you?"

"No way his lawyers would have allowed it. He must be feeling the heat from whoever he's working with to sell that exploit."

"That's strange. Something doesn't add up."

"When that NSA detail gets here, I have only one question," Segreti said. "Governments buy cyber weapons to stockpile them. They're not in it for the money; they're in it to destroy things. If the Russians already possessed Red Fidelity, and it's the real deal, why would they put it on the market?"

She leaned back in her chair. "The clock's ticking, Ed."

Chapter 15

Ram clocked out around ten, feeling like a punching bag. Some nights he took stoic satisfaction in the day's list of accomplishments. Tonight, he was only debating which was worse: catching the subway at Fulton Street or just doing the twenty-minute walk down to the ferry at Whitehall.

He adjusted his cowboy hat and walked slowly across City Hall Park as if he didn't already know the answer, then headed over to the Nassau. Archetypical New York dive, with grungy booths, red-soaked bar, "Support the Troops" in uneven children's artwork strung between the shelves of liquor. Mostly a cop hangout but sometimes the coeds from Pace University wandered in looking for an authentic night among the working classes.

It had been a while since Ram had gotten lucky in a place where luck was rarer than a winning lottery ticket.

"Hope springs eternal," he mumbled as the flinty bartender set before him a Jack and chaser.

The first shot didn't make him stop thinking about Sammy. Another promise of his down the river. They had accumulated like leaves in autumn, bobbing on the water as it carried them out to some sea.

Work. Big case. Boss under stress like Ram had never

seen, Segreti practically aging in front of them all like some animated character. NSA assholes in their dark suits and striped ties giving the Bureau the hard time. *It's your exploits you let get stolen, and you're giving* us *shit?*

Had to file those last reports, clear the deck for tomorrow. It was interagency combat now. And maybe it was his boss's fault. Tremain was out there, the Russian was out there, and Segreti had blown their cover and...

Fuck it. Ram finished his beer and signaled for another round.

While waiting, he checked out the action. A couple of off-duty beat cops in uniform, a few government workers in suits, and some of the barely-hanging-in-there types in jeans and unbuttoned plaid shirts, somberly assessing the remaining balls on the pool table. No coeds tonight.

The door opened. Ram had to look twice. Segreti headed for the corner of the bar closest to the door. Too late, they locked eyes. No pretending. They both knew they didn't want to hang out together, but they also knew that was exactly what the Nassau was dishing out tonight.

A few heys later and the bartender gave them each a Jack and a Molson's. Segreti didn't ask him why he wasn't going home to his family, and Ram didn't ask him why he had decided to unwind here instead of taking the fifteen-minute walk to the Lower East Side.

Segreti tried to make small talk about sports. Said ever since the Bullets left Baltimore, he hadn't followed basketball, and the Orioles were in fifth place, and it was another two months before the Ravens hit the gridiron. Ram bleated rote mythology about the Dallas Cowboys. That got them through most of their beers.

"Gonna hit the head and go," Segreti said.

Ram watched his boss disappear into the men's room and wondered why it felt like a struggle tonight. He had worshiped Segreti; the guy was a Bureau legend and getting onto his task force when Segreti had transferred to New York had been the pinnacle of Ram's career. The energy when they had begun to sink their tentacles into Tremain had crackled. Now they might lose handling the case and, more importantly, fail to nail a guy they knew was a traitor. You had to be careful with a word like that. A *traitor* was the most dangerous and infuriating kind of enemy. You couldn't afford to let them get away with it.

And that made him think about Sammy and Sissy, and why he had become a Fed.

He resolved to make this has last drink. He closed his eyes and thought of his house and the squeals of his kids in the backyard pool and the pride he and Blessy had felt at this world they had made for themselves.

Blessy's parents, from the old country but barely acclimatized, didn't come round so much, now that the kids were older. But their Indianisms still made Ram smile. Blessy's father tended to badmouth everything about their life in the US, so one evening Ram—maybe a little drunk—had challenged him. "If it's so great in Kochi, why don't you go back?"

His father-in-law had regarded him with disinterest. "Just like that," he told Ram, the words practically shrugging by themselves.

Why are you a hypocrite? "Just like that." *Why am I a Fed?* "Just like that." *Why am I here drinking instead of taking care of my family?* "Just like that."

"Just like what?" Segreti asked.

Ram hadn't realized he had been speaking his thoughts. "Nothing."

Segreti threw down a pair of twenties. "Well, good night."

"One for the road, chief?" Ram didn't know why he had suggested it. But he did know.

Segreti looked reluctant, but whatever he didn't want to face at home must have been something. He checked his watch and sat back on his stool. "Last one."

They stared at the bartender and clinked shot glasses. Ram barely noticed it go down.

"Something you want to talk about?"

Ram shrugged. "Not work, if that's what you mean."

"Things okay at home?"

"Yeah, things are okay."

"How's Blessy doing?"

"Still running the show." He took a sip of anemic beer. "They're growing up fast. My kids. Too fast."

"Sissy's what, sixteen now?"

"You remember."

"Just a guess. Tough age."

"You know?"

Segreti cradled his bottle. "Not yet. Jake's twelve...or thirteen. Sorry, thirteen."

"You're in for a ride."

"Yeah." He forced a laugh. "The way things are going, I'm looking at some family time."

Ram felt a chill. His boss never revealed weakness. He was always perking them up, exhorting them to be their best selves. And no complaining allowed, especially about anything above their pay grades. That was Segreti's problem, not theirs. Never complain down the ranks, just up. It was good advice.

"Things that bad?" Ram asked.

Segreti shrugged. "It'll work itself out."

"Caviar not crumbs," Ram said with a grin.

"You got it, Bhav."

They clinked glasses.

"So you found me at this bar when I should be home with my kids," Ram ventured.

"Yes."

Ram paused. The music changed, from stuff he knew—Pearl Jam, The Strokes—to something electronic, stuff his kids probably recognized. He decided he needed someone he could trust, and that person was Ed Segreti.

"I hate going home. I don't know what's wrong with me. I should want to just hang up my spurs at the end of the day and be with them."

"Sometimes the work is ugly."

"They mean everything in the world to me, they really do. It's not that I don't love them. I love them like nothing else. But I can't...I find it really exhausting to leave this...job...and just go home like it's been a normal day at the office."

Segreti nodded. "Same here."

"After this case is over, I'd like to put in for leave. Before the school season starts, take them somewhere. The Poconos or something."

"You should do that."

"I don't think this city is a good place for them. The other night Sissy got home later than me. Dressed like a whore."

"She's just a teenager."

"Yeah, but do these scumbags care?" Gesturing to the bar's other denizens. "The shit we've seen, Ed, we know what she could be getting up to. And with what kind of guys. You wouldn't know, you've just got a boy. Girls, man, whoa, totally another level of stress."

"Yeah." Segreti looked blank. *Just like that.*

"Sorry to go there," Ram said. "I'm boring you."

"No, you're just reminding me of my own decisions. As a father."

"Never mind, chief. All this talk. My father said the same things, and his father said the same things. And here we are."

Segreti clasped Ram's shoulder. "It's all right if you need to talk, Bhav. You can always come to me."

Ram smiled at Segreti's sincerity. "Thanks, chief."

"And if you need something more, some counseling or something—"

"No. I don't."

"The Bureau has—"

"I said I don't."

"Okay."

Ram said, "I love being FBI. I don't think I ever told you that, but I do. I put in the crazy hours because I love my family, and the shit we see out there scares me. I'll do whatever I have to, to keep them safe. But when the day's done, I just can't deal with them."

"Sammy and Sissy need their dad."

"Yeah, I know. I'm lucky to have work at the New York office. Your family's far away."

Segreti nodded. Just like that.

"I don't know how you do it," Ram said.

Segreti swiveled to face him. "When the call comes, I respond. Doesn't matter when, where, why, or what. It's more than country. It's fidelity. To something bigger than me.

That's it."

"But faithful to what, Ed? To who? My world's my kids. They're the ones that I do this for. When I was younger, sure, it was the action, the status, the pride." The pussy too, but he didn't say that. "But these days it's for them. Country, duty, they're nice words, but I don't know what they mean anymore."

Segreti's stare was baleful. Then he finished his final beer. "That's the difference between you and me."

"So let me ask you a question. A building's on fire and Katie and Jake are inside, along with a bunch of other people. You can either run in and save them and let the building burn, or you can run to the firehose and try to save as many people as possible, even if it puts your family at risk."

"The firehose."

Ram shook his head. "No way. I'm getting my family out of there. I'll do my best afterward, you know me, Ed, but when the chips are down, it's family first."

Segreti pondered this. "I guess I look for the bigger picture, Bhav. Go home, get some rest."

Ram watched Segreti leave. The bigger picture? What the fuck was that?

He decided to walk it off and headed towards the forest of Lower Manhattan skyscrapers, half-lit and looming. He took out his cell to call his wife, let her know he was homebound, tell her he was going to hold her in his arms.

Chapter 16

Helen Taylor swelled her twenty-six-year-old chest as she glided back to the computer forensics lab. This morning had been good. Great. Amazing. Being here, in the New York field office, was amazing. The lab was *amazing*, an entire floor of ceiling-high shelves and racks containing hard drives, monitors, phones, wires, watches, any kind of electronic device that had come in for scrutiny. The stuff they had let her play with at Quantico had been impressive. But this, this was the real deal.

Except her report, Shaun Cahill, was out sick, and the other agent was on assignment somewhere in Ohio, and now Taylor was the only person assigned to the lab. She had been here for all of two weeks, minus the three days the Bureau had given her to find a place to live, and she barely knew where to find everything: disk and data capture, file viewers, email analysis, mobile devices analysis, database forensics...

Each station had its own PC and software, a networked computer and an offline one, all the way to the air-gapped systems, some even surrounded by Faraday screens that were the cyber equivalent of biohazard isolation containers. But Taylor especially loved the OG stuff: the pliers, the magnifying glass, the tweezers. She had delicate but steady fingers. Agent

Cahill had said so with a laugh, holding up his meaty digits on her first day.

She had come with esoteric knowledge learned after six months of intensive training and a comp-sci major at Carnegie Mellon. She knew the software, both from vendors and what the FBI had developed itself, and had studied how to extract, decode, and analyze data from phones, SIM cards, cloud servers, you name it. She could bypass a screen lock, ferret out passwords, dig up deleted data. And she wasn't just an agent like Cahill, trained and employed by the FBI to be an IT specialist. No, she was Special Agent Taylor, a law enforcement officer, allowed to carry weapons and make arrests.

However, she was also a rookie, and Cahill's absence had intimidated her. She hated to admit it, but it was true. She was tall, played center on the basketball team, but being left alone in the lab made her feel small. This was New York—the biggest field office in the country, supposedly a hotbed for the cyber teams. And there were no computer nerds, except her.

Nothing transpired on her first two days by herself, but yesterday morning, one of the agents working cyber had brought her a big carton full of phones and a server. The tag said North Brother Island. The agent was a Rubenesque white woman with hair dyed black and aggressively red lipstick. Special Agent Chlebek, Miriam.

"I need everything," she had told Taylor.

The jumble of electronics was an invitation and a warning. "What am I looking for, may I ask?"

"Everything! The Special Agent in Charge wants the report by five."

"Five today?"

Chlebek's look had been withering. Taylor had encountered this in her training, but there was something frightening about experiencing it and knowing this was no drill.

"I'll do my best," she had promised, and then heard Chlebek's "Fucking rookie" as the agent left. Taylor was pretty sure she was meant to hear it. She wasn't sure if 'rookie' was a substitute for something else. Well, never mind. Taylor was all about positivity. Determination had made her an FBI agent, hadn't it?

Before disappearing, Cahill had cleared her and given her a dongle with her own password that unlocked the software she'd need to run tests. She removed the items, still individually bagged in plastic, and placed them neatly on a wide, empty table. They were all tagged and dated; Chlebek's team had collected them during the bust on the island. Taylor knew there had even been a shooting—it had made the local TV news, and she'd heard Chlebek's superior had pulled the trigger. A cyber-crimes unit that pulled triggers instead of white-hatting networks; no wonder the FBI was struggling.

She had spent the day prying secrets from devices, but these processes took months to deliver preliminary results: what images or other data was found, describe their metadata— time, location, other buried treasures—and note any other illicit material. The best Taylor could do was submit a Streamlined Forensic Report with the basics, and wait for the Special Agent in Charge to approve a deeper dive. Physics was physics, as her favorite instructor at Quantico had observed, but time was also time, and she found that the investigators at the field office expected her to ignore Einstein and Newton and get results faster than the speed of light.

Special Agent Chlebek hadn't yelled at her, necessarily, but the woman had come down at the end of the day, and when Taylor began to explain the situation, Chlebek just pointed out mistakes in the workspaces. Taylor didn't have a rejoinder; there were some messes on the table. She wanted to say, I'm just one person—but she was not about to do that. Not today, not to this agent, not to anybody. Not to herself.

Helen Taylor asked for a three-hour extension, worked as fast as she could, and emailed Chlebek an update before clocking out at nine. She hadn't even stopped to message Javon and tell him she'd be working late. After he had gone to sleep in their one-bed Brooklyn hovel, she had stayed up, staring at the shimmering gold badge, hers for only a few weeks and still a treasure.

This morning, she was told to get to the auditorium, mandatory for anyone under one year's experience. She filed in with twenty or so of her cohorts—fresh-faced, eager patriots. ADIC Deborah Church came in and delivered a welcome speech to the new agents.

Taylor hardly heard the ADIC's words. She didn't need the pep talk. She had made it this far—getting into Quantico, the physical training, the crammed lessons, practicing field work, learning how to disable a gunman after getting pepper-sprayed in the face—and standing before her was a Black woman running the biggest field office in the country. Taylor couldn't have wiped off her smile if she had wanted to.

The ADIC invited a few questions and Taylor's hand shot up.

"As the first Black woman to run New York, what's your advice to someone who aspires to be the second?"

Church smiled. "It would be the same for each of you, because all the Bureau cares about is defending our country and our Constitution with integrity."

Taylor returned to her lab feeling ready to put in as many all-nighters as it was going to take. She had already ensured her workspaces were in good order. No more complaints from Special Agent Chlebek. Now it was time to…

She heard the heavy door behind a ceiling-high stack of equipment open. She looked up and saw Deborah Church.

Taylor straightened. "Ma'am, how can I help you?"

Church was practically half Taylor's height, all curves and sass in her high red pumps to Taylor's skinniness and sensible rubber-soled shoes. The ADIC may have been short but she dominated the room. Maybe it was Taylor's awe. But she sensed ADIC was not altogether pleased.

"Special Agent Taylor, right?"

"Yes ma'am."

"I wanted to see how our lab is going. I understand you're the only one here."

"It's a good opportunity to work on cases," Taylor said. "There's plenty to do." She tried to sound confident instead of overwhelmed.

Church nodded, looking around like a tourist. "I'm requesting additional resources for the computer science lab. As you know, the Bureau's a little short on people with your skills."

"That would be great, ma'am."

"Are we going to identify any individuals with this stuff? The Brother Island case?"

Stuff. Taylor had learned to elide the details with superiors unfamiliar with technology. "With time."

"The one thing we don't have. Taylor, how many programming languages do you know?"

Maybe Taylor had misjudged the boss. "Besides the usuals like C++ and Python, I'm proficient in Go and Solidity, and I can find my way through Lisp."

"Any of those work on quantum computers?"

Taylor hesitated. This was unexpected. "No, ma'am, I don't think so."

"Get up to speed. Might come in handy."

She was both thrilled and wondering when she was going to find time to study a new language by herself. Whatever—she recognized an open door when she saw one. "Yes, ma'am. Permission to speak freely?"

Church nodded.

"I just want to say you are my role model."

Church hm-hmmed. "That stuff I said about the Bureau being color blind?"

This was an unexpected comment. Taylor furrowed her brow. "Yes?"

"That's what assistant directors are meant to say. I don't need anyone throwing around my color, especially you. It's hard enough to convince these people that I'm not just a PR story cooked up in Washington. You got that?"

"Y-yes, ADIC."

Church gave her a long look, her own face slowly de-icing. "To answer your question, someone like you will have to prove yourself two, three, ten times more. You learned that growing up, and nothing's changed just because you're FBI. And computer folk like you, you're like the school librarians thrown in with the jocks. You request a resource, like to learn cutting-edge code, I'll see what I can do. You get into trouble with one of our white colleagues? Don't come running to me. That'll just make it worse for both of us and all our people."

Taylor sensed this was her first encounter with office politics. Perhaps she could learn something from Church's ambition. "I understand."

Church gave her a sympathetic smile and took her hand. "This country needs more patriots like you, Taylor. I do wish you very good luck."

"Thank you, ma'am."

Church made her way back out, pausing to say, "And we never had this conversation."

"No, ma'am."

The ADIC left the lab, leaving Helen Taylor wondering if this was the dream job, what kind of dream was it, exactly?

Chapter 17

Segreti looked at the photo of his family, the only personal touch in his apartment. Looking at the faces of Katie and their son, Jake, last night's conversation echoed in his head. It didn't exactly play because he and Ram had been drinking, but he remembered what he had said. *Duty, country, that's it.*

The big picture.

He had taken on a vital job. A gigantic responsibility. Sworn fealty to something bigger than himself. If the country wasn't safe, how could he think his family would be?

But now as he gazed at the faces in the photograph, he wondered how he'd feel about being back home with them. Full time.

He should call Jake. He wanted to speak with his son.

When Segreti was transferred stateside from Asia, he had called home to let Katie know. Their marriage was already moribund, but they had felt duty-bound to patch things up. So, he had called home; and when a strange man picked up the phone, Segreti almost responded with four-letter threats. But then this strange man asked, "Dad?" Jake's voice had cracked. Another milestone in his life that Segreti had no clue of.

Sometimes he was grateful for the oath he had taken—the one to the government. It was an escape hatch. Some escape.

The day had been grim. He had already filed his shooting incident report, which went outside the Bureau, to the Department of Justice's Office of Inspector General. He had also notified the Civil Rights Division's criminal section of the shooting. He supposed he should be losing sleep over the man he had shot and killed in the line of duty. The T-shirt-clad bodyguard had been ID'd as Drew Kovicec of Springfield, Missouri. Segreti would have been following the leads to tie the dead man to the organization that brought him to North Brother Island, but that was now considered a conflict of interest, so another unit in the Bureau was following up.

Segreti could be lighting candles in cathedrals for this young man and whispering confessions to his priest. But he truly was unmoved by the man's fate. It was police work, and the idiot had jumped knowing full well who he was tangling with.

Now the OIG was receiving a flood of paperwork: autopsy reports, witness accounts, the Bureau's diagraming of the scene, Segreti's firearms qualifications, and more detailed reports on the context of the situation. FBI rules said everything had to be filed within two weeks, but Segreti wanted this over with, so he had spent the entire day finishing his paperwork.

He knew what was in store. A grilling before a Shooting Incident Review Group. Deborah Church would be on it. So would DOJ, CRD, and a mix of Bureau people from New York and DC. He'd probably have to truck down to Headquarters, and he had no idea what he was going to tell Katie.

Hi, honey, I'm home!

This sword of Damocles would be hanging over his head for a couple of weeks, while Tremain was out there, the Shadow was out there, and bad things were happening.

So no, Drew of Springfield, Missouri, Edward Segreti is not weeping for you.

He turned away from the photograph and decided to go for a run. The rainclouds had given way to pleasant weather, and there would be a breeze off the East River. Segreti half-jogged out of his building, phone strapped to his forearm, earbuds piping in his workout mix, and his route took him to the Essex Street Market. The big glass windows blazed with life tonight, and he could see everything inside. Foot traffic appeared moderate. He searched for it, but he couldn't see the wine kiosk.

This was stupid. He wasn't going to try anything with Isabella, even if she'd give him a chance. Which she wouldn't. He was still a married man, and a vow meant something. He had strayed once, and he didn't know what to make of that, other than strange land, exotic woman. He had caught a bullet for her. That had meant something to him, before she vanished and he'd been repatriated.

But if one vow didn't mean anything, then no vow did; and then he wouldn't truly be an FBI agent. He'd be just a fraud who had murdered a kid from Missouri.

Segreti shook his head violently, as if to eject his silly thoughts. They weren't helping him stop the Shadow or bring Tremain to justice.

He continued on past the Market until he reached the East River Greenway, a running trail that ringed lower Manhattan. He turned right onto the esplanade and began running faster towards the regal Brooklyn Bridge and the brightly lit skyscrapers guarding Battery Park, about two miles away. As he crossed beneath the bridge and came to Fulton Street, his phone buzzed. He slowed to a walk and checked. It was a new Android model given to him by the Bureau, and he had received an encrypted message from work.

Tremain had promised an SMS and here it was, rerouted to him via his original device now in the computer forensics lab. It was a photo of Segreti running along the Greenway.

He took stock of his surroundings and removed the earbuds. Ever since Tremain's call, he had assumed he might be under surveillance, but it hadn't hit home like this.

The next message was a text: STATEN ISLAND, TOMORROW 9PM.

The night seemed to darken, the lights of the cars on the FDR blurring into a receding scream of red.

Segreti forwarded the messages to the lab. He'd alert his team separately from a different device. He wanted to finish his run. Staten Island was plenty big, but Tremain was giving him enough of a heads-up to be ready to chase instructions tomorrow. He was tempted to take the ferry over, start thinking of exit points. But, maybe better to have Ram check it out. Ram had said he'd be working at the office late tonight, and Segreti had left him at his desk. He hadn't asked about Ram's family. Or his state of mind. Their drink together had fallen under omertà.

Whatever the excuse, he resumed his run towards the tip of lower Manhattan. Maybe he'd catch Ram headed home on the ferry. Maybe he'd just finish out his last mile before turning back.

He ran harder, using the exercise to keep his mind clear. Maybe Tremain wanted to come in. Or maybe Tremain was full of shit.

Segreti finally reached Whitehall Terminal and considered taking the subway back home. He walked inside the terminal's main building—a giant glassy box, brightly lit, with a giant

American flag hanging over the escalators, electronic bill-board posting the next sailings for Saint George. At this time of evening most of the traffic was weary commuters headed back to Staten Island. He weaved through office workers waiting for their boat and made for the 1 and 9 trains. The atrium was split by a long row of wooden benches and seats, and something sparked in the corner of his eye. He arced that way and took a beat to confirm what he saw.

The girl was French kissing a somewhat older male, college age. He was white, brown hair, sparse beard, tattoo visible on his neck above the collar, dressed in a fatigue jacket, loose dark trousers, Doc Martin boots. The girl was about sixteen, brown skin, black hair in a double ponytail, heavy makeup, platform shoes, black skirt that barely counted as clothing, denim jacket, unbuttoned, and just a black halter top below, where the man's hand was squeezing a breast.

"Sissy, stand up."

The couple parted, the man lazily, the girl abruptly.

"I said stand up."

Her eyes, bloodshot from drinking, narrowed. "I know you."

"Ed. I work with your father."

"Oh, shit," the man said, suppressing a giggle.

"Are you spying on me?" she demanded.

"No. But your...friend...has to go. Now."

"Hey, man," the kid said, "I don't have to go nowhere."

"Jim, don't," Sissy said.

"Your old man isn't going to do nothing," Jim said. "You're allowed to be with whoever you want."

"Jim," Segreti said, "See all these people? Lots of witnesses. So there's no way that I would dare lay a finger on you, right?"

"Yeah, man, that's right. So why don't you just beat it, okay?"

"Stand up. Just for a second. Come on, Jim, stand up and look at me. Look at me."

Jim gave Segreti his most bored look of indifference, but he stood up. "What?" And then his eyes bulged and his entire body quivered. He hadn't had time to see Segreti poke his throat. Segreti made the next strike to his solar plexus look like he was helping out a man bending over sick. Jim obliged by throwing up on the gleaming floor tiles.

Segreti set him down on the bench while casually removing Jim's wallet from his rear pocket. "Maybe you're right. Sit down and get some rest, Jim...Fiorinetti. My paisan. Come on." The New Jersey driver's license number memorized, he tossed the wallet back in Jim's lap and grabbed Sissy by the arm. She didn't resist as he marched her toward the ferry pier.

"What the fuck?"

"Watch your mouth."

"My father's going to kill you."

"No, he's not. You're lucky it was me who saw you, not your dad. Otherwise, your ex-boyfriend would be in lot more trouble, believe me."

"Jim's not my..."

"He's not anything anymore. Forget him."

"You're not my father!"

"No, but I rely on him at work, and I can tell you, Sissy, he is very worried about you. Your father loves you, and if he had just seen that...well, I think we both know how he'd react."

She pulled herself free. He could smell booze and cigarettes, but he didn't think she had taken anything worse. "He doesn't give a shit about me."

"That's not true. Listen, please. I'm not going to patronize you with some speech about how I know what you're going through. I'm just asking you to understand your dad is a good man, and there are better ways to get his attention than making out on his commuter route with men who should know better than to touch a girl your age."

She snorted.

"Tell you what," he said. "I'll make you a deal. I'll talk to your dad, not about you, not about tonight, but about working less and getting home earlier. And you...you'll be home to see him. How's that?"

"You're an asshole."

He smiled. "Guilty."

She made a big sigh. "My ferry's about to leave. Can I go now?"

"Sure. Have a good night."

"Whatever." She joined the crowd of commuters. He waited until she had passed through the turnstiles. Returning to the atrium, he saw a janitor pulling a mop and bucket toward the mess, but of Jim there was no sign.

Chapter 18

Justine took the subway to Morgan Avenue. Ascending the steps, she felt that summer had finally arrived. She was wearing her aviators but had to squint against the glare.

This section of Brooklyn was still transforming from warehouses and trucker stops to a hipster hangout. Having journeyed here for a gallery opening, she knew that a few blocks away was the local historical district known as "Little Poland". But this borderland of the neighborhood formally called Greenpoint was short on trees and long on concrete. She walked past some of the city's wildest graffiti art and headed towards the yellow-brick edifice that was the fine arts center—a warren of workspaces, showrooms and ateliers. Checking the GPS on her phone, she crossed the street and headed towards a chalky side street where a forest-green van covered in dust was parked illegally near a fire hydrant. She paid it no heed as she walked past, but she was relieved it was here. Bert would be inside, keeping an eye on her. Fearing surveillance, she had asked him to drive separately. But she would want a haven to run to, if it came down to that.

A few blocks further on and the landscape became the unforgiving steel shutters and brick walls of industrialism. Construction machinery buzzed lazily to one side, cleaning out rubble to make way for something new. That was the only sign of life here. No tattoo parlors, vinyl shops, trendy pizza joints or art galleries. At the end of the street a huge garage door trundled open. By the time she reached the corner, an eighteen-wheeler emerged, its noise and exhaust adding to the grime and the heat.

She trotted around the truck and made for a lifeless street of closed garages and chain-meshed windows. There wasn't any graffiti here, not even the banal kind. The truck coughed, startling her, and rolled past her in a crescendo of noise and dust. She looked for street numbers until she came to an unmarked steel door painted brown. The door blended into the rest of the street, but she identified small camera bubbles mounted above it, small enough to go unnoticed to anyone casually passing by. The door's buzzer looked old and battered, operated by thick numbered keys from another century, but embedded above this, at about chin height, was a small electronic screen.

She pushed the buzzer. Static, and then a barely intelligible man's voice. "Yes?"

"I'm here to see Walter Klinger."

Static.

"I have information about Red Fidelity," she added.

"Wait."

The sound went dead. She stood for a long minute.

"Scan your retina."

The screen in the wall lit and a bright green line scrolled down its face.

She bent forward so the green light blinked into her eye. What kind of database did these people have? What biometric secrets had she just divulged?

The door hummed and she heard a lock turn. Justine pushed on the brown door. She gave the street a final look, but it remained desolate.

She folded her shades over the top of her T-shirt as she walked through a typical apartment building hallway with linoleum tiles below and fluorescent lights above. Except here the doors were unmarked. The hallway led straight to a waiting elevator that stank of cigarettes. When she stepped inside, the elevator's door rattled shut. The buttons went from B to 6, but before she needed to guess, the elevator wheezed upwards and took her all the way to the top floor.

She stepped into a brightly lit loft, like a thousand others throughout New York, with brickwork and crisscrossing vents and pipes in the ceiling. The windows were all glazed, though, letting in light but no views—and blocking anyone eager to peer inside. Metal desks and expensive chairs, whiteboards, and lots of computers. It could be a trading floor or a design studio, but it was empty, except for one man lounging in a black mesh chair. He was white, middle-aged and paunchy, wearing charcoal slacks and an ugly striped shirt beneath a seer-sucker blazer that didn't match. Black curly hair going gray, a bushy mustache competing with fleshy jowls, and thick square glasses with clear frames.

"I figured any chick that actually found me deserved five minutes of my time," he said.

Justine nodded, trying not to look nervous. "Thank you."

He kicked a chair that rolled towards her, its wheels making banshee squeaks. "Make yourself comfortable, sweetheart. You want a coffee?"

"No, thank you." She moved the chair towards him and sat down out of his reach.

"You come with a name or do I just call you Blondie?"

She could imagine how Klinger's idea of chitchat wouldn't have gone down well with the people at Columbia.

"Blondie's good."

He shrugged. "You consented to a retina scan. I'll know your name soon enough. But Blondie it is. OK, you found Q-Vectors, you found me, and you know the name of interesting software. Ask whatever you came to ask."

"Who else is interested in Red Fidelity?"

"Who isn't interested?"

"You're a specialist in quantum computing. There's a quantum zero-day exploit loose on the market. The people who possess it tried to sell it at an auction last Friday, but there was a fight. I don't know if there was a deal. I want to find the people who have it."

He snorted. "You a buyer?"

"That's right."

"You could be a Fed."

"I'm not."

He scratched his head through the curls. "Maybe not. You don't strut like those assholes. Still, it's a funny ole world. Man can't be too careful."

"I'm not recording this. I'm not wearing a wire."

"It wouldn't matter if you were. The elevator is equipped with electronic-cancelling devices. Anything electronic on you is erased."

She pulled out her mobile. It was dead and it wouldn't turn on. "You can't just..."

"Sure I can. Tell me again, Blondie, what you've got to trade."

"I was prepared to pay you," she said, improvising, "but

without my phone, I can't."

Klinger chuckled. "That's exactly what the last guy to come here without an appointment said."

"Who was that?"

He shrugged. "Nigger. Little light in the loafers. Dresses like a swish, anyway."

Klinger's N-word was like a slap in the face, but she had to ignore it. "Dresses how?"

"Like he's ballroom dancing."

Her mind raced to Bomber's group at the island. The Black man, beautiful in his sports jacket and pocket square.

"This guy come with a name?"

Klinger shrugged. "You're Blondie. He's Braun."

"That's the name he used, Braun?"

"That's the name he used."

"But you have a retina scan of him, too, right?"

He smiled. "You're a little sharper than the other bimbos in this town."

"What's his actual name?"

Klinger leaned back and stuffed his fists into the pockets of his seersucker. "Now *that* is a very expensive question. But your phone's fried so you can't pay me. Braun had the same quandary."

"What did he want to know?"

"A description of Red Fidelity. How to know if it's the real deal. And if I knew about some other people who might be involved in it."

"How would you describe Red Fidelity?"

Klinger eyed her with a lizard's patience. "I admit my knowledge is speculative."

"I could tell you what I think I know. Is that a fair trade?"

"Tell me and I'll think about it."

"No, we make a deal or I take the fire stairs out of here."

He licked his lips, thinking. "All right, I'm enjoying your company. Tell me what you know about Red Fidelity, and I'll tell you what I know about Braun."

She told him what Clement Ang had told her, without mentioning the mathematician's name, and about what had gone down at the auction. She didn't mention Bomber or Blond Ambition—or Mr. Ballroom Dancer. While she talked, Klinger got up and walked to an espresso machine and hissed out a doppio.

"Interesting theory," he said. "Q-Vectors has some research that I'm sure these folks would like to buy."

"I might be able to make an introduction."

"I'll bear that in mind." He sipped his espresso. "Guy's name is Malcolm Belmont. Georgia driver's license. There's more, but if you want it, you'll have to take off your clothes."

She stood up. Klinger was several steps away, and nose still in his cup, so he didn't feel like a threat. But who knew how this place was booby-trapped?

"Thank you for your time."

"I didn't say you could leave."

"I don't need your permission. Don't come near me."

He ambled to the workstation he had been sitting at. "Relax, Blondie, you'll find I'm a nice guy...Who's this?"

He swiveled a screen around. It was a closed-circuit camera aimed at the street. Bert loomed, and despite the fuzzy screen, she could see the anxiety in his face.

She reckoned he must have tried calling her and her fried phone gave him a nobody-home answer that had scared him enough to break instructions and come after her.

"One of my team. There'll be others."

"You said you're not a Fed. I don't forgive liars. I go after them."

"I didn't lie."

Klinger looked her over, then typed on the keyboard and she heard the elevator open behind her.

"Have a good day, Blondie."

She hurried to the elevator.

As the doors groaned shut, Klinger called, "Next time we meet, I'll know your name."

Chapter 19

Segreti sat in the passenger seat of Belmont's government-issued Dodge Charger with a Bureau earpiece connected to his phone. He beheld a river of headlights and heard the rush of the traffic along South Avenue. To one side the blazing lights of a Sunoco gas station defied nighttime, washing him and everything else in a cold pallor. Belmont sat still behind the wheel, waiting like a monk. But instead of a robe, he wore a well-cut two-piece suit and tie.

"All units in place," crackled a voice in Segreti's ear. The time on his phone said 8:39.

They had Staten Island locked down tight. Teams were ready to close any of the four bridges. Police speedboats circled offshore. Two helicopters were fueled and ready to go at the Linden airport, across the water.

Segreti and Belmont were parked at the biggest intersection central to the island, with the Staten Island Expressway's heavy concrete bridge above them intersecting with Route 440. From here they could reach any point on Staten Island within fifteen minutes. Ten if Segreti were driving.

Ram and Chlebek were in another car at the intersection down by Pleasant Plains. They were prepared to intercept in case Tremain wanted to send Segreti on a wild chase. ADIC

Church was listening in from Manhattan.

Segreti didn't trust Tremain or believe the guy would expose himself this way, but he wasn't about to surrender any opportunity. Beside him now, Belmont just breathed, eyes open, not moving a muscle otherwise. Segreti admired his colleague's repose. It wasn't something he could ever replicate, but he resisted the urge to tap his fingers or fidget.

"It's twenty to," Ram said over the encrypted line. "Is this guy going to show?"

Segreti smiled at the impatience. Let Tremain drag this out. Enjoy his freedom while it lasted. "Stay off the line," he said.

He and Belmont listened to the traffic, watching cars and rigs pull in and out of the gas station. And then his cell phone lit up and he plugged in. "Segreti," he said.

"Fort Wadsworth," Tremain said. "Don't be late or I'm gone." He hung up.

"Fort Wadsworth," Segreti said into his encrypted line as Belmont turned the ignition. "Backup units keep a one-k distance. I want boats there, and birds in the air but stay over Greenbelt." They were screeching into traffic. "He's right under Verrazzano-Narrows Bridge, so stay awake there, people."

As Belmont aimed at the next on-ramp to the Expressway, he wondered at Tremain's choice of location. Fort Wadsworth was a decommissioned military base that was now a park, located on one tip of Staten Island, across from Brooklyn. But it was easy to shut down. Two units along New York Avenue could stop any road traffic. Unless Tremain intended to go by boat, but then Segreti had that sewed up. And Tremain wasn't stupid.

"We'll be there in plenty of time," Belmont said, weaving

between the array of red taillights.

"This seem like a strange place to do a meet?" Segreti wondered.

"It's empty at night. Plenty of privacy."

Segreti grunted and let Tremain focus on the road. His cell rang again, showing a different number. "Yeah?"

It was Tremain, using a different phone or SIM card. "You know I'll expect you to be alone, Ed."

"You know I'm not."

"Park at the museum gate and tell your people to keep their distance. If I see them, I'm gone."

"All right."

"You, alone, walk to Weed Battery. I'll know if you send anyone in."

"Weed Battery."

The line went dead.

Segreti said to the encrypted channel, "All units stand by. Maintain one-k distance. Boat units, lights off, stay close to Weed Battery. I'm going in on foot. Chlebek, call the park, tell them to get any workers out of there."

Belmont angled towards their exit. "You want me to circle around?"

Segreti pulled up a Google Map of the site. "He might have eyes on the entrance, so park just outside and then run north until you find a way in. Stick to the perimeter but close in behind Weed."

His earpiece crackled. Chlebek: "There's a Coast Guard station there."

"Good. Alert them. I want any active-duty personnel armed and positioned along the beach on either side."

Belmont ignored a do-not-enter sign and pulled up to the

park entrance. He turned two corners to an empty parking lot and rolled to a stop.

Segreti checked his gun out of habit. "This feels too easy. He's surrounded."

"Be careful, sir."

They both got out of the car.

"You too. I'll give you some time."

Belmont nodded and set out on a trot back to the road, jacket flapping. Segreti checked his watch and walked briskly alongside the darkened visitor's center, and then cut into a flank of trees. He was wearing a dark blazer, jeans, dark shirt, and rubber-soled boots.

There were no lights on along the ground, but the Verrazzano Bridge loomed almost directly overhead, glowing like a great green steel monster, casting an eerie glow across the grounds. In the distance a police siren wailed, attesting to some other nightly tragedy.

He came to Tompkins Street and jogged along the sidewalk. Five minutes to go. The roads then took long diverging paths, so he crossed more undulating grass and trees. The land rose and he breathed heavier. By now he had a good view down at Weed Battery, a turn-of-some-century fortress, half a hexagon, its three sides facing the river. They rose as three levels of column-covered halls, looking like the Roman Coliseum sheered in half. In bygone days those halls would have bustled with Union troops and their cannons, but they were dark now, their stories held close. The fort's interior ground was a grassy courtyard but it was defended by a wall too high for Segreti to scale without a ladder.

8.59.

He reached the wide central doors leading to the courtyard.

Railway tracks emanated from the entrance and ended behind him at a high hill, where they would have kept munitions: cannon balls, breechloading Sharps rifles. Those multiple tracks converged on the courtyard entrance like a dead end.

The doors were unlocked. How had Tremain managed this? Various theories drove a chill down his spine. Whom might Tremain have hurt to arrange all this?

He passed through a modern covered entrance for visitors and stepped onto the grassy courtyard. Dozens of darkened archways faced him from three directions.

"Okay, Tremain. You wanted to talk? Let's talk."

The fortress remained silent.

Then his cell buzzed and he answered it.

"Throw your gun away," Tremain said.

"I don't think so."

"You've got an itchy finger, Ed. Throw it where I can see it."

He pulled the Glock from his shoulder holster, held it outstretched, and tossed it. He still had the Sig P365 cuddling his ankle. "Enough games," he said. "Show yourself."

Tremain emerged from Segreti's left, ground level. He wore a black T-shirt and black jeans, his blond hair bobbing like a golden crest in the half-light. The bridge's greenish light cast his shadow long.

Segreti murmured, "Tremain's here. All units stand by." To Tremain he called, "I can arrange for Witness Protection. Something comfortable."

"That's very kind," Tremain said, closing in. "But you're dealing with forces that are beyond whatever help you can give me."

"Bobby, you're looking at treason. That's the death penalty. You think your fancy lawyers are going to keep us from arresting you and charging you?"

Tremain looked around and Segreti did too. The open mouths of walls remained dark and still. So what was Tremain looking for?

Segreti added, "When that time comes, there won't be any deals. No plea bargains. You're the guy I want. Turn yourself in and testify, and I'll do everything in my power to—"

A glint of ruby from above Tremain.

Laser.

"Gun!"

Tremain seemed non-plussed. As if he had been waiting for this. Segreti rolled, not knowing if there had been a shot. Tremain stood grinning like an idiot.

He heard a faint "Drop the weapon" as if carried on ether. It sounded like Belmont.

A second red dot appeared—on Tremain's shoulder. Two gunmen. It crept towards his skull.

"Get down!" Segreti shouted, springing back to his feet. He ploughed into Tremain and this time felt the bullet whiz past his ear. A divot of grass exploded.

Tremain was solid but not braced for the tackle and they hit the earth. Lasers from the two ends of the fort, levels above, formed a shifting X in the air. Another shot like a bark, and one of the lasers spun into the sky. Now a different kind of firing, pulsing, but within the fort, not aimed at the courtyard—at Belmont? Segreti rose to a kneel and fired to his left, the other threat.

Tremain bolted back towards the fort. Bullets danced at his feet. He made it as far as the archway when something knocked him to the ground.

Segreti rushed toward the right, away from Tremain, to deny

the shooters an easy target. He fired as he ran, not wanting to give the attacker a moment to take careful aim. Tracers lit up the air, but he reached the archway and the safety of the corridor. He saw Tremain in silhouette: he had gotten up and was leaning heavily against a column.

"Stay there and wait for the medics," Segreti called, checking his Sig's magazine. Two bullets left. He ran down the corridor and was rewarded with stairs leading up to a void. He ascended, daring the dark to trip him, and heard breathing. When he reached the second layer and poked his head around the corner, a dim green light off the bridge gave the corridor a fuzzy visibility. There was a shadow, wielding a rifle—turning toward Segreti.

Bright blossoms set the corridor ablaze. Segreti ducked back as chunks of brick hurled into his face. He turned and heard a different kind of bark. The attacker clutched the column and fell into the night. Then another figure came running, crisp shirt visible, green gleam of regulation pistol raised in his hands, and the whites of his eyes flashing.

Belmont peered over the edge. "He isn't moving."

"What about the other shooter?" Segreti asked.

"Got away."

"They wounded Tremain. I'm going back to get him."

As Belmont ran back the way he had come, looking for the second attacker, Segreti hurried down the steps, nearly falling on his face in the darkness and jumping when he saw the bottom was near. He landed and saw the shooter's corpse sprawled on the grass. No sign of Tremain.

He ran to where he had last seen the man. Looked like a blood stain on the slate floor—touched it, yes, warm blood. He viewed an empty courtyard, hearing the FBI chopper a moment before it popped into view above the outer wall, searchlight sweeping the fort.

Segreti jogged to where he had thrown his gun. It wasn't there. Tremain? He paced, looking for signs of blood; spotted one and decided the closest exit was a small tower at the fortress's edge. He ran there and found stairs leading both up and down. Up looked like it would go to the fort's roof. Down, he didn't know, but he saw a black dot that was probably blood. He scurried down circling steps, going so fast it made him dizzy, until bang! He slammed into something. The collision sparked stars. A dull pain soon set in. He reached out and felt a wooden door. Fumbled for a knob, he found a latch, and gave it a shove.

Emerald light flooded his vision. He was at sea level, on a coarsely sanded beach. The bridge and its lights filled the sky. The waters were black and swift: here the bays opened to the unforgiving Atlantic. Here was the last embrace of the city: Brooklyn shimmered beneath the far side of the bridge; and northward, he could make out the distant towers of Manhattan, the Statue of Liberty visible against the horizon, lamp raised. Lady Liberty was a tough gal, but she had been betrayed, and Segreti had come up empty. He felt sick.

He jogged along the beach and his toe kicked something hard and unrelenting. Not a stone. He bent down and lifted a gray orb. It was heavy enough to require some back muscles. It was part of a linked set of heavy oblong spheres...a belt of weights. Divers wore these belts to control their buoyancy.

Segreti looked out to the waters. By the water's edge, where the sand was wet and hard, he saw a triangular print, like a flipper.

Had Tremain escaped underwater, or had the other shooter?

Or both?

He called it in, telling the boats to search for scuba divers, the choppers to find nearby piers. The Coasties emerged from either side of the beach, and he told them what to look for.

Then, exhausted, Segreti headed back to the courtyard. Empty-handed, his suspect missing, his firearm stolen.

One question blazed in his thoughts as he marched up the stairs. One of those bullets had been for him. Had the other been for Tremain?

Chapter 20

Justine, bleary-eyed, stared out the window at the brown-stones, now turned orange by the streetlamps. Decatur Street was not quite asleep, but Bert snored in the driver's seat. They had seen a few people walking with relative ease, a drunk shuffling from one stoop to another, and a man scurried down his steps carrying a bicycle and then sped past the van. But at this hour, no children played along the tree-lined street, the bells on the corner church didn't ring, and the cocktail lounge at the other end had shut its doors.

Justine had snuck back to Steve's apartment to grab one of her other phones. She was relieved to find he wasn't there, must have been working in the office. She checked her messages and got Patty's update that she and Josh had found four Malcolm Belmonts in the New York City area. There wasn't much on Google—a few photos that she couldn't tie to anything solid; no one with Ballroom Dancer's looks or style—but their four Malcolms did come with addresses.

One Malcolm was listed as 82 years old—scratch that one.

Justine and Patty had gone to check out the other three, Patty insisting someone go with her after hearing Justine's story about meeting Walter Klinger. "This city's full of pervs," she'd said.

The Malcolm in Jersey City was an obese white man who answered his door wearing a crumb-covered bathrobe. Scratch him.

The one in Astoria was a middle-aged Black man who greeted them in a reverend's robes and a wicker basket with a "Donation$" sign pinned to it. The beard told her this wasn't Ballroom Dancer, but she had to be sure. Could she ask him some questions? Ten minutes and twenty bucks later: scratch.

Having spent most of the day crisscrossing New York, they were exhausted, but that only left one Malcolm, in Brooklyn's Bedford-Stuyvesant neighborhood. He lived on the second floor of an old, gorgeous brownstone bounded by a wrought-iron fence, fronted by a row of tall trees. But even though it was seven p.m., no one answered the buzzer.

Patty had suggested they call it a day, but Justine had decided to wait it out. So Patty insisted Justine needed company. They walked two blocks to Peaches Hothouse for fried chicken, and when Justine came back from using the bathroom, Patty informed her triumphantly that Bert was on his way.

"You can't just tell Bert to drop everything," Justine said. "He's got a family."

"Yeah, us."

Her cell rang, cutting the argument short. It was Steve. When was she coming home?

"It's going to be a late night," she told him, and finished with a "Love you too." To which Patty made a face.

Bert's green van rolled up. And when Justine apologized, he just said, "I might need to drive around. Till a parking space frees up." It took him almost half an hour before he secured a spot along Decatur, a few doors away from that Malcolm's apartment. Justine brought him takeout: blackened catfish and cornbread.

"Well, see you tomorrow," she said to Patty.

"And leave you alone with this lug? I don't think so."

She was still there, behind Bert, high tops kicked up on the seat beside her, Rangers cap covering her eyes. At least she wasn't snoring...

It had been a long, boring night that Justine had passed by questioning the wisdom of staking out this stranger's place. They could come another time. Maybe the guy was traveling. Or at a friend's place. Or he was a hermit who didn't answer the door and kept the lights off.

Anyone who had gone to Walter Klinger asking questions about Red Fidelity was probably not the nine-to-five type.

Her body ached and the soul food felt permanently stuck to her ribs. She could barely focus on the street, must have dropped off, because when she looked out the window, there was a man walking up the brownstone's steps. A trim Black man wearing a dark suit. Clean shaven. She couldn't be sure, but...

She pressed Bert's arm. "Hey, wake up. Someone's here."

He woke up with a snort. Patty stirred and lowered her feet.

"That him?" Bert asked.

"God, what time is it," Patty moaned.

"That's him."

"Sure?"

"Pretty sure." Justine got out of the van.

"Where the—hey, where are you going?" Patty hissed.

Justine crossed to Malcolm's side of the street. He was fumbling with keys at his door. She had worked out an opening gambit, something about losing her phone and not knowing where she was, but by the time she reached his building he had shut the door behind him.

In the heavy exhaustion of the wee hour, she realized it would be beyond weird to ring his buzzer. But she had gotten enough of a glimpse. This was her guy.

* * *

They slept and waited more. The van stank of discarded deep-fried food and body odor. Patty smoked outside, leaning against the van but facing away from Malcolm's place. Bert returned from a breakfast run with coffee and pastries. Justine rubbed her eyes and recoiled at her greasy skin. As she scrolled her news apps while drinking the coffee, she saw mention of a shootout last night on Staten Island, big manhunt for suspects on the loose.

Bert said, "Hey," and she looked at the house for the thousandth time and saw Malcolm hustle down his stoop, dressed in a light gray blazer and dark pleated slacks, sunlight bouncing off his polished shoes. Behind him they saw a second man in the doorway, light brown skin and a rambunctious afro. The man retreated inside and shut the door. Malcolm walked their way.

"Let's follow him," Justine said. "I'll go on foot; you bring the van."

"Stay in touch this time," he said.

"I will. Patty, you with me or sticking with Bert?"

Patty screwed on her baseball cap. "What do you think?"

"Then come on."

For a moment she froze as Malcolm walked past, looking right at them. He kept going. She waited a beat and then got out. She and Patty trailed him, watching as he turned at the church onto Lewis Avenue.

"There's a subway station on Utica," Patty said.

But Malcolm walked past the subway station to a garage advertising valet parking.

"Bert," Justine said into her phone, "I think he's getting a car."

The green van appeared just as Malcolm appeared in a squeaky-clean sedan. Patty waved at Bert and he rumbled to a stop nearby. They ran for the van as Malcolm drove past, going straight down Fulton Street, a long, straight artery that bisected Brooklyn. Now full of rush-hour traffic. As Malcolm kept a straight line to the Manhattan Bridge, Justine typed his license-plate number onto her phone's notepad.

They crossed to Manhattan—sunny day, glamorous views. Malcolm turned north into the Lower East Side, swerved abruptly and snuggled a sidewalk along Allen Street. It happened so fast Bert had no choice but to keep driving, but Justine saw a man waiting at the curb where Malcolm had stopped.

"Holy shit, that's him," she said.

"That's who?" Patty asked.

"Bomber. Bert, turn around. Next block, can you turn?"

"*Who?*"

"It's a one-way," Bert said.

"Dammit, we're going to lose him."

"Who's *him*?" Patty demanded.

"Stop the van." Bert protested but he obeyed. Justine got out and ran back down Allen, among tenements and Chinese noodle joints and bars serving coffee and eggs. She almost crashed into a Hasidic family, the black-clothed couple pushing a baby stroller. "Sorry, sorry" versus Yiddish epithets.

By the time she returned, Malcolm and Bomber were long gone.

Chapter 21

Dawn found Tremain on the Arab's yacht staring at the Atlantic coastline. The pain in his thigh was excruciating, even after swallowing the pills, and the bobbing of the ship made him queasy.

He was alive, great, but he was done with being used as bait.

Even though he had taken a chance on returning, and Volkov's team had patched him up as best they could, Tremain *knew*. It wasn't an FBI bullet that had grazed his leg. She had wanted to tie up loose ends. All of them.

He hadn't had time to think this through. Once he was back on the yacht he had passed out. Waking up was the surprise.

The seas were subdued, accommodating. Not like the last time he had been here. Not like what he sensed from last night. But that turmoil hadn't been the water. He didn't want to dwell on it but the memories pressed images on him. Adrenaline had gotten him to the beach at the foot of Fort Wadsworth. Two sets of scuba diving gear, as promised. The second gunman was already pulling on his wetsuit.

Looking back, Tremain realized he had gone into shock. He didn't know how much blood he had lost, but he had known that everyone was an enemy, and he pointed Segreti's Glock at the Russian gunman.

The gunman, a rugby player-sized blond, had merely walked up to him, ignoring the gun, and knelt to examine the wound. He drew a knife, picked up the other wetsuit, and sawed off the arm. He turned this into a foam neoprene tourniquet and winched it around the top of Tremain's thigh. That probably had saved his life. It might still save his leg.

The wind was imbued with the saltiness of the sea. It came and went with no pattern, a random force bearing oceanic taste. It shifted and bore him something else, the acrid smell of cigar.

Volkov scared him, but right now she scared him less. She had taken her shot and missed.

Of course, he was helpless on board this yacht. He couldn't run—hobbling was about the best he could manage. One snap of her fingers and several muscular deckhands would seize him. Maybe just a quick bullet to the head. Or tie him up in a sack and toss him overboard with a couple of weights. Or arrange something creative, as she had with Dimitri, assuming she had yet another guest to intimidate. Tremain reckoned he was already a dead man so long as he remained in her orbit. All that remained was for her to follow through.

"Your men can't shoot for shit," he said.

"An FBI agent disrupted them. And you obstructed their view."

"Uh-hunh." Fake agreement. The wound was burning and he was too tired to argue. His brain had been reconstructing the scene in the fort's courtyard. Had the bullet that passed through his thigh, just missing the femoral artery, been aimed at Segreti, or at him? Did he owe his life to fucking Segreti?

Assembling memories was more a process of jerry-rigging

than anything methodical. He kept coming back to that darkened beach, the wetsuit foam squeezed tight around his thigh, wearing nothing but his flippers and the scuba tank, stumbling weakly after the gunman. Beyond that he could remember the violent grip of the Atlantic cold water and the helicopter spotlights crisscrossing the bay's black surface. Then underwater, feebly kicking with his one leg, trying to follow the gunman, unable to see a damn thing. Then below him, a flare, a hazy red beacon. The current happened to be going his way and he let it carry him. He feared hitting rocky bottom, but he hadn't put on the buoyancy weights, and his problem was struggling to go deeper. Without the wetsuit he was freezing. Hypothermia would kill him before the bullet wound ever could.

The last thing he remembered were the lights of the submersible, arranged on twin metal columns flanking the big acrylic window. Inside, the silhouette of a man behind the controls. Tremain couldn't actually see the submersible's body, but remembered seeing it in the yacht's hold, like a black cyclops. The lights illuminated the submersible's two claw-like arms, forward in half bends. The gunman pulled him and he clung to the steel arms of the sub. Another glimpse through its window, and he realized the driver was no man...

Then Volkov had killed the lights and the forward motion nearly tore him away. He couldn't do anything but hang on, breathe through his regulator, listen to the sound of his exhales and the subtle throb of the sub. And shiver to death.

And now here he was, sitting on the middle deck, by the white railing, bad leg extended, leaning on his hands. After nearly freezing in Raritan Bay, he welcomed the sun.

Volkov pulled up a chair from the tables in the shade and sat high beside him. "Segreti is alive. Yet you set him up," she said. "This is bad for you."

"I did what you asked. Your sharpshooters weren't too sharp, and I took the bullet for your mistake."

"Maybe is another bullet. Waiting to blow your fucking brains out."

He looked up at her, but she was just minding the sea. She could be talking about the nice cloudless day.

"Then get it over with."

She smiled and drew on her cigar. "I don't have to be the one with this bullet, Tremain. You now have many enemies. Many."

"Which is why we're going to sail back to the Gulf, and you're going to set me up in a sweet apartment in Dubai along with a fat bank account." He could plot his return from the UAE in comfort without fearing extradition.

"If this is what you want, then you must sell Red Fidelity."

"Jesus, Volkov, it's an NSA exploit. That's all. Lots of sellers and buyers. One of them will have the right cloud access. Get... I don't know, get Klinger to do it."

"Walter Klinger." She said it like she had taken a bite of something slimy. "How much does he know?"

"Not much. He helped write the quantum piece when we were at NSA Hawaii. He'll do anything for teenage pussy."

"And you have been in contact?"

"No, not for years. But he's in the area. Made the papers a few months back."

"Why?"

"Something about sleeping with students, or trying to."

"You were friends with this man?"

"No, never. Klinger's an obnoxious slob. He knows his

way around computers, but he lacks self-control." Klinger's dishonorable discharge had been as predictable as the sunset.

"So why trust this to him?"

"It's easy to push his buttons. You wouldn't even need to pay him much. He'd do it for the excitement. He's got no moral compass."

Volkov emitted what he took to be a laugh.

"If that's directed at me," he said, "I believe in greed as a calling, not an impulse."

While Volkov puffed calmly, he noticed how green her eyes were, and the way she wrapped those succulent lips around the cigar shaft. Never mind the ravaged face, the manly haircut. He couldn't help but get ideas. At least it was a sensation that distracted him from the ceaseless pain in his thigh.

"Tremain," she said, "you are fucking idiot. But with a useful reputation. That is your only value." She looked at him the way a cat might regard a wounded mouse: with amused patience. "You need hospital. We can take you, make sure no problems. You keep your leg before it turns green and smells like a frog's cunt. No Walter Klinger, he is reckless. You do this alone. And if you sell Red Fidelity to right people, then Dubai, okay, sure."

Chapter 22

Volkov's idea of 'hospital' turned out to be a backwoods clinic upstate. She had the chopper take Tremain most of the way, landing in a fallow field bounded by trees—presumably a place the Russians had used before. He was too tired to care. The wound hurt like crazy, and a fever had snuck in and was now consuming his consciousness.

The chopper touched down long enough for him to get out. There was no dignity in this. He couldn't stand and toppled over as soon as he put any weight on the shot leg. The pilot didn't wait, the updraft of the chopper blades kicking up soil and dust. Then the helicopter was gone, and he thought he really was going to die right there on this plot, half-buried as he was.

It was still daylight when someone came for him. Car engine, the pain of rough handling. That was all he remembered.

Then waking up here, in a room of gray walls, harsh lighting, and a terrible painting of kittens. His thoughts sloshed around, wondering who would pay for such a cheesy illustration, who would spend time making it? He vaguely decided he was high, here on a bed, under a thin blanket. He pulled the blanket aside and saw he was wearing somebody else's undershirt and nothing else. His right thigh was wrapped in gauze and his penis limply looked the other way.

"You're awake," said a white guy wearing a lab coat. So, sure, Tremain guessed he was a doctor.

"I've given you ten migs of Percocet and started you on antibiotics. Don't let the wound get wet for forty-eight hours, then clean it twice a day with clean water—don't use alcohol, it'll slow the healing—and wrap it up. Put a little Vaseline on first so the gauze doesn't stick."

"Am I going to walk again?"

"Sure, pal, you'll walk just fine. Just take it slow and elevate the wound to keep the swelling down." The doc handed him a plastic baggie of pills. "This is enough Percocet for a week. After that you'll need a prescription."

Meaning, this guy wasn't putting his signature on anything. Not for Tremain.

The doctor smiled. "Of course, if you keep taking this stuff, you'll end up a tweaker. Your choice."

"That it?"

"That's it." He gestured to a chair with a pile of clothes. The only thing Tremain recognized was Segreti's Glock. Volkov had told him he should chuck it into the Atlantic, but he wanted to keep it, at least so long as he was in her orbit. "You can wear those. Get dressed, I'll drive you into town and you can take it from there."

He needed help pulling on the trousers, but he was able to manage bending over to tie the shoelaces of the sneakers. The quack had given him a cane before leaving the room. And now he looked at himself in a mirror, light flannel shirt over a T-shirt, pants—just another schmuck in the big ole US of A. His ID, any item that could identify him as Bobby Tremain, was back in his penthouse. He imagined himself home, meditatively rubbing his feet over the Persian silk carpet, sipping a shot of Four Roses on the rocks. *Soon*, he promised himself.

The sun was headed for the tree line by the time he emerged from the rural clinic. The parking lot was barren but for the buzzing of flies. 'Margaretville Family Clinic' was stenciled on the front door, right above the sign that said 'Closed'. The quack drove a dinged-up Ford SUV. Tremain was able to hoist himself into the passenger seat. He hoped his exit would be smoother than his entrance from the helicopter.

The drive was twenty minutes of darkening woods, mountain cabins, and sagging houses set too close to the road. No small talk. Tremain knew there was no point to asking the doctor about who had paid for his services.

The town was small, basically one main street. They passed a proper hospital, and then some cafes, tourist shops, and a bowling alley. The quack pulled up beside a CVS, killed the engine, dug into a pocket and handed Tremain a bunch of folded twenties. "Oh yeah, and this." Another pocket yielded a tear of paper with a phone number. "That's the Catskills taxi service. There's a phone in the drug store. It'll take you anywhere within an hour's drive."

Tremain counted two hundred bucks. Enough, he supposed, to get him back to the city with a stop to eat along the way. The pain in his thigh was dull, and his empty stomach now demanded his attention.

"Do you need to take out stitches, anything like that?"

"No. And don't come back. Ever, for anything. If the wound bleeds or becomes infected, or if it becomes cold and numb, go find help somewhere else." The man's voice trembled. Whatever deal the doc had made to oblige him to patch up a stranger—perhaps one struck long ago—he was regretting it now. Men with the jitters could be a risk. "I never saw you, okay pal? And you definitely never saw me."

Tremain grabbed the quack's lapel and pulled him close. "I know where to find you. Just remember that."

* * *

Tremain changed his mind as the taxi driver neared Pough-keepsie, getting off in town to find a new ride. He was acting on instinct, which he trusted, and his memory, which was trained.

After using a phone at a dry cleaners' to get a new taxi, he filled the wait time by grabbing a Big Mac. Then he instructed the new driver to take him to Short Hills, New Jersey. By the time he completed his journey, he had exchanged the melancholy homes on isolated Catskill Mountain roads for this suburb's six-bedroom modern mansions atop sweeping lawns. His destination, a farmhouse bereft of its fields, felt a little less prominent than its neighbors and slightly less tended to; a memory of an earlier community before all the New Yorkers had moved in. The house sat in a basin rather than on high ground, with a barn on the property; a reminder of what this place once was.

Tremain considered his options and ruled out the direct approach. The barn door was locked, but there was a narrow side door, also locked but with a latch that felt loose. He walked around, not sure what to look for, and came across a flower bed overrun with weeds, ringed by fist-sized rocks. He hefted one—it would do. He removed his shirt, wrapped it around the latch, thumped it off and chucked the rock into the grass.

Then he wandered a safe distance away and waited for an hour. Nothing happened; the barn wasn't alarmed. He went back and entered, making out the shape of two cars in the converted garage. One car sat low and the other stood tall as a sentry.

He awoke to his second strange dawn. The barn door and cracks between the planks of its walls glowed. He had caught sleep in the passenger seat of a BMW luxury SUV. The other car was a Porsche Boxer, and with his injury, Tremain doubted he could winch himself in there.

Now he popped a Percocet and ignored the rumbles in his stomach. He waited with the gun on the dashboard. Before long, electricity hummed and the barn door ground open along metal tracks.

Tremain slid out, using his cane, and raised his gun hand to shield his eyes from the sunlight. As he hobbled backwards into shadow, a man entered. He had a slouch and a paunch, a head of frizzy hair and fat glasses. He walked toward the BMW; then he stopped, saw the line of sunlight ending right on the mouth of the Glock, and raised his hands.

"You won't find much worth to steal," the man said. "But go ahead."

Tremain stepped into the light. "Hello, Walt."

Walter Klinger squinted. "Jesus fucking Christ."

"Lovely to see you too."

Klinger relaxed his arms, but Tremain gestured with the pistol. "Where I can see them."

"Really, we're going through this charade?"

"Tell me about Red Fidelity."

"What kind of question is that?"

"When you release it, it's not a worm. It's not Stuxnet or something that takes out a power plant."

"If I slow clap, you going to shoot me?"

"You wrote it using quantum computing languages. Do we have the hardware to execute it?"

"Finally, someone asks me the right question." Klinger seemed genuinely pleased.

That sent a chill down Tremain's spine. Who else had been asking questions? "You're a popular guy now, hunh? What's that mean?"

Klinger shrugged. "It means if you're asking about Red Fidelity, get in fucking line."

Tremain was tempted to pull that thread, but he'd come back to it. He knew too little about the zero-day. "Who does have that kind of hardware?"

"The Chinks. Our big tech companies. Maybe the Aussies and the Japs."

"Russians?"

"In their dreams."

"If I sold Red Fidelity on the black market, how would someone use it?"

"Using a classical computer, it's your average unstoppable ransomware. Well, maybe more than average. Probably put a few banks out of business."

"The NSA developed something to bring down our financial system?"

"Not ours. China's or whoever's. But of course, once something like that's released in the wild...it's like chemical warfare, blows right back into our trench. Depends on how good Wall Street's been at patching their tech stacks."

Tremain guessed that was what Volkov wanted. Sell it into the market, no Russian fingerprints, and trigger a financial meltdown in the West. Payback for Ukraine, or just because

Russia under Vladimir Putin had become a big North Korea and was in the chaos game.

He didn't mind selling this thing on the black market, of course; everything has its price. But the foreknowledge was helpful. Anyone who hardened their systems in advance would make a killing on the rebound.

"And if someone ran this program in a quantum computer?"

"Ever hear of Peter Shor?" Klinger parried.

"Famous math guy. MIT, right?"

"Right. Back in the 1990s he developed what's now known as Shor's Algorithm."

Tremain had spent his time in Hawaii doing ops, not the nerd stuff. He waved his gun. "Skip to the sexy part, Walt."

"Whoever's first with that algo and enough qubit power can unzip every secret that's been encrypted digitally. Unlock the deepest, darkest secrets, from bank accounts to nuclear codes."

Tremain didn't have much time to think this through, but it was obvious why the Russians would want this. But they *had* it. Tremain had bought it from Klinger thinking it was malware and sold it to them, basic middleman stuff. Then Dimitri Mahalin had entered the picture—Dimitri and Annika Volkov—and asked him to set up the auction.

"How do you make it do that?" he asked.

"Bobby, it's been great seeing you and all, but can I put my hands down and go to work?"

"How does it do that, Walter?" His shout made Klinger flinch. Good.

"There's no way to test it with the limited hardware we've got. I modeled it. But that's back when we were in the Firm. When, as I recall, you made me promise never to try to find you."

"I am aware that this meeting is a risk."

"Oh, you're aware. Gee, how comforting." Klinger put his hands down. "Fuck this, man. We did what we did, we got paid, end of story."

"Do you have the hardware?"

"Q Vectors? We have prototypes, cloud-based services. We sell time to Big Tech, some universities." That unhinged grin of his. "The coed interns are a major perk."

"What would you do with Red Fidelity if you had it?"

"Nothing. Wouldn't make me any money, and my idea of retirement doesn't include being forgotten in a CIA black site."

"How many people know what Red Fidelity's real purpose is? Not as malware, but a decryption protocol?"

"Couple people from the old days. That's it, far as I know." If Klinger was telling the truth, then the Russians hadn't known what was embedded in the code when Tremain sold it to them. Now they knew.

Time to wrap this up. "You said someone was asking questions."

"And making educated guesses," Klinger said.

"Who?"

Klinger stuffed his hands in his blazer pockets. "Enough, Bobby. You want that information, make me a deal."

Tremain knew he could have shot Klinger. Popped him in the gut—not immediately fatal, just a slow bleed out. Prove he wasn't bluffing. *Talk and live, bullshit me and die.* But it was too risky. Even one isolated gunshot would attract attention in this neighborhood. Besides, Klinger was already frightened; the chest-puffing was a feint. If Tremain shot to wound, Klinger might think he didn't have a chance.

He kept the gun up but lowered its angle. "Okay, Walt. I'm in the broker business. Red Fidelity's come back to me and I'm looking to sell. Malware version. Help me and get a cut. I'm talking a million bucks here."

"The original buyer made a copy? And sold it back to you? Anyone will be able to tell. It's damaged goods, Bobby."

"The malware version is. Maybe not the quantum side."

Klinger shook his curly head. "How do you know it's the real deal? You analyze the code yourself?" Knowing, of course, Tremain couldn't read code.

It didn't matter. If the Russians had bought it and were now asking him to put it back on the market, it was either junk and they wanted to screw somebody else to recoup their investment, or they knew exactly what Red Fidelity could do. And they wanted Tremain to find a way to unleash it.

"I know it's attracting bids," Tremain said.

Klinger stepped forward and leaned on the hood of his BMW SUV. Tremain retreated a half step and Klinger noticed the cane. "Looks like you're attracting more than business offers," he said.

Tremain nodded. "I have enemies, sure. Like I said, this exploit's generated a lot of excitement. The offer is twenty million dollars. My cut's fifteen percent. Help me, Walt, and a third of that is yours."

Klinger guffawed. "We're going to sign a contract, Bobby? Should I have my lawyers check it out?" His fear was sub-siding, and he was still leaning against the hood, but half a step closer. Tremain was aware he couldn't pull back further. "I like my money, sure," Klinger said. "Geniuses deserve their rewards, and the Firm was never going to give me what I deserved. But it wasn't my idea to sell anything to the

Russians. Yet I'm the one who gets hounded out of my career, my name smeared in the press."

"You passed that shit to me for cash."

"And here you are, the golden boy—the golden sellout who deserves the electric chair—hiding in my garage, barely able to stand straight, thinking he's going to tell me what to do. Fuck you, Bobby."

Tremain pressed the snub of the gun against Klinger's forehead. "Don't," he said.

Klinger tried to sound brave. "You're on the run, Bobby. You can't help me. You can't help yourself." His voice was shaking.

"Tell me who else is asking about Red Fidelity."

Klinger's eyes crossed on the metal shaft pressing his skull. That lopsided grin again. He backed up a step. "One's a Fed. The other's a reporter."

Tremain pulled the gun back. Its snout glistened with Klinger's perspiration. "Go on."

"Fed's named Malcolm Belmont. Goes by the name—"

"Braun."

"You're acquainted."

"And the reporter?"

Klinger was restoring his courage. "Fine piece of ass named Justine Jarman. Pretending to be a buyer. A little old for me, but I'd still do her. What do you say, Bobby, did I earn my mil?"

"Sure, Walt." Tremain was ready to make his peace and his exit, thoughts already jumping to make sense of this information, when Klinger's fist came out of his blazer pocket with a car key wedged between his fingers and he slashed it across Tremain's face.

Klinger's weight sent him crashing against the barn wall, cane gone. Klinger followed the key with his other fist, a haymaker. Tremain was on the ground now, everything spinning, Klinger's shoe smashing the back of his wounded thigh, lights popping, pain unleashed like a writhing eel, mouth agape, eyes hungry.

Flopping arms and hands, knuckles grazed the cane. Klinger stooping to get the gun. Tremain didn't have leverage on the ground, but he didn't need it—just a snap of the cane, like a bunt, right between Klinger's spread legs. A whack on the testicles was a guaranteed showstopper. Tremain was already dropping the cane and reaching for the Glock. He didn't have time to fix on a target but at point blank it was hard not to hit something.

Klinger collapsed back onto the hood, which was now splattered with his blood. Tremain, ears blown, sat up as Klinger staggered toward the open barn door. Now he took the time to aim.

Chapter 23

Justine walked into the *Archer's* office, the elevator dinging behind her, and made a bee line for her desk. She was wearing leftovers from her apartment: ripped jeans, boots, white crewneck T, and a cropped blazer the hue of a cigar. Sporty enough for walking in Manhattan, yet comfortable enough for a day she intended to spend at her desk.

Since Covid, the once-hectic buzz had become a somnolent hum, forlorn desks waiting like jilted lovers. Paul Chow was there, of course, in his glass-encased chrysalis. He stared at his computer screen with a look of weary resignation— probably budget time.

The office had gone open plan years ago, when she, Patty and Bert had occupied a corner table and dared anyone to usurp their turf. She had adopted Josh when he was an intern; he was their junior associate now, and it was his turn to bring the bagels.

"What do you have there?" she asked, setting down her shoulder bag. "Any onion?"

"Onion?" Josh's smile faltered. "Uh, I got poppyseed and sesame, and, uh, plain."

Patty smeared cream cheese on hers, shaking her head. "Kid wants to be a reporter but doesn't pay attention to what people order."

"Sorry," Josh said.

"It's all right," Justine said, taking the sesame. "They're all good."

Bert put down his coffee and patted his mustache with a napkin. He was wearing an orange and white trucker cap with the Gatorade logo. "J.J. always gets the onion."

"Onion. Next time," Josh said.

"And I get the Everything," Bert said. "Remember that too." He took a big bite.

Justine picked up the latest print edition of the magazine—fresh out of the box, distributed around the office. A janitor in overalls was already hanging up a framed copy a few desks down, filling in the last corners of white space. Taylor Swift regarded the office from her new perch on the wall.

"What's Paul got for us this morning?" Justine asked, flipping through the pages.

"Gotham Gossip," Patty said.

"I thought that was Ben's beat," Justine said.

"Ben's on vacay. Remember those?"

Justine spread cream cheese on her bagel. Gone were the days when an investigative reporter focused just on her project. Paul Chow still had an edition to get out every week, and the senior correspondents and their teams were expected to contribute. Most of Patty's time was spent condensing features into online stories, and Bert was usually off turning city anecdotes into video clips.

They had spent extra hours on Justine's quest because they were loyal to her, knew it was an incredible story, and were also transfixed by its quixotic nature. She was going on year three of trying to pose as a buyer in the black market for oh-days, and suddenly after being a curiosity, the auction and the shooting had busted the story open.

But Paul wasn't about to give them too much leash.

"All right, what tidbits have we got?" Justine asked. Gotham Gossip was a six-page roundup of weird anecdotes from around the city. *Archer's* staple. She hadn't missed this part of the job.

Josh was scouring his mobile. The dailies were one source, although *Archer's* staff writers were supposed to leverage their curiosity and social position to find their own juicy tales. Josh paused to read something.

"Find anything good?" Justine asked.

"What was the name of that guy again?"

"Guy, what guy?"

"The sleazy guy you visited the other day. Downtown."

"Walter Klinger?"

Josh held up his mobile. "That him?"

She read the local police-beat story from New Jersey. It might not have gotten mentioned except that Short Hills was such a wealthy area.

"Well, what?" Patty demanded.

"Klinger's dead," she said. "Shot twice in his garage."

"Holy shit," Patty said, coming around to peer over Justine's shoulder.

"Good work, Josh. Patty, Bert, let's go," Justine said. "We need to find out everything we can." She was already crossing the office.

"But what about Gotham Gossip?" Josh wondered.

"*Buena suerte, amigo*," Bert said, pushing aside his unfinished breakfast.

"You're in charge of that now," Patty said.

"Me? But, but..."

"This is your big break, kiddo," Patty told him as she hurried after Justine.

* * *

They reached Klinger's house just before eleven, Bert having the benefit of going opposite the end of rush hour traffic. The barn was latticed by yellow police tape, and a cruiser sat in the driveway. Unmarked cars lined the suburban street.

"Take photos of everything," Justine said.

Bert nodded, removing the cap from his Nikon, which looked like a toy in his beefy hands.

Patty, in the van's rear, had a laptop open and was typing furiously.

"Bluetooth on?" Justine asked, shifting her mobile from her jeans pocket to one inside her jacket. Patty gave her a thumbs-up and she got out of the van.

Patty had already filed a request to interview the officer in charge from the county police's public information officer, but she had warned it might not get approved before the evening, if the PIO approved it at all. The richer the district, the less likely the cops felt like talking to reporters.

Bert took snaps of the barn as Justine walked down the long driveway, noting the farmhouse and the disheveled grounds. Newer, bigger McMansions towered over the scene at a distance. A young, white uniformed policeman met her halfway to the house. Good. Justine hadn't wanted to tangle with a female.

"I'm sorry, ma'am, but this is a crime scene. Gonna have to ask you to leave."

She presented him with her business card. "Officer, my name's Justine Jarman. I'm a reporter at *Archer's*. I've filed my PIO, and they've assured me it'll get approved."

The cop handed back her card while checking her out. "Sorry."

"Are you the officer in charge?" She didn't take the card back.

"No, ma'am, but it doesn't matter."

"Doesn't matter that I'm from *Archer's*?" She flicked her hair. "You've heard of *Archer's*, right?"

He looked uncomfortable, then sighed and clicked the mic strapped to his chest. "Lieutenant Lewis there? I got a lady out here, says she's a reporter from…" He had to squint at her card. "Archie's." Then he saw Bert taking pictures. "Hey, sir, you can't be there!"

Lieutenant Lewis was a plainclothes investigator—forties, white, with a hangdog look and eyes that had seen too much. He came out from the farmhouse and crossed the unkempt lawn. "You'll need permission first," he said.

"I know," she said, "and I've got my POI in, but this is an *Archer's* story, and I want to make sure we're as accurate as possible. Isn't that what you want too, Detective?"

"I hear that one every day from you people," he said, but added, "*Archer's*. What's this to a society magazine?"

She wanted to tell him it wasn't a society magazine, it was a literary pillar of New York and American cultural life, but she smiled and said, "We've been looking into Walter Klinger. Want to trade notes?"

"You first."

"He ran a secretive technology company called Q-Ventures that specializes in cloud-based applications for quantum computer researchers. He was hounded out of Columbia University for sexual harassment. And he's ex National Security Agency."

The detective lifted an eyebrow but didn't give away anything. He let out a long sigh as he looked beyond her shoulder. She turned and saw people walking from one of the unmarked cars. Upright, they strode with purpose, one carrying a large steel box, both wearing ties and sunglasses and dark blue windbreakers marked with a big yellow FBI.

"That's interesting," Detective Lewis said, "and I didn't know that, but they do."

"What's the FBI doing here?"

He shrugged. "They took over the case half an hour ago."

"Did they say why?"

"Nope. And that's all I can tell you, Miss...Jarman. I'm no longer the officer in charge."

* * *

Night fell and the offices of *Archer's* turned ghostly. Only Paul remained in his illuminated office, rubbing his eyes beneath his glasses. Justine powered down and stuffed her laptop in her shoulder bag. She, Patty and Bert had spent the day like crime reporters: asking the neighbors what they had seen or heard; going to the Short Hills's coroner's office; checking whether Klinger had any attorneys representing his estate. The police POI request came back declining their request for an interview, so Patty filed one with the FBI, but no one had much confidence in that.

At the end they didn't have much more than was officially reported on the police website and what she could find on

LexisNexis. Someone had broken and entered the barn. Two shots fired a little after seven that morning. Cops were reviewing any nearby street cameras for clues. Nothing about what else may have gone down, if Klinger had been robbed, or any physical evidence from the murder scene. The scandal from Columbia was mentioned, but no comment on whether that was a line of questioning.

What the police website didn't mention: that the case had been turned over to the FBI.

Her feet ached and she was suddenly starving. She messaged Steve to tell him she'd be home soon, asked if she should pick up anything. No, he'd eaten. She took the subway, one hand in her bag clutching her bottle of pepper spray—she had once trusted this city's byways with her life, but those days were long gone—and picked up Chinese takeout on the way to the Gramercy apartment. She unlocked the door and found the duplex's downstairs quiet. "Steve?"

"Up here."

"I'll be down here."

Moo shu pork straight out of the white carton box, a Yuengling beer from Steve's fridge. She was halfway through when he came down, beard needing a trim, in his Rolling Stones T-shirt and shorts. He paused to appraise her.

"What?" she asked.

He folded his arms and leaned against the doorway. "Just wondering who this beautiful stranger is in my kitchen."

"Whoever she is, she's exhausted."

He stepped behind her and began to massage her shoulders. "Ace reporter crack her case?"

It felt good so she paused her eating and closed her eyes. "Not yet."

"Getting close?"

"I thought so. But one of my contacts was killed this morning."

His hands stopped. "What?"

"It might not have anything to do with anything."

He faced her across the table. "Justine, tell me this is going to end."

"Do I tell you to stop working for those asshole clients of yours?"

"I haven't seen you in three days, and now you tell me one of your sources is dead?"

She took a swig of beer, regretting having said anything. "It's not like that."

"What's it like, Justine?"

"I'm tired. Can we not talk about this?"

"You can't disappear and then pop up and tell me someone's been killed and not talk about it."

"Fine." She got up and put the takeout box in the trash. "Then I'll leave."

"Justine, come on."

"I'm not having this conversation, Steve."

"I'm asking because I'm worried about you. I love you. And now you're turning your back on me."

"I'm cleaning up after dinner."

"Goddammit, Justine! When are we going back to normal?"

She whirled on him. "Back to what?"

"Normal. You know, when you lived here and we were a family and we spent all our time together."

"That was during Covid, Steve. The city was shut down."

"Covid? You shacked up here because of Covid?"

"No, that's not what I mean."

"Jesus, Justine, I was your Covid fuck buddy, was that it?"

"Steve, don't be a child."

He fumed. "You're something else, you know that? You're really something else."

She remembered when he had used almost the same words, a long time ago, in the aftermath of their first kiss.

"Okay, then I'm something else," she said. "Where's Zach?"

"I don't know. Out."

"Is he alright?"

"I'm not sure it's your business anymore."

"What does that mean?"

"You know what he's going through. What I'm going through. Between him and the school principal, it's like I've been on eggshells."

"Sorry. So is he okay?"

"Honestly, Justine, I don't know. He comes home, *if* he comes home, goes straight in his room, shuts the door and plays video games."

"And the school?"

"There's a hearing tomorrow. Whether or not to kick him out."

"Oh jeez."

"Yeah."

He was now standing in front of her. He stroked her cheek, pulled away a strand of her blonde hair. "You had a bad day too..."

She nodded. "Exhausting."

He traced a finger down the spine of her ear. "So tell me about it."

"No. Too frustrating."

He took her hands and kissed her. She kissed him back, but she was too tired to get into it. When he squeezed her breast, she pushed him away.

"Why not?" he asked.

"I'm too tired."

"Maybe you could use some Stevie wonder."

"Not now." She brushed past him for the stairs, thinking she should have gone to her own place.

"Okay," he said, "we'll save it for the morning."

"Please, Steve. I need to stay focused."

He was bewildered. "You can't have sex because you need to stay focused?"

"That's right. So long as I'm undercover, I need to stay sharp."

"Why, so you can sleep with another source?"

At one point he would have been cute, with his beard and his not-bad dad bod, the trendy architecture job and the grit to raise a child alone, and she would have probably pulled him close or pushed him against a wall and gone in for the lunge. But he had decided to dredge the ugly stuff. Nuclear option.

"To give people the truth."

She walked upstairs, not interested in hearing his rebuttal.

Chapter 24

"What are we missing?" Segreti asked.

It was the nine-a.m. meeting, downtown in the windowless conference room that Segreti's team had made their own. Beneath the unforgiving fluorescent lights was a cork billboard illustrating what they knew about Robert Tremain and a zero-day allegedly stolen from the NSA— "allegedly" because the DOJ had said it maybe, might be, and the NSA had refused to say anything. Didn't matter that someone had tried to assassinate a federal agent; NSA wasn't fessing up to losing their top goods. Segreti found it easier to get mad than to contemplate the sound of the bullet whizzing past his head.

He added a new photo to the board. "Walter Klinger, murdered yesterday at his home in New Jersey between seven-oh-five and seven-ten a.m. Former software developer at NSA." He tapped the dead man's picture. "His time on Oahu overlaps with Tremain's."

Ram, Chlebek, Belmont. Open files occupying the conference table, marred by the stains of vending-machine coffee. Belmont with a notebook, Chlebek with a laptop, Ram with a hangover.

Chlebek typed. "He had four partners in Q-Ventures. And he got fired from Colombia on a harassment charge."

"Find those partners. Interview the school, and whoever accused him."

"On it, sir."

"Ballistics filed their report last night," Segreti said, pawing through his manila folder. "Two shots from a single weapon. One frontal, very close range, the second from ten feet, kill shot to the back of the head. Signs of a struggle. We think the perp shot Klinger the first time from the ground, maybe after fighting over the weapon. The second time looks like Klinger was trying to get away before the perp shot him again."

"Any DNA?" Belmont asked. "Seems messy."

"Forensics says it hasn't found anything. The perp was methodical. Wiped his prints and took the cartridges. We only have the bullets and Klinger's body. The first bullet was lodged in a ceiling beam, and the second one's in Klinger's skull. They're nine-millimeter, and from a Glock, probably the nineteen, gen four or five, but possibly from the seventeen."

"There's a lot of Glocks out there," Ram said.

"Yeah," Segreti snarled, "including mine." Pointing at Tremain's photo. "I think Tremain's the shooter."

"Any DNA traces on the bullets?" Chlebek asked.

"Still running tests," Segreti said. "That takes time." They all knew the tests would probably prove inconclusive.

"You're going with that theory to ADIC?" Belmont asked. "Sir?"

Segreti walked to the map filling most of the corkboard. "Tremain was wounded by sniper fire two nights ago here. We think he and a shooter escaped with Scuba equipment. So in the space of two days, Tremain somehow disappeared into Raritan Bay, got himself patched up, and appeared here, in Short Hills, yesterday morning, and killed a former colleague."

"Forgive me, sir, but that's a stretch," Ram said.

"Not if he's working with these people," Segreti said, tapping a yellow Post-It Note, on which he had written: *Dimitri Mahalin – Shadow?* Beneath it was the rendering of the woman, presumably Russian, also seen on the Arab's yacht, presence unknown. "The Russians are using a yacht big enough to have a helicopter pad. What else is that thing carrying?"

Ram rubbed his temples. "Occam's razor, sir. The simplest answer is that Tremain washed up on land and somehow avoided law enforcement."

"How would they get to the yacht?" Chlebek asked.

"He thinks they have a submersible," Ram said.

"It's a theory," Belmont said. "But do these pieces really fit? We don't know how the Russians got a hold of an oh-day developed by the NSA, but they hire Tremain to sell it on the black market. We arrest Tremain and his lawyers spring him. A Russian diplomat is linked to the yacht, and maybe that suspect at the auction was Russian, but we have no other information on his whereabouts. Tremain calls you, asking to meet. At the meeting, two snipers open fire. I tag one, the other one gets away, along with Tremain. That's all we've got, sir."

"That's not all we've got, Belmont. You questioned Klinger shortly before he was killed."

"As part of a canvassing of anyone whose profiles include cybersecurity and quantum computing, yes, sir."

"How many of these people have you identified and con-tacted?"

"Contacted, three. Identified, more than fifty from our

records.”

“But only Klinger ends up dead.”

“What about that shooter that Belmont took out?” Ram asked.

Segreti thumbed through another file and pulled out a biopsy. “Here’s our John Doe. Coroner’s got no ID. Asian male, mid-thirties, five foot eight, two hundred pounds. A little facial hair. No tattoos or markings. Prints not in any of our databases. Doesn’t smoke, last meal was a burger, high concentration of alcohol in the bloodstream. Genome test suggests ancestry in far northwest of Asia. Siberia?”

“Doesn’t tell us anything about where he’s actually from,” Chlebek said. “He could be a US citizen who just never got into trouble.”

“Or he infiltrated our borders via a submersible,” Segreti said. “The same sub that carried Tremain and the other shooter away. Tremain was brokering a sale of that oh-day for a Russian. And we know the Russians are on that yacht. Tremain requests an exchange of information, but we’re attacked at the meet, Tremain takes a bullet, and leaves with the other shooter. Back to the yacht. He then appears in New Jersey with a Glock, maybe mine, and shoots Klinger.”

“Maybe Klinger had something to do with Red Fidelity?” Ram wondered.

Belmont said, “When I interviewed him at his office, Klinger said he was under oath to never disclose his work at the NSA. I asked about the quantum angle, but for someone meant to be a leading expert in the field, he had nothing to say.”

“So what the fuck *is* this thing?” Segreti shouted. “Whatever Red Fidelity is, the one guy who might have told us is now dead, and the guy selling it probably killed him. That’s probable cause for a warrant."

"A warrant for what?" Chlebek asked. "We've already got arrest warrants out for Tremain."

"For a wire on that yacht and everyone who's aboard."

"Church won't go for it," Ram said. "We need more."

"What we need is to establish a Moscow connection. Link their consulate, something like that... ID somebody."

Ram buried his face in his hands. "I know where this is going."

"Not a stakeout," Chlebek protested.

"Stakeout," Segreti said. "We keep an eye on Russian properties in the city."

"You want us sitting on our asses for how long exactly?" Ram asked.

"Until I get Church to open the electronic cookie jar," Segreti said.

Belmont, softly, mused, "Sir, that could take..."

Segreti raised a silencing finger. He picked up the conference room's landline and punched a number. It rang twice.

"Computer forensics lab," replied a young woman. The rookie.

"Agent Taylor, right?"

"Special Agent," she corrected him.

"Special Agent in Charge Ed Segreti from the cyber unit. I'm in meeting room three oh two. Can you come up? Now?"

"Yes, sir."

Chlebek frowned. "Last time I spoke with her, she didn't know her ass from her elbow."

"She's young," Segreti said. "She'll get the hang of it. Like we all did."

"But we need her to get us answers now," Chlebek said.

"Your hearing—"

"I'll worry about bureau politics," Segreti said. "You stay focused. Who wants another coffee?"

After a few minutes someone knocked and he told her to come in. Helen Taylor entered with a nervous grin. She took a seat, ramrod straight—a tree amid slouching bushes.

"Okay, Taylor, all of those devices in your lab, the haul from North Brother Island... What can you tell us?"

"Well, sir, I've filed my Streamlined Forensic Report and a request for further data investigation—"

Segreti pushed a folder across to her. "Which you'll find signed."

"Thank you, sir." She gave the cover page a quick glance. "I'll get to work at once."

"Wait, before you go. We need some help. The metadata. Where those phones have been."

Taylor surveyed the room and saw jaundiced impatience. "It's against best practice to speculate without a proper accounting of the data," she said. "Sir."

Segreti took a seat opposite her and leaned in. "I know, Taylor, and you have a lot of work left to do. But can you tell us if those phones were purchased outside of the US?"

"Tracing devices is a lengthy business."

"But you can tell if they've traveled."

"Geolocation, of course, but the warrant..."

"Look, Taylor, we need to know if any of those devices have been used in the past three months in Russia, Cyprus, or from a boat in the Hudson River or Raritan Bay."

"I..."

"Have you unlocked those devices?" Chlebek asked her.

"I know how to. I'm just waiting for the proper authority."

"Taylor, look at me," Segreti said. "I'm the proper authority, and I need to know, today, if any of those devices have traveled to those places. Do you understand?"

Taylor took another account of the room. "Yes, sir. I'll get you a report by lunchtime."

"I don't need a formal report," he said. "Just...I'll come by around one o'clock and you can fill me in. Got it?" He gave his team a wink.

Taylor stood up. "I think so."

* * *

Segreti went out for lunch after filing a request for any info on James Fiorinetti or anyone with his driver's license number. Probably nothing to it, and no need to tell Ram about his daughter's boyfriend. But Segreti wanted to be careful. The paperwork took only ten minutes, and then he had a pile more to clear. And now he needed a break from the building, from the chaos on his desk, from the update that ADIC Church had sent him last night about the bureau's hearing on the shooting on North Brother Island. His fate was to be decided on Monday. Tremain's lawyers were filing motions naming the FBI and Segreti as defendants. And the NSA was working the corridors of Washington. They really wanted to get their code back.

The bravura from the conference room wilted in the summer humidity.

The Shadow had disappeared. Tremain was on the loose. Klinger was dead. Red Fidelity was waiting to be triggered.

And all of this might get taken away from him.

He went to a nearby Chipotle and ate a taco bowl. The fine weather had turned muggy, as if conspiring with his circumstances to add to his heaviness. It was time to broaden this thing, go to the SIGINT unit tasked with spying on foreign consulates.

As he returned to Javits, he was intercepted on foot by a bike messenger in bright canary and orange cycling gear with a pouch Velcroed across his chest. "Agent Edward Segreti?"

By instinct he reached for his sidearm, forgetting that he hadn't been issued a new one yet. Daylight out front of FBI headquarters—uniformed police officers, plenty of pedestrians.

"Who wants to know?"

"Special delivery," the messenger said, ripping open his pouch. He withdrew a fat envelope. "I just need to make sure it's for the right Edward Segreti, of four thirty-one Dorchester Street in Chevy Chase, Maryland."

"Yeah, that's me," Segreti said.

The messenger threw the envelope and it struck Segreti in the chest.

"You been served."

He knew what it might be. But he forced alternatives to the front of his mind: a gift from Jake. Or maybe a problem at school. Or the update to her will Katie had been talking about ever since her father died. A medical emergency?

He bent down and used his apartment key to slice through the tape. From Katie, all right.

He read the words but didn't process them. The idea seemed like gibberish. They had been through too much. Plenty of arguments, tears—mostly hers, but still—and some histrionics. Hers. His too. Slammed doors and reconciliations. For Jake. Always for Jake.

But for more than their son. For family. The bedrock. That's what he had pledged. Across the altar. Taking communion. The family was the first society, the start of the Church, the bedrock of believing in Jesus Christ as his redeemer, the ultimate granite of America.

All that and...the humiliation, which burned through him now, hollowing him out. Like a goddammed enema of fire and resentment.

He noticed the people going in and out of Javits, but he didn't see them. Lawyers, cops, the luckless and the unloved, they were just a hive of scorn poised to jeer.

Segreti returned the divorce papers to the envelope, obscuring their heresy, and stalked back inside.

Chapter 25

Justine overslept and was relieved to awake to an empty bedroom. Steve's desktop monitor was blank. He must have gone to the office.

She made a coffee downstairs and flicked through her messages. Paul Chow's reminder about filing expenses. Josh's Gotham Gossip piece, awaiting an edit. And from Bert: he'd been pulled onto another assignment.

She called him and he picked up. She could hear the hum of his van's engine.

"Hey, what's up," she asked.

"Paul put me with Gregor on this royal visit thing."

She squished her eyes and took a deep breath. "You're my videographer, Bert."

"I know. But, Justine, there hasn't been any video. I haven't shot a single frame. Not even B-roll."

She knew he was right. Bert was loyal but he was a cameraman, not her chauffeur.

"Can you help me out tonight?" she asked. "I want to get some shots of Belmont."

"Um, leave Marta with the kids on a Friday night?"

She wanted to say, yes, of course, but she knew that was both wrong and stupid. "Sorry. I forgot what day it is."

"Take a break, J.J. Seriously."

She went back upstairs to collect her laptop. Friday already. Should she come back for dinner? See how much of yesterday's argument could be unsaid? Or maybe just go back to the Upper West Side, get takeout pad thai and watch a movie on Netflix. And then, after midnight, take the train to Brooklyn, put on a pair of gloves, and go through Belmont's trash bin to see what she could find out about the guy. She'd already looked it up: Bed-Stuy trash got collected Saturday mornings, so tonight he'd have a container full of clues.

As she came back down, laptop in its satchel slung over her shoulder, she saw Zach's bedroom door ajar. She knocked. "Zach?"

"Yeah."

She let herself in. He was on his bed, still wearing his sneakers, scrolling his cell phone.

"Your dad's at work."

Grunt. Language of a sort.

"Your hearing was today, wasn't it? Want to talk about it?"

Shrug. For a teenager, almost verbosity.

She set her bag down and planted herself in his desk chair. "It's okay if you don't want to tell me. But you'll have to tell your dad."

"Maybe you can tell him."

"Me? No, hon, you need to tell him yourself."

His eyes were languid beneath the fiery curls of his hair, as though he had reached a peace. Or a resignation.

"Besides," she added, "I might not be around tonight."

"Your case?"

"Yeah—no. No, not work. I just feel like a little me time, you know?"

"You guys fight again?"

"No, nothing like that." Her lie was so obvious that it sparked his interest.

"He's a dick," Zach said. "I get it."

"No, he's not," spoken with enough conviction that she believed it. "I'm the dick. I haven't been around."

His phone was pulling him back in. "Whatever."

"I have to go to work. You going to be okay?"

A nod.

"Call me if you need anything." She picked up her satchel.

She was opening the door when: "Justine?"

"Yes?"

"They didn't expel me for drugs."

"Oh, that's a relief."

"They expelled me...for something else."

She froze. Although his eyes bowed down to his cell, he wasn't looking at it. He was staring intently at an invisible charm located somewhere around his knees. Part of her wanted to run. Let Steve deal with his son. Get the ex, whats-her-name, back if the kid needed a mommy. But she had befriended him. At first, just to get into his graces so she could date Steve. Along the way, though, the buddy act had matured into something better. "If there's something you want to say, you know I've got your back."

"Thing is, you can't tell Dad."

She was wading in deep now, should have just left Steve's apartment instead of butting into Zach's business. But she couldn't just switch him off—not now. "Is it something you're going to have to tell him eventually?"

He nodded. "Yeah, I believe so."

I believe so. He sounded like an adult. "Then you can tell me first, but whatever it is, you're going to have to be the one to tell your dad too."

He bit his lip, but he looked as though he had already made up his mind to trust her. "That's okay," he said. "But maybe if you're there. You know."

"I will be. Promise."

He looked her in the eye. "I'm gay."

She almost choked because she had feared something horrible had happened. It was obviously difficult for him, but she had to repress a look of relief. "That's cool," she said.

"I figured you'd be okay with it."

"Is this something that just happened?"

"No. Just something that I have to, um, talk about now."

"Okay. Well, Zach, honey, I'm proud of you for being open about this. Do you have a boyfriend?"

"I wouldn't call him that."

She showed her palms. "Hey, it's none of my business. I just want you to be happy and safe."

He picked up his phone again. "Yeah, well...."

This wasn't over. "But you said you were expelled. Want to tell me why?"

His face flushed. He had that long stare again. Whatever he needed to say was having a hard time convincing his mouth to let it out.

"We got caught." He attempted a veneer of defiance, but she could see right through it to the shame. "At school."

This could be serious. "You and...another student?" Please let it be another student.

"Yeah."

"And it was...consensual?"

He nodded.

"Nobody touched you or did something—"

"It was consensual."

"Okay, okay." She felt her heart skip ahead, grateful that he didn't feel inclined to share the details. "So now you're going to have to tell your dad. Is that it?"

Zach nodded.

"Well, look... your dad loves you and he won't care if you're gay. I'm sure you don't have anything to worry about." Except the part about getting expelled, but one thing at a time.

Barely a nod. The incipient adult was ceding back to the teenager.

"When do you plan on telling him?"

"I don't know. But you have to be here." He reached for his PlayStation console.

Conversation over.

* * *

Staking out Belmont's brownstone was a lot harder without Bert's van. Justine and Patty couldn't just stand on his street for a couple of hours. She didn't even know which apartment belonged to Belmont. A1 to B4, take your pick. Patty counted the apartments with lights on inside, which narrowed it down, but they couldn't be sure Belmont was even home.

She suggested they walk a loop, returning to Decatur Street in twenty-minute intervals, peering into the alley behind his building to see if the trash had been taken out. By the third or fourth shift, she realized they must stick out—a white blonde woman and a Japanese woman in a Black neighborhood appearing over and over.

An old lady in a ragged coat and winter woolen cap seemed to own the stoop a few doors down, and she cackled at Justine's latest walk-by. The street seemed to close in, and she began eyeing the other passersby with suspicion.

"Do you know how stupid this is?" Patty asked.

"Yes."

"Honestly, J.J., I don't know what you would do if I had a love life."

They walked it one last time, determined to hit Belmont's building and turn around rather than chance the lady on the stoop. They were rewarded with what looked like a fresh dump of garbage bags in the wire mesh cans.

"Okay, so now what?" Patty asked.

"We go through it looking for receipts, bills… a bank statement."

Patty looked at her with disgust. "I thought you said you knew what you were looking for."

"I do. Some way to identify this guy."

"Do you know what year it is?"

Justine folded her arms, trying to close the conversation.

"It's the year when the whole world gets their bills online, that's what year it is," Patty finished.

"You don't have to help with this part."

"And you're what, gonna go through his trash right here, with the neighbors watching?"

Justine said, "Yes," but realized she hadn't thought this through. "Or we could…take it back."

"On my Kawasaki?"

She surveyed her folly and saw a blur behind Patty. "Holy crap, I think that was him." She ran to the alley's end. Sure enough, Belmont was jogging down the street at ten thirty at night. Even if she hadn't quite seen his face, how many people in Bed-Stuy wore a tailored summer gray suit late on a Friday night? "He's in a hurry."

Patty sighed and flashed the keys to her motorcycle. "All right, let's go."

Chapter 26

Segreti took a cab to Queens, got out ten blocks from the covert site and walked the rest of the way, moving circuitously, keeping an eye out and following ADIC Church's advice to *Practice tradecraft if you go there.* From outside it looked like just another warehouse and office build along Van Dam Street in Long Island City: steel-shuttered garages, two stories of grimy windows and yellow brick, the ground level tagged with graffiti.

Companies operated actual businesses here: "Kratz Self Storage". "Chau Elevator Components". "Oak Global Logistics—family owned since 1994!" All of them were FBI fronts. But even at this late hour, they were active, with trucks coming and going. Some of these things made good money, he was told.

He showed his badge and the workman in his mesh baseball cap and plaid shirt waved him through. Segreti hadn't bothered with a costume; his jeans, dark blazer and a black shirt were nondescript enough. Beneath the jacket was a newly issued Glock.

He was met by a forty-something white woman with graying hair in a no-nonsense bun and wearing cargo pants and a T-shirt. Her broad face expressed Midwestern politeness mixed with a skepticism honed in New York. "Well, well, Eddie Secrets has entered my lair."

Her nickname for him, from Academy days. Hers had involved sexual innuendo, which he judged would not be remembered so amicably. "Good to see you, Agent Towers."

Jessica Towers smiled and shook his hand. "Welcome to the Warehouse."

"That's what you call it?"

"An honest name for an honest job."

She led him through the ground-floor shops and their everyday affairs involving grease and forklifts, to an elevator bank, one of them chained with an 'Out of Order' sign stuck on its door. She used a key to unlock the chain and ushered him inside. Ignoring the row of rusty floor buttons, she put her thumb on a dark glass panel. It flashed once and the elevator rumbled down.

"Ever get a customer who wanders the wrong way?" he asked.

"We have an entire team managing street traffic, twenty-four-seven."

He followed her into a gleaming hallway of stainless-steel partitions, giant tables showcasing unrolled blueprints and schematics, and glass-encased offices. The basement was buzzing with people as if it were one of those high-powered offices in a Manhattan skyscraper, mid-day.

"Coffee here any good?"

Towers laughed. "Bureau-issued." They detoured to a vending machine, same as the one at Javits.

"Twenty years and I didn't know you were such a big deal," he admitted as they drank.

"That's my classmate, always reminding me why I asked

for that transfer."

"I meant the divis—never mind."

"Breaking and entering into foreign embassies and consulates requires extraordinary resources." Towers chucked her now-empty cup and walked with her memorable briskness. She pointed to an office with closed steel doors and frosted windows. "That's the NSA's corner. Code-breakers." She paused at a large table and checked a clipboard bustling with notes. "East Sixty-fourth Street. This one's for India."

"That's their consulate?"

"Great views from here," she said, stubbing a finger on an unscrolled architectural blueprint. "They say when they open this window, you can hear the lions roar in Central Park Zoo. We had a team in there last week."

"My interest is north of that."

"So I gathered. This way."

The basement seemed endless. It must have occupied more territory than the real estate above. In fact, from the soaring ceiling, he guessed it must poke up into an adjacent building. She led him into a vast hangar-like space filled with a maze of walls, doors, desks and computers. "This is the mockup of the Russian consulate, all three floors. We use it to train our burglars. They Russkies are always redoing their interior, so we're never certain."

"I'm looking to identify two possible enemy agents." He pulled out two photos from his jacket's inside pocket. "This one, Dimitri Mahalin, has been identified with the consulate but has disappeared. This other one... well, you couldn't tell by looking at this, but she's female, brown hair, masculine cut, last seen in Cyprus."

Towers frowned. "You got a problem with butch-looking

women, Eddie?"

He raised his hands in supplication. "C'mon, Jess, don't take it that way. I'm just saying, she's a she. So far, surveillance hasn't found anything. Anything from inside that you could share?"

Towers snatched the photos from his grip and looked at the faces. She shoved them back against his chest. "You sure it's to be found in their consulate building? Russia also owns a twenty-story building uptown on Riverdale, and two properties on Long Island."

"What's the most hardened facility for comms?"

"Probably the consulate. We have an asset that has access to the first two floors—a maid. Depending on what I tell you, it could compromise her cover."

"There's a yacht offshore, Emirati-flagged, but I think she's on it. I think it's got a submersible and a helicopter. I think she's using it for infil/exfil, running their own asset. I need something to justify a move."

"A move, like a B&E?"

"Whatever they're up to it has to be GRU-run. What's on the third floor?"

Towers regarded the mockup of the consulate's interior. It looked banal without the people, the machines, the security. "A shit-ton of comms, signals, cryptographs, and an incinerator. Plus, there's a basement we've never been able to crack. We've got listening devices in all the nearby buildings, but the Russians are very good."

"Something like this wouldn't be communicated directly. They're using Yacht Woman to run their asset, and their asset is, uh, very familiar with our policies and procedures."

Tower raised an eyebrow. "I see."

He risked a glance at the corner office silent behind closed doors. "He's one of theirs. Ex-NSA. Robert Tremain. You want to help me nail this son of a bitch?"

"Policies. Procedures."

"It's not like you're waiting for a warrant to break there."

"No, Ed, but I have my mission and you have yours."

"I've got a detail keeping an eye on their consulate and their UN mission office. But we're probably spinning our wheels. You've got these places covered inside and out. Can you give me a heads-up if this lady shows? Or better yet, look for chatter about her and Tremain?"

"I'd need an official direction from Quantico—"

"Come on, Towers." He tapped the photos in his hand. "I'm talking about a major cyber breach and treason." She looked dubious, but she hadn't told him to get lost. He played his final card. "ADIC will deny ever having suggested I come to you, but who'd need to ask her, anyway?"

"Do what I can, Segreti."

"Thanks. And thanks for the tour."

"Deb Church and I go way back." She smiled. "Seems like you've pulled every string to get into my panties here. Word of warning? Deb doesn't take to being made a fool of. We have that in common."

"I owe you one. I'm good for it."

Towers led him back the way they had walked. "Are you?"

The steel door shouldering frosted windows opened. Two people emerged wearing jeans and T-shirts—a skinny East Asian woman with a moony pout, and a solid Latin-looking man with a buzz cut and a face that had taken a few punches.

"You Segreti?" the woman asked.

To Towers, Segreti mumbled, "Do NSA usually mix here?"

"Nope," Towers said. "And, gee, they know your name."

"Mind a word?" the Latino said, gesturing to the open door.

"Sure, guys, whatever."

"Enjoy your chat," Towers said. "I'll be sure someone can see you out."

Segreti followed the two NSA agents into their office. The Asian woman shut the door. The interior looked like a command room: two long tables were flanked on both sides by rows of computers and monitors, and an enormous screen occupied the opposite wall but was dark. Segreti assumed they had turned it off before calling him in.

The National Security Agency was the nation's specialists in signals intelligence and cybersecurity. Best toys, smartest people, didn't play well with others.

"You know my name. Care to share yours?"

The two agents replied with stony stares.

"All right," he said, telling himself to stay calm, "what do you want?"

"Your unit has something that belongs to us," the Latino said.

"Above my pay grade, guys."

"That so?" answered the Asian woman. "Well, what we know about your case is also above your pay grade."

Segreti folded his arms and took the Fifth.

"What we're saying," her partner said, "is we appreciate your service, but we can take this from here."

"Because," Segreti said, "it would be so embarrassing if it turns out one of your people was responsible for the worst security breach in American history."

If their expressions were rocky before, now they congealed into granite furies.

"You don't know what you're talking about," the man said.

"Or how close you are to fucking yourself," his partner added.

Segreti gestured at the computers, the screens, their setup. "Heartwarming, this inter-agency cooperation. I'll see myself out."

Chapter 27

"What is that place?" Justine wondered aloud.

She was on the back of Patty's motorcycle, visor up. They had followed Malcolm Belmont into Manhattan's Upper East Side. He had parked along East Sixty-Seventh Street and then stayed put. The street was quiet, mostly residential, lined by squat white-bricked blocks from the 1950s. A few doors down, one of the blocks had a steel canopy shielding its sidewalk and a pair of flagpoles.

"What flag is that?" Patty said.

"Let's drive by, get a look." She lowered her visor as Patty swerved alongside Belmont's car, but she didn't get a look at him. Instead, they ambled alongside the apartment block. It was a quick enough look. Patty pulled over on the next block and Justine searched Google, just to make sure.

"That's Russia's property," she said. "It's where their UN delegation lives."

"You're shitting me." Patty cut the engine. "J.J., we getting, uh, in over our heads?"

"No such thing." She tried to connect the dots. Braun and Bomber were at the auction where somebody was selling incredible zero-days. Walter Klinger, ex-spook, had probably had some kind of hand in designing this one. Now he was dead, and Braun was casing a Russian ambassador's residence. "Go back around. We need to keep an eye on him."

Patty sighed. "You're really something, you know that?" But she started up her Kawasaki. It took a few turns to get back to where Belmont was parked.

He was just pulling away.

"Follow him!" Justine shouted.

It was a straight shot up Park Avenue. Patty hung back, and the longer Belmont maintained his course, the safer it felt to put some space between them. His taillights became a blur in the traffic, but at this hour, the street was not that busy, and they could keep an eye on him. The silent glass towers of banks and Fortune 500 companies gave way to stylish apartment blocks and the darkened windows of expensive restaurants.

"He's turning!"

Patty followed Belmont onto East Ninetieth and then up Madison one block. He pulled over too quickly and Patty kept going.

"We have to turn back!"

She sped around the block and then trundled onto the sidewalk. She lifted her visor. "I'll hang here. You go see what he's up to."

Justine swung off the bike, put her helmet in the Kawasaki's backseat storage, and trotted back to Madison. Cabs drove past, a woman was walking her dog, an elderly couple walked hand in hand. She crossed Madison and was about to turn onto Ninety-First Street when Braun and his party walked around the corner, practically crashing into her.

She didn't know what to do so she just kept going, hoping they wouldn't recognize her. But she definitely recognized them: Braun, the curvy white woman, the South Asian man...

and Bomber. The whole gang. They were marching back the way Braun had arrived. She cursed her luck. A minute earlier she could have identified them from a distance and continued to follow them. Now she couldn't do anything but keep a straight face and carry on down the street. Had any of them stopped to get a look at her?

She was now on a quiet street of old brownstones and mansions from the turn of a lost century. But as she progressed, she noticed one of the fine old stone houses boasted a large flag overlooking its entrance. The same white, blue and red horizontal stripes she had seen before. She fished out her phone as she hustled past it, just to be sure. Yep, the Russian consulate-general.

She dared to look over her shoulder. At the far end of the block, she saw a lone figure in a dark outfit and blazer, motionless, watching. She had gotten Bomber's attention.

Justine looked away and called Patty. "We're done tonight. I'll find my way home."

* * *

She returned to her Upper West Side apartment building feeling like the city had given her an extra coating of grime. There was no doorman here—she didn't have that kind of money—and the entrance involved two doors with their own keys and, inside, fluorescent ceiling lights that made everyone look like they had consumption. And of course, the elevator was out of order. Again. "Didn't they just fix this thing?" She was so tired that she was mumbling aloud. She pushed into the fire stairs, an uninviting concrete ascent.

Fourth floor. Justine practically fell against her apartment's door with keys in hand. Inside at last, she flicked on the light, moved robotically toward the bedroom, and then something made her freeze. The skin on her neck crawled and she swung around.

The man was sitting on her couch, out of view from the front door.

She screamed. It wasn't deliberate, but she was terrified.

He sighed and pointed at the gun on her coffee table, raising his other hand's finger to his lips.

She clasped her hands over her mouth, but the only reason she stopped screaming was because she began to hyperventilate.

The man nodded. "Sorry I frightened you."

Justine looked back at the door.

"Sure, run. I won't chase you."

She bolted for the door.

"But, Justine, hear me out."

She flung the door open and halted.

There is a strange man in my apartment.

With a gun.

And he knows my name.

She gasped for breath. He might be a thief. A rapist. A killer. All of the above. But he was there for a reason. She took a deeper, slower breath, shut the door in front of her and turned around.

He was white and blond, with a preppy sweep of hair that partially obscured one of his blue eyes. He wore a loose button-down short-sleeve top with a blue and white pattern, baggy trousers, and white sneakers. His physique was good—big shoulders, strong arms, not much of a belly. His bronzed skin suggested outdoor sports. His hands were encased in a doctor's prophylactic gloves.

"Good decision. You want to sit down? In that chair."

"No, I don't think so."

"Suit yourself." He pointed at the coffee table with his blue-encased finger, but not at his gun. The glass tabletop held its usual items: a ceramic bowl where she deposited pens, keys to Steve's place, bills; and a pile of books and magazines. On top was a recent *Archer's*. He picked it up. "Must be rewarding, seeing your byline in such a prestigious magazine."

"Who are you?"

"A concerned friend," he said, flipping the magazine's pages. "You know, this story on Taylor Swift is really intriguing."

"I didn't write that."

"I know." He threw the magazine in her direction, and she flinched as it fluttered to the floor. "You write investigative pieces about technology and national security."

She realized with a whomp in her chest that she knew this man. Blond Ambition. The guy with Bomber at the auction.

"I'm easy to look up online," she said. "How about you?"

"Let's talk about you, honey. You're a big deal, star journalist. Working on a story about quantum computers, is that it?"

She wondered how he had connected those dots. He was working with Bomber and Malcolm Belmont. Had she given herself away, following them? Who else would know that... Professor Ang...Walter Klinger.

The dead Walter Klinger.

"Why do you ask?"

"It so happens we may have a common interest."

Or he could have learned it from one of her colleagues. From

Paul Chow...or Bert, or Josh.

"I'd like to understand where you got your information."

Blond Ambition weighed her demand. "No. Let's stick to how I can help you."

"If you hurt anyone—"

"Relax, honey. If I wanted to hurt someone, you'd know."

"How did you know I lived here—how did you get in—"

He shook his head. "I thought you were a hotshot reporter. But you aren't asking the interesting questions."

"Okay. Let's say I'm working a story on a cyber-weapon that uses software written for a quantum computer."

He gave her a big, sunburned grin. "Ask away, honey."

"It's called Red Fidelity. Someone stole it from the government and tried to auction it off last week. Things went wrong, though, so maybe the thieves still have it. Most zero-day exploits find vulnerabilities in software, cloud hardware, PCs, anything that the tech companies don't know about. Red Fidelity's like that too, but it has a different effect if you run it on a quantum computer."

"Sure, honey, but you have to ask me a question."

She eyed the gun on her coffee table. "Did you steal Red Fidelity?"

"No comment."

"Who's that other man, with the dark complexion? I saw you together at the auction. You came in on the same boat, and left together."

"He's a corrupt FBI agent named Edward Segreti."

"Why is he corrupt?"

He spread his arms wide. "Guess."

"And Malcom Belmont?"

She noticed him twitch, just once. She had surprised him.

"Ditto." He recovered his flow. "The others are Miriam Chlebek and Bhavin Ram."

"They're all dirty?"

"They're loyal to Segreti. Bhavin Ram's an alcoholic fuckup, a chink in the armor, so to speak. Just a tip."

"Are they selling it to the Russians?"

He stood up, slowly, and she had to force herself to remain steady. "That's for you to find out. But Segreti killed a man on North Brother Island. Maybe he wanted to keep some people silent."

"You two had a falling out?"

"Who said we ever were an item?" He fished a phone out of his pocket and tossed it to her. She caught it.

"What's this?"

"A burner phone with one number on it. Get them on Messenger. You're on the cyber beat, you'll figure it out."

The phone was an old, scratched-up clamshell.

Blond Ambition picked up his gun. Pointed it at her. Her reflex was to cower.

"Move back that away, so I can see myself out."

She backed up into the doorway to the bedroom. He moved with a limp, his other hand holding his thigh. That was new. She despised herself for cringing in front of this man, gun or no. And she found some courage.

"Who killed Walter Klinger?"

"Interview's over."

"Was it you?"

His smile was like an invitation from an old friend. "Keep up the good work, Justine."

Chapter 28

It was pushing three a.m. when Segreti found his team within Central Park. They had agreed to break up and meet here, along the northern edge of the reservoir. They'd only be disturbed by the odd jogger or junkie at this hour. The lights of Manhattan, though reduced in number, still defined Midtown at the far end of the water.

The others emerged from the shadows and cohered on the running trail along the high iron fence that ringed the lake. They came together with a furtiveness that he imagined his quarry would recognize. He couldn't make out their expressions in the dark. Chlebek's broad pale cheeks, the whites of Belmont's eyes, Ram's ragged breathing. It was enough that they were still here. Because it was important that he speak with them now, out of sight. Home—a cold apartment with divorce papers burning a hole on his kitchen counter—had to wait.

Segreti considered thanking them, or apologizing for the crazy hour. They had all been working non-stop for more than twenty hours and the coming day would be no different. But now wasn't the time for that.

"Things are going to get messy," he told them. "The NSA wants me off the case."

"They said that?" Ram asked.

"They weren't subtle. Plus, we're being tailed. I think we've been under surveillance for a while."

Belmont said, "I think someone's been hanging around my place."

"Caucasian female, blonde?" Segreti asked. Pretty? —he didn't add.

"Not sure, sir."

"She approached me at the auction," Segreti said. "I brushed her off. I didn't think she was significant. But I saw her tonight, outside the Russian consulate."

"Think she's one of them?"

"Russian, NSA, one of Tremain's people... I don't know." He gritted his teeth at his ignorance.

Chlebek asked, "Can you tell us what the NSA actually said?"

"Two of their liaisons at the Bureau's Long Island City facility told me to give back the Red Fidelity code, stop investigating, and otherwise avoid career suicide."

"Did you tell ADIC?" Belmont asked.

"No." Church had gone out of her way to get Towers to receive him in her secret lair: what the burglars did was a secret even to most other Bureau personnel. Need to know, etc. The metadata that Taylor had scrubbed from those phones had given Church a simulacrum of cover, and she had put her name on the line to get him the electronic surveillance on the Russians. But ADIC had been plain: Segreti was out of favors. "And I'm not going to."

Ram stuffed his hands in his pockets. "So, where we at, chief?"

"I've skated so close to the edge I can't see it anymore," he confessed. "Tremain's a traitor, and the Russians are up to something that could do real damage to this country. Damage I can't add up. But we're getting spun. By the Russians. By our own people. By Bobby fucking Tremain."

"What's the play?" Belmont asked.

"The play is that from here on out, I'm not concerning myself with diplomatic immunities. Or complying with bureaucratic niceties. Which means I'm going to be damaged goods, and Deborah Church might decide to hang me by the balls. But I'm nailing that sonofabitch. You guys should go home, take tomorrow off, stay the hell away. I won't hold it against you."

The other three exchanged glances in the dark.

"If it's all the same, sir, I'd like to see this thing through," Belmont said.

"You could get fired. They'll haul you in, question your loyalty, question everything."

"I know, sir, but if this threat is what we think it is—I'd rather try to stop it."

Chlebek asked, "Exactly what bureaucratic niceties do you think you'll ignore?"

"State Department protocols and whatever Internal Affairs tells me to do."

She nodded. "You'll need somebody who can access IA files."

"If you get caught trying to cover for me, or covering your own ass, Miriam..."

"I won't get caught."

Ram coughed. "I'm in."

"Bhav, no. You've got a wife and kids. I don't want you messed up in this."

"I said I'm in. This is what we signed up for. What we *really* signed up for."

Maybe he should have felt grateful. Relieved. Proud. But something nagged him.

"Remember what you told me, family comes first?"

Ram hung his head, as if being scolded. "I remember."

"So?"

Ram wasn't ashamed; he was embarrassed. But he spoke the words. "This is family too."

Segreti finally said "Okay" and fought the urge to throw up.

* * *

Ram had already messaged Blessy to tell her he'd be working all night. As the meeting broke up, he contemplated the convoluted commute. He'd get maybe an hour's sleep before dawn broke.

Segreti must have recognized the exhaustion, or maybe just the despair. "There's a sofa with your name on it, if you want it."

Ram nodded and wordlessly followed his boss back to a shiny new apartment hoisted high over the Lower East Side. It was bare-boned, as he'd expected, but even so, the coldness of the place was enough to make a man shiver. He slumped on the couch facing the cityscape, the towers hushed as tombstones, as Segreti brought a blanket in from the bedroom.

Ram didn't move.

"You want this?"

"Okay, thanks." Then Ram added, "I'll sleep better if you got something to take the edge off?" Maybe it was a dumb thing to ask your boss, but the idea had trailed him all the way back here.

Segreti threw the blanket onto another cushion and walked to the kitchenette. He pulled out a bottle of Jack Daniels, poured each of them a finger, and put the bottle and the drinks on the glass coffee table. He followed this with his gun and badge, then sat on a chair by his lonely dining table. "Cheers."

Ram shut his eyes and savored the firewater. He felt its tendrils seep through his chest and shoulders. Coming here had been the right call; having a much-needed drink at home these days got him nothing but shouting matches. When he opened his eyes, he saw Segreti had turned his back. He was brooding over a bundle of forms on the table.

"Don't tell me you're doing paperwork," Ram said, suddenly feeling tired. Maybe just another drink before stretching out.

Segreti reached an arm back to show him one of the documents. The all-upper-case title, Complaint for Absolute Divorce, was enough.

"Shit, Ed, I'm sorry."

They had another drink. Ram's brain was softening into a tired mush, but he wondered how much of Segreti's talk of going rogue was the job and how much was this. He wondered about following someone disintegrating like that. Then he thought of yesterday's argument with Sissy about her dating some college-aged scumbag. He felt a heavy regret in his chest. Whatever Segreti was fighting for, it seemed a million miles from the patriotic family schtick that he liked to preach. Blessy, Sissy, Sammy. They were real. Sometimes a real pain in the ass, but they were his everything.

He could get shot. Get cancer. Get whatever. But one way Ram didn't want to end up was head in hands at a kitchen table empty of anything meaningful except divorce papers.

Segreti turned in and Ram laid down on the couch. In the darkness, the lights from nearby towers hovered like lonely motes. His mind replayed the pledge he had made to the others. He wondered how to account for the damage that was sure to accrue. Assets and liabilities. Bills bills bills; the bills were going to come due, just like that...

He squinted in the heat of the morning sun. Cotton mouth, spinning head. By his standards, not a bad hangover, but it felt worse because for a minute he didn't know where he was. Then he saw Segreti's badge and gun on the coffee table. The bottle of Jack was gone but had left a sticky ring on the glass.

Ram sat up. Segreti was already dressed and scrubbed. The aroma of coffee delivered a semblance of comfort. "What time is it?" he asked.

"Nine."

"Shit."

"I went for a workout and you were snoring away, so I left you alone." The coffeemaker beeped. "Milk or sugar?"

"Sugar." Ram got up and used the bathroom. His reflection reported back a tale of woe. He went back out, drank his boss's coffee, and decided he'd message Blessy once he was on the ferry.

"Take the day off," Segreti said. "We all need a rest."

On his way out, he was going to tell Segreti that he was out. That he would step up to that invisible line; however, if he thought it would harm his family, he wasn't going to cross it. But Segreti was at the table, face robotic, eyes vacant, signing papers.

Ram left and made his way home. He lined his stomach for the ferry with a greasy sandwich, and spent the ride going through emails on his phone. The house looked quiet, but when he stepped inside, he heard music from upstairs.

"Blessy?"

But Blessy wasn't a Taylor Swift fan, and she didn't listen to music amped up like that.

He climbed the stairs and knocked on Sissy's door. The volume suddenly dropped. "Who is it?"

"Three guesses."

She opened the door, dressed in T-shirt and cutoffs, hair done up, makeup on.

"It's algebra," she said, gesturing to her computer monitor and its grid of young faces.

"You're not at school?"

She sighed like a princess, a gesture he found both infuriating and charming. "Friday classes are online, Dad, remember?"

That it was Friday was news to him. The past week had been a blur. He didn't understand why teachers and students wanted to continue lessons as if Covid still raged. Whatever. Just add it to the list of domestic matters he didn't get.

"Does the teacher recommend blasting music? Is that some new form of learning? I missed that one when I was your age."

She eyerolled like the best of them. "It's a ten-minute quiz time. Mrs. Pearson isn't, like, even talking."

"Keep it down."

She wrinkled her nose. "You smell disgusting, did you know that?"

"Yeah, I know. When it's your lunch break, want to have lunch with your dad? Promise I'll shower first."

She looked like he had pitched selling the Brooklyn Bridge. "Uh..."

"We can grab a pizza in town."

"I got to, you know, do this quiz."

"Sure, honey."

When she came out a few hours later, he had mowed the back yard and cleaned out the gutter like Blessy had been chasing him to do—the work and the sun like a detox. She watched him take the detritus to the trash can in the garage. "So, like, Pier 76?"

"I was thinking Tony's."

"That's where the old people go."

He didn't mind her little dig. Pier 76 was twice the distance and more than twice the price, but her acceptance filled him with a glow.

Walking with a teenager required a patience he still didn't appreciate. She travelled with cellphone in hand, and every corner was a chance to dash messages back and forth. As they ambled among the leafy detached houses of Crescent Street, talking about the minor iniquities of school life, Sissy checked her phone again. Puzzled, she halted.

"What is it?"

She scrunched her face and, to his surprise, handed over her phone. "It's for you."

"What?"

"Why someone would be messaging you on my phone is beyond me."

"Give me that." She was on Facebook Messenger. Had clicked open a message from an account called Ellie.

Hey, I'm looking for Bhavin Ram!

"Who's Ellie?"

Sissy shrugged. "I don't know."

"You answered a message from someone you don't know?"

"Maybe she's from school and I just forget. Besides, I didn't answer it."

But she had clicked on it. Did that mean anything? He hit the call button. It rang.

When someone picked up, he said, "I'm looking for Ellie."

A woman's voice responded. "Are you Bhavin Ram?"

"Who's asking?"

"Someone with a mutual interest in Red Fidelity."

He froze.

"Who is it?" Sissy demanded.

Ram stayed her with a finger. "Who are you?"

"Someone who knows you have an interest in things like that."

Ram looked around to see if he could identify a spotter. "I don't talk to strangers."

"Then we should meet."

He put a protective arm around his daughter. "How did you get this number?"

"You want to meet or not?"

They were calling his daughter's phone. His blood was up but he kept his tone even. "To talk about..."

"Your involvement with Red Fidelity."

"Sure, we can meet." *So I can shoot you, involving my daughter like this.* "How's downtown at three?"

"Starbucks, the one on Astor Place."

The line went dead.

"Shit."

"Dad!"

He went to the call record, number without ID, tried to get the woman to pick up, but he only got a disconnect signal.

"I have to go," he said. "And you need to get back to the house and stay there."

"What? You promised lunch!"

He held the phone up high as she jumped to snatch it. "And I have to take this."

Chapter 29

Justine stared at the burner phone in her hand. It was the only thing she was keeping still. The rest of her was shaking.

"Well?" Patty demanded.

They were at their cluster of desks at *Archer's*. The windows blazed with late-morning sun, yet the fluorescent-lit office interior seemed impervious to the outside's warmth. As if they were functioning in some kind of tomb.

Patty leaned across her desk, eyes blazing beneath her Islanders cap. Josh had stopped typing on his laptop, fresh-faced and unsure of what meant what. Bert was here too, leaning against the wall, nursing a Styrofoam cup of tea, his graceful bulk filling Justine's awareness of her colleagues, her team, here, witnessing her utter fumbling.

"I didn't expect him to call," she admitted.

"Nobody actually makes calls," Josh said. "It's like... so creepy."

"Nobody asked you," Patty snapped.

Justine said, "He suggested meeting downtown at three."

"And you said Starbucks?"

Justine shrugged. "Public place, lots of people coming and going, and plenty of directions to run."

Bert wiped droplets from his mustache. "If you can make it

outside."

Justine bowled the burner across the desk to Patty. "Blond Ambition talked about dropping a pixel. What do you think?"

Josh said, "No way you can get hacked just by answering a call."

"He's right," Patty said.

"What about Pegasus?" Justine suggested. "That Israeli spyware can get into your phone if you click on a WhatsApp message."

"But you used Messenger," Patty said.

"They're both owned by Meta," Justine said. "WhatsApp relies on a mobile account. Messenger's a Facebook account. No one's come out and said they've hacked Facebook, but that doesn't mean no one has."

"You're telling me a stranger breaks into your apartment and gives you a phone with spyware that even the Israelis don't have," Patty said.

"Maybe?"

"And this intruder says, hey, call this guy, and you call that guy and make a date for coffee."

Justine covered her face and groaned. "Was I really bad?"

"You were bad," Bert said, dipping his teabag.

"I thought you were fine," Josh declared.

"You were shit," Patty said. "But now what?"

Justine glanced across the office. Paul Chow was in his glass enclosure, engrossed in his desktop. Probably editing something. "Now we have to get down to Astor and see if this is going to work."

Before heading out, Patty cobbled together a tiny micro-phone and wire. In the ladies' room she taped this to Justine's sternum. Outside, Bert donned headphones and gave them a thumb's up. He got his camera equipment and headed down to his van.

Justine took the Number 6 train with Patty and Josh, but she got out early at Union Station and walked the rest of the way. Josh and Patty were going to check out the Starbucks, pounce on advantageous seats, and find a nearby place where they could regroup.

The summer day was hot but fine. She was wearing a sleeveless blouse, Capri pants and flats. She had her shades on but felt an extra precaution might help, so she bought a bland white baseball cap with a Nike swoosh. Her purse was a supple, lightweight bag, but she still felt the burden of the burner phone inside.

She had Googled Bhavin Ram, narrowed it for New York, and still faced a selection of men's images and bios. None of them purported to be FBI agents. Of course, she had searched for Edward Segreti, shortly after the intruder had left her apartment. She had been so scared, she just wanted to get the hell out of there and go to Steve's. But it was so late, and the man hadn't hurt her. He was gone and this phone was now in her hands. She also looked up all the names he had spilled, and only after half an hour of fruitless searches had she been able to fall asleep.

The brief exchange with Ram played in her head. She felt like an ignoramus—playing spy-girl with strangers, not knowing the rules of the game. Even after three years of passable undercover work, she still felt out of depth. These people are trained, she thought, as she reached Strand Books.

Blond Ambition had said these feds were crooked. But Justine knew the opposite could also be true. At least she would have a chance to ask some questions, even if that meant confessing some sins. Who knew, maybe she'd even get a straight answer.

The Starbucks overlooked a busy square: NYU kids, a couple of guys pounding rhythms on arrays of plastic buckets, skateboarders, and tourists giving the black Cube sculpture a spin on its corner axis. When Justine entered the café, she saw Josh and Patty were near the back, occupying a pair of large reclining chairs bracketing a small table. Two-thirty.

Justine bought a coffee. Josh stood and gravely walked out, like a general leaving the field of battle.

"This seat free?" she asked Patty, who shrugged and kept reading her phone.

Justine sat down and surveyed the place. "Anything I should know?"

"Bathrooms are a dead end. If it's an emergency, go behind the counter. I saw them hauling trash out that way."

"Wish me luck."

"Pray you don't have to pee."

Patty hung around for a while, just to make sure they could keep the seat. Justine kept one eye on the burner and another on the door. And then on the baristas, wondering what would have to happen for her to need to burst through their ranks. It's just a meeting with a...source.

Three o'clock. Patty had gone outside. Bert messaged that Justine's audio was coming through just fine. She knew he would be filming the entrance. She had a nervous jolt: what if Ram came through the back, where they take out the garbage?

One minute past. Two.

How punctual were these things supposed to be? She had experienced her share of covert meetings. Sometimes people were quite late, but Ram was supposedly a government agent.

Justine had the sense that they would be punctual.

Five past.

Her coffee cup was empty.

"This free?" asked a young white woman. Definitely not Bhavin Ram.

"Sorry, it's taken."

"I been waiting in line for like ten minutes and nobody's been sitting here."

"It's taken," she said, putting her feet on the opposite seat.

"Fuck you, bitch," the young woman said, but she went looking for somewhere else to sit.

Justine's heart raced, and she knew her mind would drive her nuts reviewing this meaningless exchange, but she canvassed the space with a sense of minor accomplishment.

Ten more minutes passed, and then fifteen, and she dreaded risking getting up to get another coffee. Of course, she now had to pee too. But the importance of this meeting had grown. She had come to realize that this was the closest she was going to get to Bomber. Having Blond Ambition break into her apartment proved that she was onto something big. But Bhavin Ram was the only thread she had left to pull.

After another half hour and another unpleasant customer exchange, she accepted that he was standing her up.

She group-messaged the others. "Calling time on this bullshit." Then she dashed to the bathroom.

Justine exited the Starbucks and met the others by the Cube. The black sculpture was a solid piece of interlocking slabs, spinning upright on one corner, like chaos about to break.

"Well, this sucks," Josh said.

"Sorry, J.J.," Bert added.

"No, I'm sorry," she said. "I made a play and it didn't work.

You guys should get back to your other work. I have to deal with Paul."

Patty folded her arms. "How do you know it didn't work?"

Justine was about to respond, then shut her mouth. She looked around at the skateboarders, the tourists, the street hustlers and the ordinary New Yorkers striding to their next rendezvous. She did a three-sixty, saw the Cooper Union Building across the plaza, saw the endless wall of windows in the surrounding buildings. She spread her arms wide. "Here we are!"

"Hunh?" Josh said.

Patty chuckled and pulled her Rangers cap down low. "Oh man."

Bert looked uncomfortable. "We should go."

"They've rounded us all up," Justine said. "The least we can do is express our gratitude."

Patty raised both her middle fingers and did a pirouette.

"Yeah, up yours!" Josh giggled, giving the world the bird.

Bert shook his head. *"Nosotros estamos tan jodidos."*

She put a hand on his shoulder. Her moment of bravado was melting into regret. "Sorry, big guy."

* * *

Segreti and Ram returned to the office the same time, Segreti with a Canon 7Dii slung over his chest.

"Got four suspects waving back at me," Segreti said.

"I want to know how they got my daughter's number."

"You sure they knew it was hers? Your name isn't on an account somewhere?"

Ram paused. "Good point."

"So, we know someone's been trawling for our personal information. They found something that tied back to you."

"I'm careful about these things, boss."

"Those cellular companies are getting hacked all the time. All of us have data floating in the ether."

"If I see anyone look even crosswise at Sissy, I'm putting them down."

Segreti clapped him on the back. "Come on, let's see what the others got."

Upstairs he handed the camera to Belmont. "Get me IDs on these four."

Belmont looked worried. "We're actually minus one ID."

"What's that mean?"

Belmont opened a drawer and passed him a report. "I just emailed you a copy. The guy you dropped at the auction?"

Segreti remembered. He didn't like to dwell on it. Not just because of the hearing. "Drew Kovicec."

"Looks like a stolen identity. The real Kovicec is still there, in Springfield, Illinois."

Segreti opened the file. There was a photo of Drew Kovicec, but it wasn't the man in the Javits morgue.

"So who did I shoot?"

"Working on it, sir."

"Just gets better and better. Keep digging."

He didn't know what to make of this. Better to keep busy. He called Ram and Chlebek. Time to visit computer forensics.

Special Agent Taylor met them wearing plastic goggles and latex gloves. She was gangly and nervous when they entered her lab, still a rookie, but when she bent over the table where she had dismembered Sissy's phone, Taylor was all business. "I've identified IOCs that correlate to an offshore C&C," she said.

Segreti signaled his distress. "Sure you did."

She pulled away her goggles. "Sorry, sir. I've found indicators of compromise that point to a command-and-control server that is located in Venezuela."

Chlebek said, "Have we seen an injection package like this before?"

"It's similar to Pegasus, but this isn't Pegasus," Taylor said.

"That's the Israeli malware, right?" Segreti asked.

"Yes, sir," Taylor said. "It's software that infects a phone without you needing to click anything. Pegasus used zero-days in iPhones that let it encode itself into WhatsApp messages or photo files. I've found similar vectors of communication back from this phone in the past six hours to a suspicious server. That's probably issuing commands, tracking the location of this device, and so on."

"Bhav, anything on your daughter's phone we need to know about?" Segreti didn't mention what he'd learned about the daughter's boyfriend. Drug misdemeanors. A petty hustler, but a nobody. Segreti had tucked that information away and hoped he'd never have to use it.

"I've sent an encrypted file with that information to Special Agent Chlebek," Taylor said.

"I'll go through it," Chlebek said.

"It's Sissy," Ram said, incredulous.

"The phone was probably only infected after she clicked on the message from the Ellie persona," Taylor said.

Segreti asked, "Do you think the perp thought it was Ram's phone? Or did they target Sissy because they figured she was more likely to click on that message?"

He watched Ram's visage turn angry. "These assholes are

using my *daughter...*"

"Easy, cowboy." Segreti added, "Good work, Taylor. Now I need to connect this malware to Russia or Tremain."

She shook her head. "The best I can do is find that server."

"Venezuela?"

"Yes, sir. But they'll geolocate the phone to our location. They'll know we have it. They'll cut communications, cover their tracks."

"Okay. Go dig. Remember, Taylor, we don't find crumbs, we find caviar."

She beamed at him. *Finally*, he thought as he headed upstairs, *I made someone smile.*

He wasn't at his desk for long before Belmont came over, looking pleased. "Check your email, please."

Segreti pulled up Belmont's message and opened the file. The photos Segreti had taken from the second floor of Cooper Union were blown up in fine detail. Four people, four names, four addresses, numbers, social media channels, place of employment.

"*Archer's?*"

"Looks that way."

He opened a new window and Googled Justine Jarman. Plenty of images of the pretty blonde with a fierce disposition, her book about cyberattacks, her articles for *Archer's*, *Vanity Fair*, *Wall Street Journal*.

"Jesus wept."

"Sir?"

"We've been hacked by a fucking reporter?"

Belmont couldn't hide his bemusement. "If you say so, sir."

Justine Jarman looked back at Segreti with a determination that he was now ready to match. He thought about their brushes, the auction, outside the Russian embassy. Was she an enemy asset? How did she come into possession of such sophisticated spyware if she wasn't working for the Russians?

"She wants to meet? Let's meet."

Chapter 30

Justine laid it out for Paul Chow. Her editor wiped his round rimless glasses with a cloth and said, "You didn't call the police?"

"And say what?"

"An armed intruder broke into your apartment. They can investigate, see what a security camera might have caught. You said he limps, so he can't be too fast on foot."

"Paul, he alleged that this team of FBI agents is illegally hustling cyber weapons."

"And you automatically believe him?"

"No. But what do I tell the police? What if it's even halfway true?"

"I'm uncomfortable with this, Justine. I think you should drop your story."

"Are you kidding me? This is becoming huge."

"It's becoming a legal liability that our insurance won't be able to cover."

"Wait. Did you just tell me you want me to spike an investigation into government corruption in national security because you're worried about the corporate's insurance policy?"

"You would not believe the number of lawyers from upstairs

that sat in on my last presentation to the board."

Her head was spinning. "I've never, ever, in my entire career—"

"Let me stop you right there, J.J. You're a tremendous reporter. But times have changed. This is *Archer's*. We do hard-hitting features, sure, but the P side of the ledger is from Jaime's exclusive with a certain Hollywood star's campaign to save some dolphins, okay? You understand you're on the L side of the ledger, and the bigger your L gets, the bigger I need to make the P, and I can't make the P any bigger."

"Three years, Paul..."

"Three years of L. That feature you pitched me last month on the city's new infrastructure plans, Robert Moses something..."

"'The Drowning of Moses'," she recalled with a groan.

"Finish that."

He was blurry. That's how she realized she was crying.

"It's a good story," Paul said, which at that point was the worst thing he could have said.

"I quit." She stood up, backhanding her nose. "I'm sorry, but I just—I quit."

"Justine," he said, but she was gone. Then she doubled back to her desk to get her bag.

It was sundown and the others had left, except for Bert, quietly filling the corner.

"Go home," she said, trying to keep her voice under control.

"I don't know what to say to my wife."

"Tell her it's over." She walked away before he could reply, before she had to admit what a mess she was.

She didn't know what to say to Steve. After last night, the idea of returning to her apartment freaked her out. Her sanctuary had been violated. Even the idea of picking a few personal things up was mission impossible. Most of her possessions were at Steve's anyway.

Maybe what she needed was Steve. And Zach. Put aside their arguments, maybe reconsider her hesitation at moving in permanently. What freedom was she trying to defend? What lifestyle demanded she be alone? She hadn't been interested in dealing with Steve of late, he had done nothing but disappoint, but she had to admit that she was probably to blame. She was the distant one, the one prioritizing work at oddball hours and with dodgy people.

She now realized had screwed up everything, and yet, maybe this was something she could salvage.

The summer night felt heavy. Humidity was setting in and the breeze off the river was limpid, as if daring her to take a deep breath. The walk hadn't cleared her head, but the physicality at least preoccupied her, and she'd worked up a perspiration by the time she reached Steve's.

Justine let herself in. The lights were on and Zach's door was shut. She knocked, called his name, but nothing. She considered opening the door, just to see, but dismissed the urge.

Steve came hustling down the stairs, fixing the last open button on his shirt, the black shirt he usually wore when he was going out. He looked fresh and shaved, and she could smell cologne.

"Hi," she said.

"Hi." He moved to the kitchen.

"You, uh, look nice."

"Thanks."

Pizza delivery and Netflix didn't look like it was in the cards.

At least, not together. "Been quite the day," she said.

"Uh-hunh." He was scribbling a note to pin on the fridge.

"Where's Zach?"

"Staying at Enrique's."

She wondered who Enrique was. Or if Zach had told his father. She assumed not yet.

"And you...?"

"Going out," he said, brushing past her toward the closet.

"I see."

"Problem with that?"

"No, it's just that, uh, I've had kind of a rough day. I was thinking we could, you know, catch up."

He slid on a brown checked jacket. "I'm out tonight."

"Need a date?"

He paused. "Maybe looking for one, Justine."

The words hit her like a punch.

"Then I should go," she said.

"Suit yourself."

"Is Zach okay?"

"He's fine. Have a good night. There's some leftover Chinese in the fridge."

Steve left.

Justine looked around the duplex wondering why she felt like a bomb had gone off. She couldn't go back to her Upper West Side apartment. She couldn't stay in this shrapnel-littered place. She searched online for a nearby hotel she could afford. She wanted a place with at least a doorman and some kind of security, so no Airbnb. The list was short. She booked a place on Lexington called The Freehand. It was about a ten-minute walk.

She stayed long enough to shower, change into clean clothes, and pack a small duffle bag that would last her a few days. She'd arrange another time to get the rest of her things.

On her way out, she saw the note Steve had left on the fridge. Behind it were pinned tickets. *Zach, Yankees-Angels, right behind first base. Your dad kept this promise.* She wondered what broken promises this gesture was meant to whitewash.

So this was defeat. Now for the retreat. Hefting the canvas duffle over a shoulder, Justine promised herself she wasn't going to make a fuss. But her plan for the hotel room involved a cold drink, a hot bath, and a good cry.

She walked north for ten blocks, turned onto Twenty-Third Street with its roaring busses and chain stores, and over to Lexington Avenue. The hotel's name was written in looping red-neon script. She was relieved to see a bellhop; she wanted a place with humans keeping an eye out.

"Justine."

She turned, body still taut with alertness, ready to sprint. He was standing with his empty hands loose by his waist, white shirt, gray blazer, dark jeans. Kempt black hair with a touch of steel, and eyes a surprisingly bright brown. He appeared from the shadows like a dangerous invitation.

"Let's talk," Bomber said.

Chapter 31

Segreti gestured up the block, doing his best to exude coolness while his mind furiously turned this over. The best approach was to stay professional, learn what she knew, and persuade her to quit. But Justine Jarman unnerved him—she was a surprise. As they walked up Lexington he didn't know where to put his hands or how fast to walk or whether to take the lead or linger a few steps behind.

Justine was frightened. He had pinpointed her so precisely, without warning. If he had shown up at her apartment, or Steve's place, or at *Archer's*, then that would have been fine. Well, not *fine*. But expected, after being tricked into the fake meeting with Bhavin Ram.

Frightened and encouraged. Hadn't she been trying this whole time to score exactly this? Face time with the mysterious Bomber. Her last chance to make this story—three years of effort, three years of hassle—real.

Initially she followed him to the corner of Twenty-Fourth, crossing to the entrance of one of the Baruch College buildings. Now they walked shoulder to shoulder and she became aware of his physicality, his gait. She had seen him advance before with a swagger, and she had interpreted it as overconfidence. He moved with purpose, matching her pace, not trying to force her to keep up. Not asking to carry her big bag. He was walking *with* her.

Segreti had already picked his destination. The norm for a conversation like this might be a booth in a diner or a coffee shop. He had judged this encounter would require a different touch. But exactly what to say, how to pitch it, that he was still mulling.

"How did you know where to find me?" she asked.

He smiled. "I'm FBI."

"You must have been tailing me."

"You got my attention."

Why had he said that? The question was to be expected, but his line should have been 'you got *our* attention'. Keep it impersonal, bring the weight of the Bureau into play, a subtle way to add gravitas.

They reached Twenty-Fifth Street. A few blocks to the left, the street ended at Madison Square Park, but to their right it was a pedestrianized park flanked by Baruch buildings. On the next corner was a cozy tea shop.

"I thought we could grab a drink and have a chat over there," he said, suggesting the narrow park. The street was quiet enough without cars, informal, relaxed, but public, and therefore assuring. Of course, he had also set it as a trap, in case she bolted. Ram was nearby on Fifth, Belmont out of sight towards Third Avenue.

"Here?"

"Doesn't have to be here, but I can vouch for the drinks."

Justine switched her bag to her other shoulder. The sign read Yi Fang Taiwan Fruit Tea. There was a Starbucks back the way they had come, just across Lex, but Bomber wanted this place. It felt strange.

"They serve coffee and regular tea if you don't like the bubble stuff," he said. To her he was trying to sound relaxed. But Segreti had picked this place too, to distract her.

"Sure," she said, walking inside. Other than a wooden high table running the length of the window, there was no seating. She squinted at the unfamiliar menu.

"Ever have bubble tea before?" he asked.

She shook her head. Josh liked this stuff, but it had never occurred to her to try it. She said, "I kind of pictured you as more a black coffee type."

He grinned. "No sugar, either, but exceptions can be made." He had a compelling smile. "If you want the classic, I'd go for the pearl black tea latte."

She nodded and he ordered. He kept one eye on the small crowd of university kids and tourists waiting patiently for their drinks, and the other on her. Just professionally, he told himself, but he noticed he wasn't the only male in the room clocking Justine Jarman.

He paid cash and carried both of their cups outside. The park was busy on this summer evening, but Chlebek had occupied a little table for two. She cleared out as soon as she spotted them emerging from the shop and Segreti eased into her chair. He smiled again when he saw Justine take a deep pull off the fat straw, imbibing the tea's little balls of tapioca.

"You know who I am," she said. "And I know who you are, Edward Segreti."

He had been in the field plenty. Had dealt with numerous beautiful women. The job was the job, the rest didn't matter. Besides, Justine was conventional, almost boring—a Nordic blonde, blah blah blah. But it was the sideways moments when he noticed a smoldering tenacity in the way she looked at him.

"Everything I say is off the record," he told her. "You've stumbled into an investigation. I need you to tell me what you know."

"Is this conversation being recorded? Am I being watched?"

"Recorded, no. Watched, yes, ever since you blundered into the middle of my work."

She scoffed. "Blundered?"

"How did you get that number?"

"What were you doing at that auction on North Brother Island?"

He wiped the bottom of his plastic cup where condensation had formed. "You understand, Miss Jarman, that there's a limit to what I can discuss."

"I'm a reporter investigating a story in the public interest. You can't tell me what to do."

"No, but I can arrest you for obstruction of justice."

"On what grounds?" She didn't try to hide her anger.

"Harassing government officials at their homes, digging through their trash as we investigate a case, calling their families. I don't want to go there, Justine, and neither do you."

"This your style, Agent Segreti? Sweet drinks and empty threats?" She sucked the straw loudly while he thought of what to say.

"All right," he said. "There might be a few notes we can compare. And it's Ed."

She decided to accept this as a tactical victory. "All right, Ed. I've been investigating cyber-weapons by posing as a buyer."

"Undercover work is our job, not yours."

"And how do you think it's going, Ed?"

His easy smile gave way to intensity. "The things we've

busted, the crimes we've prevented? Better than you think."

"The Shadow Brokers stole NSA weapons and sold them to North Korea. When the Koreans unleashed them, they almost destroyed Maersk, the British health system, a hundred other companies. Then came Bitcoin, untraceable made-up internet money, and ransomware skyrocketed. Ed, I believe you when you tell me you've saved the day a couple of times, but every time there's a new leak of a zero-day, it causes chaos, and each new one is worse than what came before."

"The world isn't perfect," he said. "When has it ever been?"

"Red Fidelity, though... that's a whole new level of threat."

"Yeah, you like to throw that around but do you know what it is?"

"Do you?"

"Ladies first."

"Used on a regular computer, it's a zero-day. Used on a quantum computer, it does something else. Your turn."

"Don't know what more I can say about Red Fidelity."

"Walter Klinger used to work at the National Security Agency, and someone killed him. Was he the leak?"

"Your guess is as good as mine."

"Come on."

"Tell me everything. I mean every last detail. If it's useful info, I'll share what I can."

Justine took a moment to weigh her prospects. Without Segreti's help, she was probably done—three years and her rep down the toilet. He had been showing some charm. Maybe she could volley. She smiled. "All right, Ed. My cover was good enough to get invited to the auction. I heard people talking about a quantum-related exploit, but nothing more. I saw you and that blond guy together. You disappeared somewhere in that building, then there was a gunshot, and you came out together.

"I asked around and a physicist told me about Klinger. Told me he was a nasty piece of work, but he used to work at the NSA and knew a lot about this stuff. I tracked him down to his office downtown. He confirmed Red Fidelity was an exploit that worked differently if you ran it as an algo on a quantum computer. He also told me that someone named Malcolm Belmont had been asking the same questions.

"Me and my team canvassed the city looking for Malcolm Belmonts, and we found your guy. I tried to follow him to find you. We spotted you hanging around the Russian consulate. And then someone murdered Klinger."

Segreti said, "You haven't told me anything I don't already know, Justine. Or should I say, Ellie?"

She had been dreading this part. She hadn't done anything illegal, but they could try to pin something, *anything*, on her. Justine counterattacked: "That blond guy showed up in my apartment last night."

That won a raised eyebrow. "Inside your apartment?"

"Yeah. He told me your name, said you and Belmont are corrupt FBI. Gave me a phone with just one number on it, told me to use that to open doors, get a scoop. He also threatened me with a gun."

Segreti hesitated. "You live alone?"

Justine sensed the pause in the question. Like, it wasn't just routine info-gathering. He had a trained neutral expression, so maybe it was her imagination. Or it was a trap. What did the FBI know of her private life? "Yes," she said. It wasn't a lie.

Segreti's focus had drifted before he even realized it. He

was back in his empty apartment with its cold glass views and nothing personal, just a face-down photo, a shelf of liquor and his badge and gun. Hotel rooms had more personality than Segreti's apartment. He snapped back. "This guy come with a name?"

"He wouldn't give it. But you know what it is."

"He may have aliases. You know who you called on that phone he gave you?"

"Another of your colleagues."

"My colleague's daughter."

He waited to see how she'd take that, and decided she'd make a good poker player.

"I didn't know that. I'm sorry. Ellie's just something I made up. There was only one number in the directory. That man told me to call it."

"You believed him?"

"I knew he was related to you, involved with Red Fidelity. What's his name?"

"I'd rather not say."

"Come on, Ed. I've given you something useful."

"Thank you. For your safety I think it's best you don't know anybody's name. He's already invaded your home and threatened you."

"I deserve to know who did this to me."

"It doesn't get safer, just more dangerous."

"You just don't like a reporter investigating the same thing you're chasing."

"You're right, I don't."

"Then we're done."

"Justine, slow down. This blond guy, can you describe him?"

"What's in it for me?"

"You're assisting a federal investigation into the theft and deployment of a very dangerous cyber-weapon."

"Hm. I've got an investigation of my own. Last I checked, this is still America."

"Let's skip the First Amendment lecture. This intruder, did he appear injured in any way?"

"He limped."

Segreti nodded. Tremain for sure.

"My visitor says you're crooked. Do you tell lies, Ed?"

"*He* does. He's trying to use you, get you to stir the pot, disrupt our investigation, send me down rabbit holes."

"I guess it's working," she said, followed by another sucking sound. Segreti felt a flash of anger and wondered if maybe taking her here had been a mistake. Maybe he should have thrown her in the MCC downtown, let her marinate in that cesspit for twenty-four hours. She surprised him by shaking her empty cup. "That was actually quite nice. Thanks for popping my bubble-tea cherry."

The innuendo, intentional or not, gave him pause. Katie would never say such a thing.

"But," she added, beginning to stand up, "this was just a one-time thing."

Segreti didn't want Justine to leave. Maybe because the job wasn't done yet, maybe for some other reason.

"It's very popular in Asia," he said, just trying to keep the conversation going. "Those bubble drinks."

"Uh-hunh."

"I served over there for a while. Anti-nuclear proliferation, based out of Seoul. When you ask me if I'm corrupt..."

She sat back down. Didn't speak. Those eyes, electric blue.

"In a way, I am." He was wading into territory he hadn't planned to visit. It was incognito even to him. "I was on a case. There was a woman."

"What happened?"

"She was mixed up in something over her head. I took a bullet for her, right here." He pointed to his breast, just below the collar bone. "After that, I broke my vows."

"Where is she now?"

"She had given me the keys to the case, and we rounded up the bad guys. Probably prevented a war. But I was in the hospital and then rehab for six months, and by the time I got out, she was long gone." He indulged a mocking chuckle. "I always put the job before my family. I thought maybe that was okay, that my job was to protect my family. But when I was back home, there wasn't any love between me and my wife. Hadn't been for years. So now we're getting divorced. That's a betrayal, of everything I thought I believed in. You want to catch a Fed telling lies? Well, here I am."

She wondered what to make of this. He seemed sincere: there was a trace of unease in his eyes, a hint of sadness. But that didn't mean a thing. He wasn't talking about Red Fidelity or the Russians or Blond Ambition. Maybe if she pulled this string, though, it would unthread something useful.

"We might have that much in common," she said. "I'm not checking into a hotel just to get away from an intruder. Or, he's not the only one I'm putting at a distance."

"This other man, he wasn't happy about your working funny hours?"

"No, and I wasn't happy about the way he made me feel about it."

"We're alike," Segreti said.

"We are not."

"When we want something, it's not just nine to five. We don't have jobs, Justine. We have callings."

Justine considered that. It was a point she didn't want to concede, because it meant taking the blame for everything—endangering her colleagues, or at least wasting their time; alienating Steve. She was a parasite, but she couldn't bring herself to say so.

"Then you understand why I'm not dropping my investigation," she said.

"I do. And I'm telling you, if you get in the way of mine, I'll drop you down a well so deep you won't remember what sunlight looks like."

She pursed her lips, tried on a thoughtful pout. "If you obstruct the free press, I'll raise such a stink that you lose your badge." She leaned in. "Come on, Segreti, we can either threaten each other or you can use me. Bring me in. Let me help you."

"To do what?" But he knew the answer was obvious: Tremain.

"Maybe the intruder will be back," she said. "Want to tell me his name?"

"If you know his name, he'll know you got it from me."

"So?"

Segreti thought it over. Tremain had figured out who she was and was using her to send the Bureau down a false trail. Why? Because time counted. Tremain needed to wrap up his scheme and disappear. He knew the government was on to him; he had been involved in the attempted murder of a federal agent. He might be chums with the Russians. And he knew an awful lot about a cyber-weapon pilfered from the NSA. Time was not on Bobby Tremain's side. He only needed to distract Segreti long enough to unleash havoc and get away. What if Segreti could somehow slow him down until the Bureau had assembled enough of the puzzle?

"What I'm about to say is so off the record that it cannot be printed or published in any format, and if I get even a whiff of this showing up..."

"Agreed."

"His name is Tremain, Bobby Tremain. He used to work at the NSA. We think his time there overlapped with that of Walter Klinger. He organized the auction. He's trying to broker Red Fidelity to the highest bidder. The part I don't understand is that he appeared to get it from a Russian source, not from Klinger—not directly, at least. The Russians had this thing and they want him to get it on the market."

"They want him to set it off."

"Or get someone else to trigger it. Plausible deniability. But if they want to unleash this thing, they could just pass it to the North Koreans or the Iranians."

"One of my sources told me it's not traditional malware. There's quantum algorithms. It might be a codebreaker."

He looked surprised. "Did Tremain say that?"

"No. I pieced it together myself." Had she turned the tables on him, won some leverage? "You didn't know that, did you?"

"Classified, sorry." *Too many people know about this thing.* "You said Tremain gave you a phone. Still have it?"

"Yes."

He opened his palm.

Justine noticed he had regained his swagger. This was the Segreti she recognized: Bomber, the man who got his way. Someone she was prone to dislike, and yet there was a plainness in his eyes that was not arrogant.

"That's evidence," he told her.

The facts were there: she had not found Segreti; he had found her. The cute bubble tea, the pedestrian zone... hell, maybe the fine summer evening breeze. She thought she had one-upped him, but she'd walked right into his net.

She gave him Tremain's phone.

III

The Red

Chapter 32

Tremain waited as the signal on his screen paused along Twenty-Fifth Street between Lexington and Third. The chip in the phone bobbed around on his map before accelerating along Twenty-Third and turning down Park. Headed for downtown, all the way to the Javits Federal Building.

"Segreti has it?" Annika Volkov asked, her cigar pulls giving her voice more gravel than a country driveway.

"Yep."

They were in windowless darkness. Cement walls beneath the plywood thicker than a man's body. The only light came from a pair of laptop screens on the steel desk. The cigar's tip ebbed like a demonic beacon.

The signal on the screen disappeared.

Tremain said, "They've already begun to take it apart. The phone we gave her."

"You will find this fucking reporter, make it happen?"

"She's easy to track," Tremain said. "What isn't so easy is recovering from a sniper's bullet. I'm not feeling very nimble right now."

Volkov snorted. "Fucking pussy."

Tremain smiled despite his anger. She had balls, he'd give her that. Volkov's beautiful ugly face was an impassive gauze in the eerie light.

"Speaking of which," he ventured, "when was the last time you got laid?"

Her eyes darkened in a way that he liked. He leaned back in his chair and swiped his blond locks back. "Just for the record," he added.

She tapped the cigar's ash onto the naked table. "You are fucking impertinent."

He gave a boyish shrug. "That's the nicest thing you've ever said to me, Annika."

She ran her tongue along the shaft of the cigar. Tremain leaned forward, fully alert. For the first time since he'd woken up in a quack's office, he didn't feel the pain of his gunshot wound.

"You like this, no?" She looked at the cigar. "You want to suck my cock, Robert?"

He chuckled, wondering what he had just stepped into. He hadn't been able to shake her mountainous face from his thoughts. The way she played the cigar on those pillowy lips, the ways he had imagined riding her—or being ridden by her. But he hadn't considered whether she might be trans. The mannishness was clear, but beneath that track suit she moved like a woman. And the Russians weren't big fans of alternative sexuality, at least not the ones in their fascist regime. Still, Tremain pictured what she might have between her legs and decided to de-risk. He wasn't ready for a surprise.

"My interest was purely professional," he said.

She laughed. "You are such a fucking coward." She suddenly lunged and smashed the hot end of the cigar on his hand.

Tremain yelped, pushed back in his chair and crashed into the wall. "Guilty," he said, blowing on his smoking hand. Now the gunshot wound's throb returned. Great. What else should hurt? "So now what?"

"They will rejoice," Volkov said. "They will find Israeli spyware that is new. It took FSB many months to crack this. They will know they have been given a gift. Why does Russia give the fucking FBI such a generous thing?"

Tremain guessed it was because Red Fidelity would soon render the spyware and everything like it irrelevant. He just wanted to make sure he was out of harm's way and rich as hell when it happened. Eventually the lack of secrecy would expose him too, but Uncle Sam and everyone else would have their hands full. They'd be like bayonetted soldiers trying to hold in their guts.

"Speaking of which," he said, "we need a new auction so we can find buyers who know what to do with Red Fidelity. Putting the reporter together with Segreti means they'll figure it out."

"They will be chasing their tails."

"They can close down every quantum cloud server in the world."

"Is so? Then you have one week."

"That's not enough."

"It's enough or you take a swim with Dimitri." She rounded the table, a shade in the LCD glow. She was close enough that he could smell her, a woodsy soap smell. "I want those FBI dead."

"The last time we tried that, your guy shot me." The wound pulsed and he adjusted his position in the chair. "I don't see any upside to killing them."

"Upside?" She slapped him so hard his teeth rattled. "Segreti has committed crimes."

"Do tell."

"Is not your business."

That smoldering look, he realized, was not a come-hither. It was a quiet, controlled rage. An aura of power. He had the gut instinct that he would go to great lengths to serve this woman. He had once feared her, but now it was something more like rapture. Tremain didn't feel like he was in control anymore.

Talk about scared.

"Okay, I think I understand," he said. "Segreti won't fall for it. Although…"

"Yes?"

"Justine might. And then Segreti will follow."

"So, you're not totally fucking stupid after all." She was standing right in front of him, all silhouette, a column of wood and stone. "Make this happen, Bobby. For me."

"All right," he said, his skin alive at her proximity, the hairs of his neck at attention, his mouth scraped dry, his heart competing with his wound, pounding electricity into his circulation. "I sold you a zero-day last year, that Microsoft malware. I think it's time to use it."

She pulled down her track pants and thrust her hips forward. Pubic hairs tickled his nose.

"Suck it," she commanded.

Tremain, shaking with dread and excitement, inched his face forward. She was a she. Volkov seized his hair and screwed his mouth against her pelvis. His tongue found her clitoris. His jaw ached with effort. With a frustrated tsk she released him and grabbed his crotch, found his zipper. He helped her pull down one pants leg, and then she straddled him. Beneath the woodsy soap were deeper smells, like the rotting roots of an ancient tree. As the back of his skull scraped up and down the concrete wall, he forgot all about the bullet hole and the burn on his hand. Guttural sounds, and those lips all over his, biting his until the sharp pain and the salt of his blood. She roared and pushed off. Stood straight and hitched her pants back up.

Tremain struggled to breathe while his head swam. The pain of his broken lip asserted itself. "Wow," he said, stupidly, aware that he had capitulated to her and not sure what that would mean.

"I go now," she said. "To Russian consulate."

He had assumed she had diplomatic credentials. How else could she have entered the country so effortlessly? They were on Long Island, where the Russian government owned a Gilded-Age mansion in secluded woods, bounded by a wall and tight security. They claimed to use it for family vacations for embassy personnel, but it was bristling with satellite dishes and other listening equipment. They called it the Dacha. Of course they did.

"What about me? How do I get out of here?"

"Fyodor will see to it." She walked to the room's sole door. It was a basement so there was only a single bulb hanging outside, but after the darkness it burned like a dark sun. He squinted as her profile moved to the stairs. "I must be at United Nations in two hours."

"What's your cover?" he asked. He didn't expect her to tell him, but she faced him, and he swore she was smiling.

"I am Russian delegate for Human Rights Office."

Chapter 33

Justine needed a car to get to Brookhaven National Laboratory, out near the far end of Long Island. Professor Ang had told her he couldn't answer her questions; he was just a theorist. She'd need to find someone who knew the workings of a quantum computer. Someone who got their hands dirty with the things. She had wheedled him for a contact and he put her in touch with a former student of his who now worked at the lab, Kartika Nagarwal. Kartika was a Princeton PhD candidate there on some kind of collaborative project. Visitors couldn't just stroll into BNL, but Kartika had filed an official invitation for her.

After everything that had happened, Justine had forgotten about it, but Kartika's invitation popped up in her email. She may have quit *Archer's*, but neither she nor Paul Chow had begun the process of ending her employment—Paul hoping her anger would blow over; Justine just too distracted from the encounter with Segreti. So she rented a car for the day and drove out. Traffic out of Manhattan was a snarl, leaving her plenty of time behind the wheel to think.

If the FBI agent had known how close she had been to dropping this, he might not have approached her. If anyone was responsible for this new determination, she mused as she steered free of the knotted byways of Queens and into the suburban reaches of Long Island, it was Edward Segreti. She daydreamed about the satisfaction of telling him this to his face. Of course, that assumed she'd see him again. And so she began imagining what that might be like. Probably awkward and horrible.

BNL's campus was among forests and fields; another twenty minutes she'd be at the beach. She parked at the visitor center where she had to show ID and fill out several forms. By the time that was done, Kartika Nagarwal arrived, a tall Indian woman in jeans and a soft blazer, wearing semi-formal black penny loafers. With her was a middle-aged white man in an off-the-rack brown suit and a friendly if bland smile.

"Joe Metzger," he said, shaking her hand, "public affairs." Routine for a visit from the media, but a hazard for her. "Welcome to C2QA."

"I don't know what that is," Justine said.

"The Co-design Center for Quantum Advantage," he replied.

"Sounds impressive. Can you tell me what that means?"

Kartika said, "Quantum advantage is the point when quantum computers can do things that classical computers can't. Brookhaven partners with several universities and companies like IBM to use this technology to transform our industries, from energy to materials."

If it were just Kartika, Justine would have told her the whole backstory. But Joe Metzger was a federal employee. She'd need to keep any mention of the FBI out of this.

They gave her a basic thirty-minute tour of the main building. Kartika was eager to talk at least in general terms about the work that went on here and her PhD dissertation.

The technicalities soon overwhelmed Justine. Scratch the surface, and quantum physics was definitely beyond Justine's comprehension.

"This story for *Archer's*," Joe said. "What's your angle, if I may ask? Happy to direct you to the best resource."

She had learned that when PR people offered help, it was a double-edged sword. Sometimes they could open doors. But they did this to steer reporters away from other portals, make sure they didn't even know what to ask.

"How would someone run an algorithm on one of these things?"

"If they have an actual quantum computer, you input it in the lab," Kartika replied. "But most services are now done on cloud, which means across a network of hardware. IBM has hardware here that's part of their cloud service."

"Can I see it?"

"We have a viewing station," Joe said. "Come on, it's downstairs. But you didn't tell me what your story's about."

"There's speculation about quantum computers being able to break all our secrets."

"Thought so," Joe said, with that ambiguous smile again. "It's a spicy topic. There's plenty of articles on it."

She followed them down steps. "Yes, I've found a bunch of them online. And videos. IBM's starting to sell the idea of protecting data. I didn't quite understand it."

"It's a genuine threat," Joe said, "but for the time being, an academic one. We're quite a few years away. BNL has people working on this, to make sure we're prepared."

"Something about Y2K?" Justine asked.

Kartika said, "That's waaay before my time."

Joe laughed. "Guess I'm the Boomer here. In the 1990s every

business and government around the world had to reconfigure all their computer systems. Turns out when we started inventing these things, we programmed their calendars thinking in terms of centuries. Forgot that in the year 2000, that first digit would go from 1 to 2. Everyone's computer was going to recalculate the first day of the new millennium as Year 1000. Cue crashing airplanes and exploding nuclear power plants. Dumb mistake, missed in the rush to jump on the computer bandwagon back in the day. The effort to avoid a catastrophe was pretty heroic, if you ask me, but it cost a lot of money. And when nothing bad happened, it became kind of a joke."

Justine asked, "So what's that matter now?"

Joe shrugged as he used his passkey to unlock a door. "Quantum computers can decrypt anything protected by asymmetric communications."

Kartika said, "Most encryption is based on factoring and private keys."

"I think you're going to have to explain that," Justine said as Joe led them along a darkened corridor. Ahead waited a high panel of windows.

"We protect data today by using private keys," Kartika said. "Let's say you bank online. To keep your account information private, the bank's computer generates two private keys that are prime numbers."

"Like five and eleven?"

"Yes. Multiply them, you get fifty-five, that's the public key. Anyone can have the public key, including hackers, but all they know is that the multiplier gives you fifty-five. You can't work out what the two private-key numbers are."

"But if you know how it works, then it's easy to work out that fifty-five is eight times eleven."

"We're talking about really, really big prime numbers."

"Oh."

"No one can factor those big primes," Kartika said. "Except a quantum computer, if it has enough qubit power, could work it out really quickly. Peter Shor at MIT was the guy who realized this first. Now we have to change encryption protocols."

Joe said, "That's one of the projects we've got going on here, making the world quantum-safe."

"It's not my area," Kartika added, "but I know some of the team. There's a whole bunch of people working on different ideas to write new algorithms that would re-encrypt data and replace the old asymmetric models."

"And here we are," Joe said. The corridor was a viewing station overlooking a lab. Computers were piled on high, interlinked by a root network of wires that would shame the mightiest tree. Three people were below, wearing white hazmat suits.

"Is it radioactive in there?" Justine asked.

"No, it's just a clean room," Joe said. "And it's cold."

Suspended above them was an elaborate golden cluster of gleaming cables, layers upon layers of them, gloriously opulent, like a steampunk version of a Victorian chandelier.

"That's it? The chandelier?" she asked.

"No, that's just the cooling system," Kartika said.

Joe pointed to a small black cube resting beneath the lustrous apparatus. "That's the computer."

"It's so small."

"Yes. That's how many qubits, Kartika?"

"Twenty-four."

Joe chuckled. "What's that story about how much it can

compute?"

"It took about a week to tell us that one times three is three," Kartika said. "It's like an idiot savant."

"But there's a lot of this hardware now, around the entire world," Joe said. "Which is linked via a cloud architecture, so that programmers can run experiments remotely."

Justine was close to learning what she wanted to know. "What if someone had a decryption algo that they ran through that cloud server?"

Her hosts exchanged an uncertain glance.

"Probably...nothing?" Joe ventured.

"Even if someone could write that kind of program," Kartika said, "we don't have enough qubit processing power to provide a meaningful answer. Decoherence is still a big challenge."

"Not even the people at NSA?" Justine asked. "Haven't they been working on this sort of thing for a while?"

Kartika shrugged. "Sorry, I have no idea."

"I get the allure," Joe said, "but that's not a real story."

"You don't think so?" Justine asked.

"It's just sci-fi stuff. A little beneath a publication such as *Archer's*. Leave that for the mobs on social media."

She pointed at the panorama below. "Just entertain me for a sec. Let's say someone with a lot of experience, maybe someone like a signals specialist, wrote a general algorithm to decrypt. To... what was it, make information symmetrical?"

"That's not what you'd call it," Kartika said.

"But you get my gist. A quantum decryption code that could be run on a collective of quantum computers using an IBM or Google cloud service. It wouldn't be hard to hide what they're doing, right? They could just make up some research-sounding mumbo-jumbo and show a credit card, and they're in."

"It's not that simple," Joe objected.

"Well..." Kartika said.

"How much information could it unlock?"

"It's preposterous," Joe said. "We're a decade away from this risk."

"It would depend on what data they already have," Kartika said. "If they had a lot of encrypted data protected by factoring, they could open it all."

"They'd have to have stolen the data first?"

"I'd say so."

"How much data has been stolen in the past few years by, say, Russian hackers?"

"Ms. Jarman," Joe said, "why don't we head upstairs?"

"I'm just, you know, trying to understand," Justine said. "If the Russians, or the Chinese, or whoever, had stolen nuclear codes or military secrets, and were just waiting to open them, and they ran that algo through your server, what could they find out?"

"That's why we're helping make the world quantum-safe," Joe said, leading the way back. "I'll help sign you out, Ms. Jarman. You'll want to get a stamp for your parking pass."

In her car, she checked her phone for messages. Something frantic-sounding from Patty. She called.

"J.J., holy shit, you're not going to believe what's going on."

"Tell me slowly, okay? What's up?"

"*Archer's* been hacked."

* * *

She bustled into her office building at dusk. The lobby was the usual post-pandemic quiet; the white-collar workers mostly stayed at home these days. *Archer's* had been different. The journalism teams felt a genuine bond, a sense of community, and liked working together. Many lived in the city or had straightforward commutes. Same for the artists and designers. It was the sales and marketing people that had never come back after Covid.

Her stomach sank as she rode the elevator up. She had been checking the magazine's app on her phone practically nonstop. Just getting a 404 error. This was bad. Her friends' livelihoods could be on the line.

The glass doors to the office didn't respond to her electronic fob. The lights were all on, but she didn't see anyone. She knocked and waited.

Josh jogged into view and turned the lock to let her in.

"All the electronic stuff's out," he told her.

"What happened?"

"Probably a phishing attack," he said, leading her back to the reporters' corner. Only a skeleton crew remained. She noticed all the computer screens were dark.

Bert and Patty were still there.

"Ransomware," Patty said, pointing to her PC screen. A blazing skull and crossbones showed over a text message. If *Archer's* wanted its data back and its systems restored, it would have to send 20 bitcoins to a specified hash.

"It's targeted at us," Justine said, "not our parent company?"

"Nope," Patty said.

"Where's Paul?"

"He's upstairs," Bert said. Meaning he was probably being

grilled by the chief operating officer and legal guys. "The police were here earlier."

"You think this has something to do with us?" Patty asked.

"It could be a coincidence," Justine said.

"And what's this about you quitting?"

Bert stuck his hands in his pockets. "I had to tell them."

"Never mind, that's off," she said. Although if the publication didn't recover their systems, they were all out of a job. "I met Bomber last night."

"No way," Josh said.

"I don't think he's dirty. I do think he's desperate. He basically confirmed the quantum angle. I think the auction we went to was an elaborate cover for the Russians to sell malware to what they thought was a regular criminal. It turned out to be the FBI, Bomber—Segreti. If you run that code through a big-enough quantum computer it can unlock a lot of information that's supposed to be protected. It's basically an all-purpose key."

"Then why don't they just use it at home?" Josh asked. "Like, if they have it, what do they need another criminal for?"

"They need someone who can access a cloud network, like the ones run by IBM or Google, or one of the big universities," Justine said. "That's the only way to get the power, the scale, needed to make it work. They don't have that in Russia. They need someone with credentials that look legit in America."

Patty looked skeptical. "I don't know, J.J. Your average black-hat jerkoff isn't going to walk into Los Alamos or wherever and say, hey, can I plug this in?"

She hadn't asked Segreti that, either. "Tremain must have vetted the buyers, thinking they were capable."

"Who?"

She realized she probably shouldn't have said the name aloud. "Blond Ambition. The guy who broke into my apartment and gave me the phone."

"So he has a name now," Bert said.

"Yeah, he has a name." Well, if she couldn't trust these three, she couldn't trust a single person in this world. "Robert Tremain. Ex-NSA. Ed says he's a traitor."

"Ed," Patty said, her eyes lighting up.

"Patty, don't."

"You two getting chummy."

"Look," Justine said, "until the company decides what to do about the hack, we're stuck. Go home, get some rest."

Her phone rang. Her desk phone, the one she never used except to field a call from reception. The blinking light said the call was coming from an outside line.

The four of them exchanged glances.

Riiing.

"Well?" Patty insisted.

"Fine." She picked it up. "*Archer's.*"

A man said, "What did Segreti have to say about me?"

She felt coils of fear tighten in her guts.

"Why are you calling me?"

Tremain said, "Come on, Justine, you can share."

"Where are you calling from?"

"He give you my name? Some backstory bullshit?"

"I, uh…" She made alarming but helpless gestures to her friends.

"Tell you what. Let's do a trade. You tell me what Segreti has to say, and I'll let you in on a little secret about that ransomware in your office."

Justine snapped out of indecision and grabbed a pen and her

notepad. "I guess a trade is okay." She bumbled for her phone but Patty was faster, calling up a recorder on her iPhone and holding it by Justine's ear.

"Ladies first."

"Well, he told me your name is Robert Tremain. Is it?"

"No comment."

"You used to work for the NSA. You're a traitor. And you set up the auction as a cover to sell Red Fidelity. You're just a Russian cutout."

He laughed. "A Russian cutout? You wound me, Justine."

"I would have thought being called a traitor by the FBI would be worse."

"It's about what I'd expect from the likes of him."

"Is it true? That you stole code from the NSA, betrayed your country, and are working with Russia to get someone in the US to run that algorithm here, using a quantum cloud server?"

He laughed again. It was an annoying laugh, all self-satisfaction and nothing funny. "You're a card, Justine."

"Your turn, Bobby."

"I'm holding another auction. This one's going to include selling the zero-day that's currently immobilizing your corporate servers. Whoever's hacked you is asking for a lot of money and no guarantees. But if you come and buy the exploit from me, it'll contain the patches you need to restore service, and it's an auction, so the price might end up being a lot cheaper."

"What makes you think I won't just tell the FBI?"

"I suggest you get some rest, Justine. You're going to have a busy day tomorrow."

Chapter 34

Segreti put on a tie before heading to ADIC's office. Formality was still expected, especially when the Bureau had visitors. Paperwork had consumed the morning, and lunch had been a poke bowl. Under other circumstances, he would have welcomed the break from routine.

Ram was in the field, monitoring Jarman and following up on the *Archer's* hack, while Belmont was pursuing internal leads on Russian activities. That left just him and Chlebek to face the music. She fell in behind him, dressed in a conservative blue pants suit, her big curves levitating on black high heels, her jet hair tamed by a chunky red clip.

He wasn't shocked to see the two NSA agents sitting on the leather couch in ADIC's office. The East Asian woman and the Latino man, today dressed in suits, but the government-standard uniforms didn't come with smiles. No, he was not shocked, but definitely not pleased to see them, either.

"Ma'am," he said to his boss.

Church indicated he and Chlebek should take the chairs fronting her desk. "I gather you have met."

"Uh, yes ma'am. But I didn't catch your names."

"Chien and Gonzalez," the NSA woman said.

"Any particular department?"

Gonzalez said, "You don't need to know that, Special Agent Segreti."

He arched an eyebrow towards his boss, which Church ignored. She was the cool professional. Segreti had the feeling that he would soon hear her say, "Nothing personal, Ed."

Church didn't sugarcoat it. "This has gone two levels above my head," she told him.

"They're the ones who lost the code," Chlebek blurted and leaned slightly forward.

Segreti put his hand over hers. She sat back.

"Sorry, ma'am. We've put a lot into this case."

"Which is going nowhere," Chien said behind him.

"Your former colleague is in New York," Segreti replied. "He broke into the apartment of a reporter who's been chasing this story since the auction on North Brother Island. He's been trying to control the narrative. Using her to play games with us. He's wounded and I'd say desperate. And likely receiving aid from Moscow, here, on the ground. It's just a matter of time before we get him."

Gonzalez said, "The whereabouts of Tremain are of secondary importance. We need to see the Red Fidelity code."

Chlebek said, "It's got Doublepulsar imprints. It came out of your labs."

Chien leaned over her elbows. "You don't know what Red Fidelity can do."

"Even the reporter knows it's written using quantum computing language," Segreti said, turning to face them. "So it's some kind of communications device. Encrypt, decrypt? Either that or a sensor."

The two NSA agents exchanged a look. He struggled to see anything human pass between them. *Maybe the robots had already come for us*, he thought.

Chien said, "With enough hardware, that code could unlock every factor-based encryption. Every single one."

"The Russians are far behind on quantum," Gonzalez said, "and the last people they'd trust to give it to are the Chinese. They're looking for a cutout to insert the code over government research lab infrastructure."

"Klinger wrote that code?" Segreti asked.

"He was part of a team." Gonzalez hesitated. "The unit director at the time decided the work was too theoretical and halted the program."

"Let me guess," Segreti said. "Klinger was pissed off. Over comes Tremain. Also on that unit?"

The two NSA agents didn't respond.

"Tremain whispers into Klinger's ear, tells him he might as well get something for all his hard work. And since it's just theoretical, what's the harm, really? Besides, Klinger doesn't have to do a thing. Tremain will handle the business end. He just needs the code. Maybe he even pays for it up front."

Chien said, "This conjecture is wasting our time. We need to analyze the code. We expect it may have been modified."

"To do what?"

"That's what we'd like to know," Chien said.

"And why the Russians are eager to execute the program," her partner added.

Church said, "Agent Chlebek will give you any help you need to take possession of the code."

"That's key evidence in our case against Tremain," Segreti protested.

"Your review is tomorrow," she reminded him. He tried to look nonchalant. Internal affairs, the shooting at the auction.

His fate. His insides shivered. "Get through that first. We've got electronic eyes and ears all over the city. If he surfaces, we'll find him."

Segreti stood up, buttoned his jacket. "Ma'am."

"Chlebek, you stay and provide assistance to our guests," Church said.

Segreti walked out of there feeling like the last few grains of sand were swirling their way down the hourglass, gravity sealing their destiny. But submitting to the flow wasn't his way. It wasn't what had made him a lawman for twenty years. If 'lawman' was still what he was.

On his way back to his desk, he decided to take a different route. He took the elevator down to the computer forensics lab. The lab was busy now; the other two technicians were back at their stations. And Taylor was at a desktop computer, her tall frame hunched over so she could read the screen's cramped lines of code. She stood up as he approached. "Sir?"

Segreti regarded the other two techs. The older one, Boston Irish, waved hello.

He crooked a finger at Taylor and she followed him out of the lab. The hallway was open space, but no one was walking through. It would do for a brief inquisition.

"Did you assist Chlebek with that code?"

"No, sir. She wouldn't let me near it. Besides, I'm not sure I would have added much."

"Did you make a copy?"

"It's highly sensitive. It's on special-purpose laptops that are in a contained room and not connected to any—"

"Yeah, but did you copy the code?"

He knew this was like asking if someone copied a nuclear bomb, just in case.

"That would be against protocol, sir."

"Let me put it this way, Taylor. I understand you did not copy that code."

"Correct, sir."

"Did Miriam?"

"Uh...I couldn't say."

"Okay, Taylor. Thanks. Get back to work."

His phone vibrated. Ram. "Jarman's on the move, chief."

So was Segreti. "Where?"

"Called an Uber from her hotel. I'm following her now on FDR Drive."

"What about those others on her team?"

"She was met in the lobby by Patricia Yamagata and Josh Friedland."

He punched the elevator button, looked at what floors the cars were, cursed his luck.

"This stinks of Bobby Tremain," he said.

"I agree," Ram said.

"Stay with them."

He was going to need manpower. He texted Belmont. No way he could get Chlebek to help him now, now that she had been detailed to help the NSA. Segreti rolled with an idea, knew it was a bad one, but backtracked anyway.

"Special Agent Taylor!"

She came at a trot.

"We're going into the field. Make sure you're armed."

"Sir?"

"Be downstairs in five."

He had one detour to make, to the armory, before he made for the carpool.

"I got a Dodge Durango," the officer said, "A Chevy Ram,

and a Jeep."

Good vehicles but they all looked a little tired. Except a pure black beauty lurking in a corner, with silver steel lines and a fan above the hood.

"What's that one, that a Mustang?"

"You bet. Impounded 1969 Boss, with a 429 V8 engine, retrofitted chassis and 500 pound-feet of torque."

"I'll take it."

"You can't sir, it's from a bust and being put up for auction—"

"I said I'm taking it."

Segreti put the cases with two M4 carbines in the trunk.

"Hurry up, Taylor, get in."

Ram once again into Segreti's earpiece, cord dangling to his phone: "They're taking the tunnel to Brooklyn. In a blue Honda Civic." He rattled off the license plate number.

Segreti squealed in pursuit but had to accept the laws of traffic when they neared the mouth of the tunnel. They emerged from darkness among the brownstones and Italian grocers of Carroll Gardens, and the road opened up, a little.

"Let's see what this baby can do."

They leaped onto the expressway and blazed a trail past the industrial park and docks hugging Gowanus Bay. The late afternoon sun bounced off the water into the car like a heat ray. Taylor looked like an astronaut pressed against her seat upon launch, as he sped along the highway over Bay Ridge. "Talk to me, Ram," Segreti said.

"Looks like they're taking the bridge."

They crossed over water, the Verrazzano-Narrows Bridge suspended high between Brooklyn and Staten Island. He caught only a glimpse of greenery below and didn't dwell on almost getting murdered down there.

"I see you," he said, noting Ram's dusty Charger a few vehicles ahead. "Belmont, where you at?"

"Ten minutes behind you, sir."

"She's staying on the expressway," Ram reported.

Staten Island's pleasant suburbs and leafy parks unfolded on either side. They followed the contours of a clover intersection and kept going through Graniteville.

"If she stays on the expressway, she goes to New Jersey," Segreti said. "Otherwise, the only other way off Staten Island is Outbridge."

"Looks like she's turning onto West Shore," Ram said.

"Belmont, you cover Goethals Bridge just in case and then head south. If she changes course, intercept her along the river."

"Where the hell is she going?" Ram wondered.

Staten Island turned to forest and then marshy wilderness. They were traversing Freshkills Park, a delta of salty waterways interspersed with forests and hiking paths.

"She's slowing down...turning off. Along the riverfront, Arthur Kill. Warehouses, recycling center...getting out at a cemetery."

Taylor said, "What's here? Seems like the end of nowhere."

He sped past Ram and pulled into the cemetery. The blue Honda was pulling out, empty aside from the Uber driver.

He parked beneath an oak tree, its serenity notable among the confusion in his head. He got out. "See them?"

"There," Taylor said, pointing.

The three figures coalesced around a filthy green van. Now four: the bulky cameraman, Bert Gomez, had joined them.

The quartet of reporters walked back out to Arthur Kill Road.

"Where are they going?" Taylor wondered as Ram pulled up beside them. He had on a shirt, jeans, boots, and a ten-gallon hat that warded off the slanting rays of the sun.

Segreti walked over to him. "This is your turf, Bhav. What's down the road?"

"Landside, auto shops and construction equipment stores. Riverside, I think that's the boat graveyard."

Segreti popped the trunk. "The Boneyard. Perfect place for an ambush."

"We wait for Belmont, chief?"

"No, but tell him to get here A-sap. Got your drones?"

"Always."

"Get eyes in the air." He opened a case and handed the automatic rifle to Taylor. "You trained on these at Quantico, right?"

She looked apprehensive, but she picked up a 30-round magazine and snapped it in.

He looked at her clothes. Chinos, button-down shirt, sensible shoes. Better than his business suit and brogues. They were going to get muddy.

"Let's go."

Chapter 35

Justine led them through a dusty parking lot towards a low white wall topped with barbed wire. The signs were clear: US COAST GUARD: NO TRESPASSING.

"Uh, J.J.?" Patty said.

She led them to the far corner of the lot. There was no barbed wire here, just an impenetrable thicket of brush. Beyond it lay the river, with New Jersey somewhere on the far side.

"Maybe you stay here, watch our backs," Justine said.

Patty didn't reply.

"It's hot," Bert said, adjusting his Pabst Blue Ribbon trucker cap.

The late day sun was brutal in that exposed lot with its chalky gravel. Its white dust covered the handful of cars, their bodies radiating heat. Justine was glad she had worn her baseball cap. Patty had sunglasses but nothing to protect her head. In her black Ramones T-shirt, ripped jeans and high tops, Patty looked perfectly suited to the streets of the Village and very out of place on this far edge of Staten Island.

Justine had told them where they were going. She was wearing jeans and hiking shoes. Bert had galoshes fitted over his shoes. Even Josh wore a windbreaker over his Lana Del Rey T-shirt, although Justine wasn't sure his choice of shorts and flip-flops was the right move. He was leaning over the wall. "That's some serious plant life."

Justine swung a leg over the wall. "Here goes nothing."

The bushes were tall and prickly. They made for a pretty good fence. But they were navigable if she didn't mind getting dirty. The summer sun was probably a blessing, because even now, the dark ground was soft with mud. It was probably more treacherous other times of year.

Josh came next, his feet sinking into the mud with a loud squish. Then came Bert, imperturbable in his rubber shoe covers, a big oasis of calm.

She heard Patty say, "Screw it," and allowed herself a little smile.

The distance through the brush was short, but the going was slow. Everyone had at least one spill, and the air shimmered with heat and the buzz of flies. By the time Justine cleared the scrub, her clothes were stuck tight from all that sweating. They were rewarded with a melancholy view. The waters along this bend in the river ran quietly. A ghostyard of ships expanded before them, silhouetted against the blaze of the lowering sun, impressionist strokes of rust and whitewashed bone against the dark browns and blues of the water. The ships were mostly skeletons now, rusted remains of steel and iron, hulks half-sunk. Whatever tales these boats could have told were washing away with the river's current, histories leaching into oblivion.

"This is so cool," Josh said.

"It's eerie as fuck," Patty said.

Bert said in his soft voice, "It's quiet."

"Yeah," Justine agreed. "There's nobody here. Tremain said there was going to be an auction."

"Let's get out of here," Patty said.

"It's massive," Josh said. "Maybe he's, like, over there somewhere."

"We're supposed to root around these wrecks, dipshit?" Patty balked. "I don't think so."

Justine thought that was exactly what they would do. She walked along the narrow bank and put a foot on the hull of what once was probably a tugboat. "Since we're here," she said, but then her phone vibrated and she fished it from her pocket. Zach. *What did he want? Not a good time, kiddo.* She let her phone buzz back in her pocket.

Accessing the boat required walking along a discarded girder, red with rust, like a pirate's plank. She carefully stepped over the remains of a railing and regarded the boat's interior. The center had long since disintegrated and was now a pool of seawater. She took slow, deliberate steps. The metal felt soft, like walking on a yoga mat, so she kept to the high edges. She didn't know where she was going, but the boat skeletons were gathered tightly, their bones sticking into one another.

Behind her she saw her companions and the wall of scrub. The road and the parking lot were probably only a baseball's throw away, but she couldn't see them. Ahead was the river, faster beyond where the hulks were berthed, but the sun was low and blinding. New Jersey was a thick dark smudge on the horizon.

She followed a half-submerged ferry and headed to a thicker cluster of bigger hulls, these with decks and the shells of pilothouses intact. Seagulls made lazy circles above, their calls the only sound other than the wind on the water not far below. And her own breathing, and the beating of her heart.

Then, a figure in the pilothouse. Pink polo shirt, the collar raised; khaki pants and tall rubber boots. The familiar sweep of blond hair and Wayfarer sunglasses. "Ahoy, Justine!" called Bobby Tremain.

She stopped. Her team was strung behind her, Josh on her heels, Bert on the previous boat, Patty cautiously close to land.

Bobby gestured for her to join him.

"Where is everyone?" she called to Tremain, cupping her mouth.

"This way!" he called back.

"What do you think?" she asked Josh.

"Totally a bad idea."

"Yeah." There was her Pulitzer-Prize story, waving from the pilothouse of a ruin. She had known he was pulling strings; that any invitation from such a man was to be suspect. But her reporter instinct had been to follow the lead. Reporters didn't drive agendas, they got close to people who did and hoped they could unearth their motivations, divine their impact on the world. Naturally, she had accepted Bobby's offer.

But this scene felt wrong. It was obvious now that he had lied.

"Come on!" Bobby called.

"You come here!" she replied. "Josh, go back. Get the others out of here."

"Okay," he said.

Bobby walked out from his perch, one hand holding a cane. He held it up and pantomimed a helpless shrug.

"Where is everyone else?" she called to him.

"Here!"

A man stepped into view behind him, half hidden by the pilothouse. Justine didn't recognize him. White, muscled beneath a black shirt, camouflage pants, wraparound shades over a thick brown beard.

"Oh, hell no," she muttered.

She heard another voice in the wind, carried softly from somewhere else. "Justine! Justine!"

She turned and saw more figures scrambling out of the bush towards the edge of the boat graveyard. Edward Segreti waving frantically. Was that a rifle in his other hand?

Something caught her eye: a long shadow thrown against the wedge of a half-sunk boat. The man it belonged to appeared, wearing what looked like a black wetsuit. If she wanted to retreat, he could easily cut her off at the flank.

She took a step back.

A long, low buzz came from the sky. Not a swarm of flies, just a single drone that appeared for a moment above her before it vanished into the unforgiving blaze of the setting sun.

"Get out of there!" Ed's call was faint, swallowed by wind and water and the graveyard's fleet of carcasses.

The brown beard behind Bobby stepped out with a Kalashnikov assault rifle that he aimed at a high angle. Justine started to run as the weapon split the blue sky with unimaginable noise. The frogman to her side had a Kalashnikov too, and he fired it at the people onshore. Her head filled with the roar of violence, thinking *Josh Bert Patty... no no no*; thinking *run, Justine, run*; thinking *oh my God*, until her foot smashed through the soft decay that had looked like solid steel and she crashed into the half-submerged deck of a long-forgotten ship and saw the drone crash like a meteor just in front of her. It bounced once and vanished into the undead craft's watery bowels.

* * *

Segreti dropped to his knee as the frogman opened fire. The man was only about a hundred feet away, partly covered by another ship's angled hull and the sun-bleached remains of antennas. He saw Jarman fall on her face. *Justine!* He didn't know if she was shot. If she was still breathing.

Segreti returned fire and, in the pause, ran for the far edge of the hulk he was on.

Civilians blocked his view of Tremain. The big cameraman, Gomez, pounded heavily as he ran. The kid, Friedland, moved nimbly despite the flip-flops. Yamagata was already behind him, close to shore.

Taylor spread out to his left, finding her way to cover, trying to flank the frogman. But Frogman wasn't having it. Lead filled the air. Chewed up boats into shrapnel, turning the hulks into grenades.

Friedland was bawling in terror, but he was close. Segreti grabbed him and hauled him to the deck as bullets ripped holes around him. He could feel the young man's heart drumming on his own arm. "You're okay, kid," he said. He popped a look over the hull. "When I fire, you get out of here."

Gomez was lumbering into view. Segreti popped up and fired at the frogman. Frogman ducked for cover. Now Taylor was shooting too. Friedland was on his way. Brown Beard was shooting back. Maybe Tremain too, with what looked like Segreti's Glock.

Bert straightened into a ramrod. "Oof," he said, and keeled over, out of Segreti's view.

"Shit." Segreti laid down another line of fire, so did Taylor, and then he ran to the body. Holes raked the back of Gomez's jacket. Blood was pouring out of him. He wasn't moving. His eyes were open with astonishment. Segreti checked for a pulse, felt for a breath. Time was short. He closed Bert Gomez's eyes.

"Justine!?" His call felt lost amid the shooting.

The deck erupted around him. Frogman was crawling behind him. Segreti turned on his back and fired the M4 until it was out of ammo. He frantically ejected the mag and felt for his reserve. More gunshots, this time from Taylor, forcing Frogman back, but then silence burst upon him. He slapped in the new mag and sat up, rifle first.

Frogman teetered. Taylor fired two more bursts that punched Frogman overboard. Segreti flashed her a thumb's up and resumed his advance. Behind him, Ram had arrived, both hands gripping his Sig Sauer. Brown Beard and Tremain had also moved in, though—they were just one boat away.

He saw her. Justine was alive, clinging to detritus in the middle of the collapsed boat, legs kicking in the water. Most of the deck was gone, the craft now just hull.

"Stay down!" he shouted.

Tremain and Brown Beard were headed for her. Segreti opened up. Taylor and Ram too. Their targets fell back. Segreti moved forward, Taylor's fire covering him. He had almost reached Justine when Brown Beard popped up from another angle, surprising him, and aimed.

Taylor was on his heels. He saw her raise her carbine and pull the trigger. Click click. She kept her cool, reaching for a fresh mag, when Brown Beard shot her once in the chest. Helen Taylor hit the deck.

"No!" Segreti cried, crawling to her body. No one was shooting at him, and he didn't care why. Helen was still warm. He cupped her face in his palms. "Come on, honey, come on."

The eyes flickered once and whatever Helen had seen, thought, felt, it was now nothing but void.

Segreti didn't have the luxury to process what had just happened.

"Ed!"

He looked up. Brown Beard had pulled Justine out of her watery pit and was retreating to the pilothouse and Tremain, Justine's legs wheeling but getting no traction to stop him. Brown Beard was a big man who half-dragged her with one arm. She looked too exhausted to put up much resistance. And now Brown Beard aimed his Kalashnikov at Segreti, the gun pointing wildly, as he made his retreat.

"Let her go!" Segreti shouted, picking up his carbine.

Tremain walked a few steps away from his shelter, one hand aiming his pistol, the other leaning on his cane. "It's over, Segreti! Put that gun down. I promise this'll be quick and painless for you. And Justine gets to live."

Segreti tracked Brown Beard and Justine along the plane of his gunsight. Ram, taking a different angle, planted his legs to steady his aim.

"That's right," Tremain called, "she was just the bait. You're the catch, Ed!"

Ram and Tremain exchanged fire, Tremain staying cool, holding his ground. Segreti didn't risk looking back. But he felt the boat rock. Ram had taken a fall.

"Bhav?" he called, his eyes on Justine and Brown Beard. "You still with me?"

"Sorry, chief."

Tremain called, "You don't want to lose any more people, Ed! Your sorry-ass life for hers, what do you say?"

Chapter 36

Justine struggled harder, legs kicking air. "Let go of me!"

Since she had fallen into the pool of seawater, she had focused on clinging to debris and trying to pull herself back out. The thunder of gunfire had overwhelmed her senses. Her hands had found solid things to grab, just ribs of the dead ship. As she pulled herself up, an unidentified force had scrunched the back of her soaked shirt and hauled her up. It took her a moment to realize Brown Beard had grabbed her. He fired his Kalashnikov over her shoulder and her ear popped. She couldn't hear a thing other than a howling ring as he pulled her back.

Facing landward, what she saw horrified her: the frogman slumped over a railing, raining blood over it; Segreti aiming his rifle at her, at *her*; Bhavin Ram stretched back on one elbow, face hidden beneath a white cowboy hat, his guts bleeding through his fingers; a young Black woman in a dark business suit lying dead on the boat behind.

She found her strength and tried to kick and squirm free. Then she saw Bert.

No. Anyone but him.

Justine stopped struggling. It wasn't that she surrendered, she just collapsed.

Not Bert.

The mouth of Segreti's rifle flashed. She felt hot rain dump on her head. They were spinning and falling, she and Brown Beard. His finger pulled the trigger of his Kalashnikov, but he wasn't aiming at anything. She registered that she was covered in blood. Soaked in burning blood.

They hit the deck and she pushed him off. He gave no resistance. That's when she realized he didn't have a head. Just a pulpy mess. Half of his head was clinging to her. *Fuck! His* gore, his fucking brains stuck in her hair—

She freaked out and shrieked, even though she could only dimly hear herself. She scrambled away and almost crashed into Tremain, who had retreated behind the pilothouse. She froze because he was aiming his gun right between her eyes. Now she saw Tremain mouthing words but couldn't hear what he was saying. She didn't think he was talking to her. Probably shouting something to Segreti. Bullets raked the pilothouse, smashing windows, and Tremain ducked back.

Segreti was at her side, trying to pull her out of Tremain's sight. Then Segreti was up again, chasing.

She stumbled after him and saw Tremain dive into the open river. He swam towards a bobbing black sphere. A submersible.

The vehicle turned and, for an instant, the final gasp of sunlight struck its acrylic window, and she saw the profile of a square-faced white woman at the controls.

Segreti aimed his rifle as a trunk hatch on the back of the craft opened. Tremain swam for it as Segreti's shots chopped up the water, but suddenly he ran out of ammunition.

They watched the submersible descend beneath the waves.

Segreti slung the rifle's strap over his shoulder and held her.

She could see his lips ask her if she was alright, but she still couldn't hear clearly. And she sure as hell wasn't alright. She shook her head and pulled away.

The rest of the day was a long series of aftershocks. Ambulances, helicopters, speedboats, whose wails she gradually heard again. She was checked and checked again by medics, when what she needed was a shower. Giving statements. Watching cops lift Bert Gomez onto a stretcher and march him into an ambulance and shut its doors.

She had said she'd be the one to tell his family. Marta and his two kids. But the medic had said no, a police officer had already been tasked with that.

The sun abandoned the scene, leaving them in afterglow. The ghostships were invisible against the dark river when Segreti approached. She was sitting on the back edge of another ambulance, had a blanket over her shoulders and was sipping from a plastic cup of tea. His expression was blacker than the coming night.

"We're done here. You need a lift?"

"I'd rather call an Uber."

He sat next to her. He seemed out of fight. "Suit yourself."

"What just happened? Why is Bert dead?"

He shook his head. He had lost someone, too. The young agent named Taylor. A rookie. Plus, Bhavin Ram was being operated on. "This wasn't about some cyber-weapon. Well, not just that. Someone's trying to kill me. They got Tremain to use you as bait."

"You don't think it was his idea?"

"No. Did you see that woman in the submersible?"

"Yeah. Who is she?"

"I think she's a Russian spook. I don't have a name. Wish I

did."

"Why does she want you dead?"

He looked her way. "Tomorrow morning, I get grilled by Internal Affairs for what went down on North Brother Island. Seems ever since I met you, things have been...out of control."

"You blaming me for that, Ed?"

"No." He stood up. "I might be taken off the case. If you need anything, Justine... if you don't feel safe...call me, okay?"

"I'm writing my story. Can I say that man is Robert Tremain, ex-NSA?"

Segreti paused. "No." He walked away from the red and blue flashers, into the night.

She'd almost died. Segreti's marksmanship had saved her, but what if he had missed, by like, an inch? 'No'?

Patty and Josh had already left. Where she was, it would take an Uber driver at least a half hour to get her. The medics and cops had all cleared out. She was left in the cemetery where they had been dropped off.

"Bert," she whispered to the darkness.

It was a long drive back to Manhattan. She checked *Archer's* website and her work email. Still all down. Maybe the patch to restore service had sunk in the waters of Arthur Kill along with Tremain and that Russian woman.

Once they crossed into Manhattan, she asked the driver to switch gears and take her to Steve's place.

Not her place any longer. Just Steve's. But she couldn't stand the idea of being alone, so even if Steve wasn't going to be fun to deal with, she could hang out with Zach. Plus, she still had a lot of her stuff there. She needed a shower and a change of clothes, and a very large glass of wine.

It might not feel like hers anymore, but she still had a set of keys. She gave the doorman a perfunctory smile, knowing she must look like a war refugee, and took the elevator up.

She unlocked the door but knocked anyway. For the first time this felt invasive. No one responded to her meek "Hello?" and she entered the kitchen. A bowl with the remains of a salad and two plates splattered with pasta sauce and breadcrumbs. An empty bottle of Zinfandel. Then she heard them in the living room. Steve and the woman were making out on the couch. Justine watched them for a slow beat. Then the two of them jumped up in terror.

"Jesus, Justine," Steve said, panting.

"Who the fuck is this?" the woman demanded, her eyes wide with fear.

Steve's shoulders slumped and he looked like he'd rather be anywhere else on planet Earth than there. "This is, uh, my partner, Justine."

"You lying asshole," the woman said. She was a plumpish brunette, a light brown, with a low-cut top that showed plenty.

"No, it's fine," Justine said. "We're not really a thing anymore."

"Not a thing, but you walk in here like you live here?"

Justine rattled the apartment keys. "I was just returning these."

"Justine," Steve protested.

"I just want to pick up a few things and I'll be out of here."

He was working out her dishevelment. "Are you okay? What happened to you?"

"She's covered with blood," the woman said. "What kind of women do you usually hang out with?"

"Lucia, I'm sure this is just—"

"I'm out of here," Lucia said, reaching for her handbag.

"No, stay," Justine said. To Steve, she said, "You couldn't wait to bring someone back here?"

"I just—I thought—"

"Yeah. Where's Zach?"

"I don't know. Out."

"Who's Zach?" Lucia demanded.

"His son," Justine said.

"I told you about him," Steve said, his voice low.

"Sure you did, my ears must be on the fritz," Lucia said. "See ya."

Justine pushed her back with the flat of her palm, sending Lucia sprawling back onto the sofa. "I said stay." She said to Steve, "Have a great time."

She stormed upstairs. She had far more clothing and toiletries here than she could take in one go. Didn't matter. She hauled a suitcase out from under the bed and threw in whatever she could grab, heedless to how necessary it was. What counted was on the desk: notebooks, USB drives, an iPad, her backup hard drives.

In the bathroom she caught sight of herself. The mess of blood and ichor darkened her hair and was smeared on her skin. Her shirt was covered in Brown Beard's gore. She looked like the girl in a slasher flick. No wonder Lucia had wanted to get the hell out of here.

She thundered down the stairs. Steve and Lucia were arguing by the door. "Excuse me," Justine said, plunging between them.

"You're leaving?" Steve asked, exasperated. "Looking like that?"

She tossed the keys onto the hallway stand. "I'm on deadline."

Chapter 37

Segreti drove the Mustang Boss to Staten Island University Hospital. The campus's big, boxy glass buildings looked like an office complex, all windows blazing with light. As he got out of the car, he saw two familiar people crossing the parking lot. The man turned back and pointed a fob, and a vehicle's alarm chirped.

Segreti knew these two. Ram's daughter, Sissy, dressed in a black skirt and top, and the paisano, the too-old-for-teenagers boyfriend. Jim Fiorinetti. Jim's other hand was around Sissy's waist. Something mean grabbed Segreti's heart and gave it a squeeze. He glanced back at the boyfriend's car. Silver Mazda convertible, top up. Expensive ride for a high-school dropout with a few misdemeanor charges. He intercepted them in front of the hospital's doors. "Hi there."

Sissy pouted. "You here for my dad?"

"You go in, Sissy. I want to talk to your boyfriend for a minute."

"Come on," the guy protested. "You're not her old man."

"My dad's been shot and you're picking fights?"

Segreti raised his palms. "No fights."

"This guy's full of shit," Fiorinetti said.

"Unless you want one, Jimbo."

The memory of Segreti's fist must have scrolled through the punk's mind. "Go on, Sissy, I'll see you in a minute."

"You're such an asshole," she told Segreti as she hurried inside.

Segreti regarded Fiorinetti for a moment. Every second he'd been around this punk, Segreti had violated the rules. The first time had been to watch his partner's back This time?

"What?" Fiorinetti blurted.

"I've seen your police record. Sissy's dad know about it?"

"Dude, like I know. Ask him?"

"You want me to do that?"

Fiorinetti shook his head. "Whatever you want to say, man, just fucking say it."

"How'd you pay for that Mazda? You still dealing, Jimbo?"

"Since you know all about it, you tell me."

Segreti reached into his jacket and the punk's eyes bulged. "Whoa, dude, easy, okay?"

Segreti withdrew his business card. "I'm not going to shoot you, Jim. Not tonight." He gave the guy his card. "I've got your number, now you've got mine. You work for me."

"The hell I do."

"Here's the deal. You treat that girl extra nice, and everybody's happy. I need a favor, you show up, and I mean immediately, no questions asked. In exchange, you get into trouble with the police, you get one phone call to me. But you make her cry, believe me, you will never see the light of day again. We clear?"

Fiorinetti took a second to consider it.

"It's a get-out-of-jail card, stupid."

Fiorinetti pocketed the card. "Okay." He strode around Segreti and into the hospital.

Segreti waited a few minutes before he followed. Inside, he found Blessy Ram walking through the emergency ward's waiting room, carrying a clutch of cans from the vending machine. "Hey, let me help with that," he said.

They embraced.

"What's the doctor say?"

Blessy rubbed her reddened eyes and slowly shook her head. "He's awake. He's stable. He's saying stupid things to his children."

Segreti grinned. "I wouldn't expect anything less."

He carried the drinks for her down the hall.

Ram was sitting upright in a hospital bed. The room was meant to be shared, but he was the only occupant tonight. The boy, Sammy, was in the crook of his arm, wearing Ram's cowboy hat, the Stetson enormous on the boy's head. Sissy stood in the corner by a vase of fresh flowers, holding hands with a sullen Jim Fiorinetti.

"Hi," Segreti said to the room at large.

"Hey, chief," Ram said.

Blessy went to the flowers. She had added a golden idol of a Hindu god to the table, and was now lighting tea candles.

"How you doing?" Segreti asked.

Ram lifted his hospital gown to reveal a big stretch of white gauze across his brown waist. "Should be out of here in a day or two."

"That's good to hear," Segreti said. He was glad to see Ram alive and cheerful, if it was only painkillers talking. Segretiy's next stop would be far grimmer.

"He should rest," Blessy said. She joined her palms and sent a silent prayer to the four-armed god.

"Yes, he should," Segreti agreed.

"I heard he got away," Ram said.

"Yeah."

"You were expecting trouble out there? Packing those rifles?"

Segreti shrugged.

"And the rookie...?"

Segreti shook his head.

Ram lifted the hat off Sammy and tousled his hair. "Thought so."

"What are you even doing here?" Sissy demanded.

"Hey," Ram snapped, "what kind of..." His admonishment gave in to a wave of pain and he sank back into his mattress.

"Sissy," the wife said.

"He's the one who almost got Dad killed."

"Your dad is a brave man who saved my life," Segreti said.

"You going to beat up anyone else?" Sissy barked.

The boyfriend reddened. "Uh, Sissy, cool it, okay?"

"What are you talking about?" Blessy demanded of her daughter.

Segreti said to her, "You know what your dad said to me recently? He told me that if it came down to country or family, he was family first, all the way."

"Not today he wasn't," she said.

Segreti put his hand on Ram's. "I think he was."

Ram was still screwing his face in pain, but he put his other hand over Segreti's. "You're going to nail him, right, chief? Tremain isn't getting away with this."

"Yeah, Bhav, I'm going to get him."

Ram pulled him in close. "Because we made a promise."

"I haven't forgotten." Segreti straightened himself and said to them, "You're my family. You need anything, anything at all, you call me."

"Thank you, Ed," Blessy said.

"Especially you," he said to Sissy. "You call me." The girl for once nodded, no drama.

"You don't know what you're getting yourself into," Ram joked.

"I've got more stops tonight," Segreti said. "Bhav, you rest up."

Bhav nodded. "Ed, Malcolm's been by, now you, but I haven't heard from Miriam."

"She's probably tied up. My hearing's tomorrow and she's trying to help me get my story straight."

"Guess that's it," Ram said. Segreti left the room.

Back in the Mustang, Segreti took no joy in the muscle car. He checked his messages before looking up Helen Taylor's address and next of kin. He noticed Chlebek had gone quiet. He sent her a message and was about to turn the key in the ignition when he had another urgent feeling. Something he had been putting off could be avoided no longer. Not without a regret that might kill him.

And so he called the house in Maryland. As the phone rang, he wondered who might pick up, Katie or Jake.

It was Jake. "Uh, hello?"

"It's me."

"Me who?"

Segreti's heart sank. "Come on, Jake, you know who I am."

"Dad?"

"Yes... Dad. How are you, buddy?"

"Why aren't you home?"

"Well, I'm not sure your mom wants me around just now."

"I know."

"You know I love you, right, buddy? I'm on a tough case. I think it'll be over soon. Then I'd like to see you. What do you think?"

"Mom's driving me nuts."

He smiled reflexively. "She's going through a hard time. Be nice to her, okay?"

"She says you're always on a case. That's why we never see you."

"Yeah, well, I'm thinking of taking some time off. Maybe we can catch the Orioles, or a Ravens game."

"Ravens? Dad, football doesn't start for another two months."

"You know what I mean. Come on, Jake."

"I gotta go."

"Hey, hang on there. I wanted to talk to you."

"About what?"

"Just to say hi. See how you're doing. Hear the sound of your voice."

"Yeah, well, you've heard it. Mom's downstairs. You want to talk to her?"

Bad idea. "Sure."

Jake called his mom. Segreti watched an ambulance blaze down the driveway, headed to clean up yet another mess. He was afraid of what Katie would say. He thought of Ram surrounded by his family. Of how he felt like he'd done more to look out for Ram's daughter than his own son.

"Edward?"

He sighed. Katie reserved *Edward* for when he was in the doghouse. Which now seemed to be his permanent status.

"Hi, Katie."

"It's late. Why are you calling?"

"I just wanted to speak with Jake. We haven't talked for a while. I miss him."

"You've had many opportunities to make him, us, a part of your life."

"I know. Look, Katie, I understand why you want a divorce. I'd like to keep things amicable, okay? Friendly."

"From now on, we should communicate through our lawyers."

"Jesus, Katie. Really?"

Cold silence.

He said, "I don't have a goddamn lawyer."

"Well, I do. His card is with the papers."

He had seen it. Hadn't thought it was more than just someone to process the paperwork. He hadn't thought about it at all, really.

"Anything else?" Katie asked.

"No. You have a good night." He hung up.

During the long drive to Brooklyn he spent the time trying to organize his thoughts. His mind had been a mess since the shootout. He hadn't wanted to deal with Helen Taylor's death. Yes, she had died in the line of duty. Then Sissy: *But he's the one who almost got Dad killed.* Maybe not Ram, but he got someone else killed for sure. And then Katie: *You had many opportunities.* So many.

There was no way to put this right. But he had a job to do. Which brought him back to the rookie. And when he couldn't bear to think about Taylor, he turned his mind to Justine. This calmed him. He didn't know why. She was probably going to write something that would jeopardize the case. Maybe get him into even deeper trouble. But he'd get to see her again.

Something she had said, though. Or rather, asked. *Why does she want you dead?* It was crazy for a foreign spook to try to assassinate a federal agent on US soil. It didn't make sense because whoever this was, she wasn't just acting on orders. There weren't many rules when it came to spy versus spy, but those few that existed did so out of self-preservation. The Russian woman was risking everything to get Segreti.

It had to be personal.

Segreti found the dingy walkup in Bushwick and parked. He checked his hair in the rearview mirror, made sure he was looking as crisp as he could manage. Then he got out and rang the buzzer. The partner was named Javon Smith. He waited a long several minutes as Smith made his way down and opened the door.

"I know who you are," the young man said. "I know what happened to Helen. Cops already told me." Beneath his politeness simmered rage and despair.

"I know," Segreti said. "I'm here to tell you that she was an exceptional agent."

Smith said, "You think I don't know that?"

"I'm sorry for your loss, Mister Smith."

Tears welled up in Smith's eyes. Segreti didn't know if he had cried already, or if the grief's wave was just now cresting. "I think it best if you go."

Segreti handed him his card. "If you need—" He stood on the stoop facing the closed door, his card still in his hand. He put it back in his jacket pocket and walked to the car. "Shit."

He checked his messages. Belmont was in the office, pulling an all-nighter, and wanted to share something he'd dug up. Nothing from Chlebek.

He called Belmont. "You hear from Miriam?"

"No, sir."

"She's not picking up. Maybe you try her. Let me know if you hear from her."

"Yes, sir. You want to see this now, or in the morning?"

"Tonight. I'll be along, if you can wait."

He looked up Chlebek's address. Greenpoint, not too far. He suppressed a worm of worry and started the car.

Segreti parked along India Avenue and trotted to Franklin Street. He had never been here before. Chlebek was from Milwaukee but had felt at home here amid the neighborhood's pierogi shops. She lived in an apartment in a three-story brick walkup, the windows boasting American and Polish flags. The street was busy, with people spilling out of a nearby kielbasa and beer bar. He rang her buzzer but no got no response. He called her again, but she didn't pick up. His heart beat faster. Where the hell *was* she?

The building had a superintendent living on the ground floor, so he pressed the super's buzzer. He did it a few times until finally a wizened old man in pajamas appeared behind the door's Plexiglas window. Segreti showed his badge.

"You got a key to Miriam Chlebek's apartment?"

The super nodded and shuffled back to his apartment. Segreti waited outside for one minute, then two, three. *Come on, come on.*

When the super emerged with a ring stuffed with keys, Segreti moved to take it, but the old man recoiled. "I go with key," he said.

Segreti considered hoisting the man over his shoulder and running for the elevator, but he swallowed his panic and walked with the old man. The elevator took its time, too.

There were six apartments on the floor, and for a while the super seemed confused about which direction to go.

"That's the right key?" Segreti asked but the super ignored him and slowly made his way to a door. Segreti knocked. "Miriam? You in there? It's me, Ed. I need you to open up."

He heard only the two of them breathing in the hallway.

"Okay, Pops, open it."

There were three locks on the door, and the super had to try a few keys for each one.

Segreti firmly barred the super from entering and pushed him aside, careful not to knock him down. "Stay back," he said, unholstering his new sidearm. Both hands on the grip, he pushed the door open.

The apartment was dark, but streetlights flooded inside. An object filled the center of the living room, something that didn't make sense.

"Chlebek? Miriam?"

He found the light switch, flicked it on.

"Oh God."

Chapter 38

Justine practically crawled up the subway stairs from the Number 1 line. The traffic along Eighty-Sixth Street was busy but the sidewalk was empty, Central Park dark and beautiful. She walked past the cafes and the shuttered shops, feeling like New York's streets were camouflage enough, and then hustled up the stairs to her apartment, exhaustion fighting with the screaming need for a hot shower. Yes, a shower and a pot of strong coffee were exactly what she needed now. Despite the horrors of the day, it was going to be a longer night.

She could have gone back to the hotel, where she still had some things—the room was hers until tomorrow morning. But she was pretty sure Robert Tremain was preoccupied and wouldn't be paying any more midnight visits. And she didn't think she could work in a strange hotel room.

Justine opened the door, quickly turned on the light and screened the living room. Good. No Robert Tremain. Aware of her nerves, she locked the door before moving further inside the apartment. She gently set down the suitcase and was about to toss her purse on the sofa, but something felt off. The bedroom was dark, but further inside she saw the outline of the bathroom light. It was on. And other things were wrong. The coffee table sat at a strange angle. And on the kitchenette counter, one of her bottles of Chardonnay stood empty besides the corkscrew.

Her heart pounding now, Justine tiptoed to the kitchen while keeping her eye back on the bedroom door. She pulled a drawer open and quietly grabbed her chef's knife.

Just get out of here.

No, this was her home, for what it was worth. She had to know who had been here...and if they still were, were they waiting for her in that darkened room?

She moved gingerly to the bedroom. She couldn't make anything out, but something smelled sharp and rank. She flipped the light switch.

Someone lay on their stomach, sprawled across her bed. A white man, jeans and hoodie, sneakers, a curly mass of copper hair...

"Zach?"

She stubbed her foot on his backpack as she rushed to his side. He didn't move. His face was buried between pillows in a pool of garish vomit.

"Zach!"

Justine pushed him over to his side. He wasn't breathing, but he had a pulse. She shook him, shouted his name, but he didn't wake up. She pushed open one eyelid, and saw his pupils dilated to pinpoints.

She called 911. Try chest compressions, they said. She turned Zach on his back and pressed her palm against his chest. The mattress was too soft, so she levered him onto the floor using the blankets. She tried again, leaning over his head, pumping his chest to get oxygen in and out. Her body ached. The repetitive motion was hell on her arms and shoulders, but she wasn't going to give up on him.

It was only after the medics showed up that she collapsed against the wall. She couldn't understand why they insisted on examining her, until she remembered what she looked like. And then she had to answer a lot of questions. About who she was, who he was, why he was in her apartment. Questions she couldn't answer. She gave them Steve's number and address.

A medic came out of the bedroom holding a plastic baggie smeared with white powder. "This yours?"

"No. I've never seen that before. Do you know what it is?"

"Ketamine, I'd guess."

"Is he going to be okay?" she asked as they put an oxygen mask on Zach and lifted him onto a stretcher.

"We'll probably get him awake in the ambulance," the medic said.

"*Probably?*"

The medic shrugged as he and his partner carried Zach outside.

"Where are you taking him?"

"Mount Sinai."

"I'm coming with you."

"Please, ma'am, let us do our job."

She followed them down the stairs, as the elevator was too small, and watched as they put the unconscious boy in the back of the ambulance. Her second nightmare of the day. The sirens wailed as the ambulance blazed down Amsterdam Avenue.

Her body wanted to sleep and nothing else, but Justine knew she had to keep going. She went back to her apartment and took that hot shower. Mud and blood swirled around her feet, and she toed unidentifiable bits of gore into the drain. After toweling off, she examined herself in the mirror. Some new scars and nicks. Mostly she looked hollowed out.

"J.J., you look like shit."

She put on jeans and a polo shirt, sensible flats, and headed to the hospital. She had her electronic gear in her bag. The idea of dealing with the puke on her bedsheets was too much; she would go to the hotel after all. After that, who knew?

The emergency ward hummed with sad energy. She saw a few doctors and nurses, but mostly the ward was filled with people, their wait for bad news filling the room with the wet smell of desperation. It was a place no one wanted to be.

A pair of burly orderlies manned a desk behind a window, keeping track of the paperwork and patiently explaining to whomever was next in line just how limited their options were. Steve was sitting nearby, his hands resting on a can of soda in his lap. He had the same long stare as the others.

Justine sat beside him. "Any news?" she asked.

"They're pumping him full of something. To wake him up."

"Okay." The exhaustion of the day weighed on her suddenly. She thought she would nod off.

"He went to you," Steve said.

"I don't know why."

"What's that say about what kind of father I am?"

"I don't think it says anything."

"Was he trying to kill himself? Or just being stupid?"

"I don't know," she said, her eyes closed.

"They say he's going to wake up... but he might not be all there. They don't know how long he wasn't breathing."

She didn't say anything. She was thinking about Bert and Marta. What did his death say about what kind of friend she had been?

"You might have saved his life, Justine."

But she hadn't. Bert was dead. If anyone's life had been

saved today, it was hers.

Ed Segreti had rescued her.

She was too tired to think of him, either.

"But he might end up a vegetable. My son. Oh God. And after we had a fight."

She didn't ask what it was about.

"Did you know he's gay?" Steve asked. "That's what he told me. That the expulsion wasn't for drugs, but for getting caught in the bathroom at school."

Justine turned cold.

"I don't care if he's gay," Steve said. "I care that he's doing stupid stuff and getting in trouble. But he seemed to think I was some kind of fire-and-brimstone asshole."

She remembered her promise to Zach, that she'd be there when he came out to his dad. That might explain a desire for him to stage a dramatic protest in her bedroom.

Her touch had become toxic; her affection a curse. Just how bad a person was she? Was the investigation worth it? It hadn't gotten her anything but ashes and dust.

A little while later a nurse approached them. "Your son's going to be fine," she said.

Justine opened her eyes. Finally, some good news.

"Can we see him?" Steve asked.

"Of course. He's groggy, though."

Steve stood up. "You coming, Justine?"

"No, I'll see him later. I think you two need some time alone."

Steve touched her arm. "You have somewhere you need to be?"

She didn't want to admit that she needed to sleep and then get this story written. That Zach wasn't the only person she owed.

He let go. "I don't know what happened to you today, but I know you think it's important. So go do whatever it is you need to do."

"Steve, it's not like—"

"It is," he said, sounding calm. "And you're right. I need to work on my dad credentials."

She turned to go.

"Justine." Steve embraced her. "Thank you."

She held him, remembering when she had loved him, like a fleeting summer.

Chapter 39

Segreti drove through the arteries and byways of New York wondering if he should put his new Bureau-issued Glock in his mouth and end it. Because what he was feeling, if you could call it that, was on the edge of unbearable.

After the shootout he had been able to operate on remote control. There were procedures. Formalities. Meetings with the survivors, the near-misses—the *whew* wasn't that close—and with the bereaved, the ones who would not get any sleep tonight and maybe not any other night for a long time. And, of course, he'd be the reason; the imp churning turmoil in their minds and in their hearts, solemnly assuring them that *country* had called and that *duty*, like a black witch, had demanded this sacrifice.

There would be plenty more officiousness and protocol, but it was the wee hours of the night and there was nothing to do but get his people safe. Round-the-clock police watch on Ram's hospital room. Safe houses for Ram's family and for Belmont's boyfriend, Darren. Agents were even in action in Chevy Chase, posting a watch over Katie and Jake.

The people behind Tremain had made two attempts on Segreti's life, and now they had murdered Chlebek. Segreti had a hunch as to why, but it didn't comfort him. Not one bit.

He parked in the basement of Federal Plaza, turned off the engine, looked at his sidearm, and felt his eyes fill with tears. He was a cheater. A sinner. His friends were hurt, dead. He was a malignant cancer. Hot tears tracked his face. His hands shook, the gun rattling his teeth.

Maybe it was a cowardly excuse, survivor's instinct, but he saw Justine Jarman on the ghostyard of ships, being dragged away by Brown Beard. He saw her in the sight of his M4, and at that moment, for the only time today, he had been calm. Like an out-of-body experience. And when she slumped over and he had the kill shot, he didn't hesitate. Brown Beard's head turned to a cloud of blood and his grip dragged her down as his body tumbled. Segreti got to her side like a shot. She was shaking, terrified, confused, and angry—at him. But she was alive, and that was the only fact that Segreti could hold onto.

He put the Glock in his shoulder holster, wiped away his tears, and clambered out of the Mustang. He didn't feel steady on his feet, but he made his way to the elevator and eventually to his desk.

The office was quiet, although there were always agents on duty. A few of them gave him odd looks. They wouldn't know about Chlebek, but they'd know about Taylor and Ram. He got a few pats on the arm, a couple of soft words, but also a few hard stares. Most of his colleagues simply looked away.

Belmont came over holding a manila folder. Even the usually impeccably dressed agent looked haggard, his shirt undone, tie askew, showing facial creases for the first time.

"Miriam," Belmont said.

Segreti flopped in his chair. "It was bad, Mal."

"Bhav okay?"

"He's going to pull through."

"That's good."

Segreti rubbed his face, tired of his own stink. "What've you got?"

Belmont placed Dimitri Mahalev's photo on the desk. It was a fuzzy portrait of a younger man in a suit and tie. "Mahalev's a director at the National University of Science and Technology in Moscow. Guess what department?"

"Mal, come on," he sighed, too tired to spell out just how exhausted he felt.

"The Institute of Nanoparticles. That's their term for quantum computing. The Russians are at least a decade behind us and the Chinese on this stuff, but if they've got someone who understands it..."

The Shadow. Segreti looked at the portrait of a younger scientist. Not a spook, at least not a professional one. A medium between Moscow FSB and the cyber world. Still missing. Back in Russia? On that super-yacht off the coast?

"Good to know," Segreti said, not caring. Like this mattered now.

"There's more." Belmont pulled another photo from his folder. It was the mystery woman. This photo was an official portrait, with her posing before a Russian flag in a military uniform.

Segreti woke up. "You found her."

"Annika Nikolaevna Volkov. Her official title is acting ambassador, fresh off the boat."

"Or the yacht."

"She's sitting in as Russia's representative on the UN Human Rights Council."

Segreti snorted. "Human rights. Pretty high-profile diplo

role for an enemy agent."

"It's just a pretext for her to be in New York. The actual representative is supposed to show up in a few weeks."

"What's her real job?"

Belmont allowed a little smile. "Deputy director at the FSB's Eighteenth Center for Information Security."

The leading cyber operations arm of the Russian Federal Security Service, the KGB's avatar.

"Miriam's research gave me most of the clues," Belmont said. "I was picking up crumbs of my own in Athens and Berlin."

"Berlin?"

Belmont nodded. "The Germans had someone in Nicosia who got on that yacht as a maid. She acquired prints and hair samples and got some of them out before anyone on that vessel got suspicious. She's missing, however, and we presume she is dead." He flourished a dense forensics report. "But this is what she got us."

Segreti was looking at DNA sample comparisons. A near match. One was Volkov's.

He remembered the meeting in DC that had started this whole affair. Being told of someone who died for vital intel. It had been a German asset.

"Okay," he said, "so we've got her biometrics..." He re-read the forensics report. "Who's this John Doe?"

"He's downstairs in the morgue."

Segreti tossed the paper on his desk, feeling a wave of euphoria tinged with anxiety. His hunch about why the Russians were targeting federal agents on US soil had been right. "That bodyguard who isn't a kid from Missouri... I shot Volkov's son." It was Segreti's turn to smile. "Fucking caviar."

"We think he's Gregor Mikhailovich Pavlova. Annika Volkov uses her maiden name, but for a time she was married to Mikhail Pavlova, a GSR general who died in Syria under mysterious circumstances."

"She ice him?"

Belmont shrugged. "Conjecture. But Gregor would have been twelve at the time. He ended up as Spetsnaz, doing special operations in Ukraine, until he got detailed to FSB."

"The black widow wanted him on this job," Segreti said. "Grooming him for something bigger. Dimitri Mahalev might have learned about Red Fidelity at his university. The NSA has been working on quantum security for several years. Walter Klinger was part of that effort."

Belmont nodded. "Maybe they were experimenting with the kind of weapons that would expose everything... thought it was in a secure lab."

"Yeah, play around with it, see what works, develop defenses."

"But then Klinger goes rogue and sells it."

"To Bobby Tremain, who doesn't know much about coding—he's a field agent—but he knows who might buy it. Or Volkov has a hunch about Tremain and sends Mahalev to make an offer."

The two men regarded each other with rising anticipation, both making the leaps of thought to work out the cascade of events.

"All that work, and Volkov's gone off the rails because her son's dead," Segreti said. "Now she's murdering Bureau agents."

"We can get her expelled," Belmont said.

Segreti's mind flashed back to Chlebek's apartment, finding her tied to a chair, gagged with her panties. Someone had thrown her back onto the floor, so when Segreti entered her apartment, he was greeted by the soles of her feet. Then he saw the jagged tear across her throat. A deliberate, vicious killing. The expression of terror frozen on Chlebek's face.

Taylor, shot in the heart, Segreti closing her eyes frozen in surprise.

Justine.

Belmont added, "We have enough for the State Department."

"We can do better than that," Segreti replied, thinking, *People are going to pay.*

* * *

Segreti walked towards the twenty-third-floor conference room, a cup of regulation vending machine coffee in his hand. Although he was wearing yesterday's clothes—the pantlegs still flecked with mud—he was freshly showered, thanks to the Federal Plaza's gym. He recognized a few of the suits headed in the same direction. No doubt his jurors, judges, and executioners. Chien and Gonzalez from NSA blew past him without saying hello.

Inside the conference room, Deborah Church was murmuring officialese to other Bureau officials. When she spotted him, Segreti saw the trouble on her face. Helen Taylor had been one of ADIC's rookies. He knew he had been cavalier with regulations when he dragooned Taylor into the field. He owed a lot lately to ADIC's goodwill, and, judging by the look he got from her now, he had definitely tapped her dry.

Today's hearing was to review the man Segreti had shot on North Brother Island. He had Belmont's report, which might not clear him of technical violations, but it would focus Bureau interest. Would it be enough, however, to keep the scales weighed in his favor?

He took his seat at the long table. A junior agent shut the conference doors, leaving him alone to face five unfriendly administrators.

Church opened her file. "Let's proceed."

Chapter 40

Later that afternoon, Justine climbed the stairs of the Hundred-and-Sixteenth Street subway station and emerged to the sounds of Latin pop and Spanglish conversations. It was high summer in El Barrio, and the basketball courts, bounded by chain-link fences, echoed with the slams of backboards and Spanish slang. The street was full of color— the red and orange hues of the buildings, the bright flags, the brilliant murals and the cacophonic graffiti—but Justine was dressed in dark navy and gray, a black handbag slung over her shoulder.

She walked towards Pleasant Avenue, past the pizzerias that reminded East Harlem of its Italian roots, past the bodegas and bakeries decorated with the red-white-and-green of Mexican flags, past the Chinese restaurants that had become the neighborhood's new calling card. Giant building-high murals of Puerto Rican mothers kept a watch as Justine made her way to a red-brick building, its façade layered with the wrought-iron ladders and landings of a tenement. She stopped at the corner grocer to buy flowers. When she explained it was for a bereavement, the old man fixed her a bouquet of white carnations peppered with yellow marigolds.

"These represent the sun," the *tío* told her, pointing out the marigolds. "*Así nos gusta recordar a los meurtos.*"

"Yes, that's how I remember him," she said. "Bert Gomez was like the sun."

She also bought some fruit and cakes. Then she walked around the corner and rang the Gomez apartment bell. After a while, a hollow woman's voice asked, "*Quién es?*"

"It's Justine."

She had been dreading this, but the writing had been a balm. At least she hadn't come empty-handed, even though she knew that there was nothing she could bring that would begin to make up for what had been lost.

The door buzzed and Justine pushed inside. She walked up the two flights of stairs and saw that Marta Gomez had left the apartment door ajar. The widow was waiting just behind it. She looked about what Justine expected, dressed all in black and with obsidian razors for eyes.

Marta received the flowers and food with indifference, and Justine followed her inside the apartment. The living room was heavy with sadness. Several black-laced relatives sat in the room, their silence pregnant with judgment as they picked at plates of tamales and fried plantains. Bert and Marta's two kids were there, too—fidgety and downcast, watching the TV news with the volume turned off. Above the sofa was a painting of a brown-skinned Jesus on the cross, and porcelain religious statues competed for shelf and table space with decorated skulls made of sugar. A portrait photo of Bert sat on the dining table garlanded with carnations and surrounded by a few of his personal effects: a trucker cap, gold chains, a video camera, and copies of *Archer's*.

The relatives greeted her politely. One old lady hidden behind a veil broke down in loud tears while her husband, a skinny waif with a bristling white mustache, held her hand. "She is glad you came," he told Justine.

Marta preferred to stay in the kitchen. They could hear her knife on a chopping board.

Justine made some small talk with the family. Bert's children, a boy and a girl, regarded her with silent hostility, their big eyes brimming with accusation. Justine could imagine what Marta must have told them.

She stayed with the family for half an hour, chatting with the cousins, greeting others who joined. The men sipped tequila and the women drank beer; the *abuela* behind the veil crossed herself every time she took a taste. Justine settled into the discomfort of being there, of being the outsider, and maybe the reason for the wake.

The gathering grew louder. While the men where exchanging stories of Bert, some of the women cried. The two kids hunched together, bored but still horrified. The uncle with the mustache strummed a guitar and sang a *corrido*. The alcohol was making the time run faster.

Justine found Marta alone in the kitchen.

"You ready to go now?" Marta asked.

"I need to ask you for something."

Marta put down the wooden spoon she had been using to stir a mole. "You want to ask *me* for something?"

"It's about Bert."

"Don't say his name in this house."

Justine opened her handbag and pulled out a clutch of papers she had printed a few hours ago at a FedEx shop. Josh and Patty had helped out this morning, reading and polishing the draft she had spent the night working on.

"This is what I'm going to say about Bert and what happened."

"The police already told me what happened."

"Please, Marta, read this. I need your blessing."

"Does this look like a good time to read your article, Justine? My husband always put you before his family. And now he's dead, but you're not done with us!"

"He loved you more than anything in the world," Justine whispered.

Marta picked up serving bowls and blew past her.

Justine waited in the kitchen, then decided she wasn't going to get an answer. But she didn't have the luxury of time. She followed Marta into the living room.

"Bert was my family," she told them. "He died trying to protect me. Like he always protected me. Not because he valued me more than you. He didn't. He was devoted to you, to Pedro and Elena. What he loved was his work. Journalism was a calling for him. You know this, you know what kind of man he was." She placed the draft story besides Bert's photo. "Publishing this story is how I want to honor him. Because it's the culmination of his work. I'm too close to this to know what's right. I need your wisdom... I need your love for Bert to show the way."

Justine left the apartment feeling flustered. She knew she was intruding on their mourning with her speech, but she also knew that she owed it to them to decide whether to publish her piece. Was she absolving herself of responsibility?

No, she thought as she headed back to the subway. She was coming to terms with the fact that this story, like every other, had never been about her.

Justine spent the evening in a daze. She had no appetite for dinner. She went to her Upper West Side apartment and cleaned up Zach's mess. The bedsheets were not salvageable—the vomit stains too nasty. There was another bottle of wine in the fridge but she didn't want to drink herself to sleep. She skimmed her phone but couldn't focus on anything, and maybe that was a relief. She did finally pour herself a glass and watched TV. The programming might as well have been static for all she cared. She dreaded the idea of going to sleep and being alone with the disgust in Marta's face.

Her cell rang.

It was Marta.

"Go ahead," she told Justine. "Publish your story."

Chapter 41

Tremain popped another Percocet. It had been more than six hours since the last one and he was feeling itchy. The gun injury wasn't intolerable, he supposed, but it was still like walking about with a poker, no longer red-hot but unyielding and jagged, stuck inside his thigh. There was more to the pills than just dulling the pain. It was everything else—the juggler losing one ball, then two, and before he knew it, the whole cosmos of goddamn balls was about to ping-pong to the ground. A man needed to clear his head, see the world in an optimistic frame. Be confident that he could rip apart Gordian knots with his bare hands—these hands and a couple of burner phones and a suitcase of cash.

He walked out of his cabin and took the stairs up to the main deck, the Percocet letting him take them two at a time. He found her sitting in the craft's spacious living room, shouting on her phone in Russian. Bloomberg still ran on the TV, its talking heads like a silent chorus, singing their songs of money, but Volkov was facing the opposite way. She wore a blood-red tracksuit and white sneakers. Two half-finished cigars smoked in the ashtray on the coffee table, their stubs reminders of her impatience.

Tremain knew not to interrupt her, but time was running

short. He signaled his desire to talk as he sauntered outside to the shaded loungers by the pool. *Maybe he shouldn't act like he owns the place*, thought that part of his mind that was always nagging him. *Nah, he has this. He just needs to work on his pitch.* He signaled to one of the muscle-bound attendants for a drink.

It was morning and the sun was high and hot, the ocean a peaceful swell of blue, with New York City just over the horizon. The attendant brought him a Bloody Mary on ice.

He paced and practiced his lines. Getting some buyer in the US was too hard. *So who's got access overseas from a trusted institution but one with security that's a little untested?* Tremain had his shortlist down to two research institutes—one in Bangalore, the other in Hyderabad. The US had a hard-on for India right now; the Indians were cocky even though they were a decade behind, and their establishment was rife with Russophiles. Now, how to make contact...

Through the open doors he could see her silhouette against the giant TV screen. She had lit her third cigar of the morning. He wondered what the sheikhs would think of getting their superyacht back with an interior stinking of tobacco. Well, the refurbishment costs would just be a rounding error below an asterisk, so maybe they wouldn't care.

Something about the image on the screen caught his eye: a fuzzy photograph, like someone had used a smartphone to take a picture of a physical image from twenty years ago. A young white guy wearing a tie, blond and enamored with his own good looks and savviness. But it wasn't that long ago. Eleven years, maybe, since Tremain had posed for his Arizona State graduation photo.

Volkov watched the news item while Tremain tried to keep

his stomach from leaping out of his mouth. Even the Percocet wasn't helping now.

He stepped into the doorway, half in and half out, trying to hear the broadcasters. Volkov walked to the bar running along one side of the living space, reached an arm behind it, and pulled out a stubby Makarov 9mm semi-automatic pistol. She aimed it at him.

Tremain raised his hands. "Whoa there." He backed out to the open deck. The slick skin of the glass slipped through his fingers and shattered in an explosion of shards and blood-colored booze.

She advanced, the gun steady. "You fucking stupid fucking cunt of a fuck."

"My cover's busted. So what? It's not like I was planning to stick around."

"Is only matter of time before you compromise my mission."

Maybe it was the painkillers. Maybe he was tired of being a plaything. "You've compromised yourself, Annika. Ever since you decided to take out federal agents. I warned you not to do it."

"You failed me, twice."

"Yeah, okay, you got me. Bobby Tremain led Segreti to your goons, and then they missed and got killed instead. What the fuck are you doing? I'm trying to quietly slip malware into a quantum computing network, and you're running around New York with a sign on your back that says, 'Russian spy, come and get me'."

"He killed my son!" She bent over double. It hurt that much to admit it.

"Segreti killed your—when?" But he knew when. "That

was your son? At the auction?"

"He was there to oversee operation." She was twisting in pain. Physical agony. She was doubled over, and the gun was pointing at the floor.

"All this has been about your revenge? Jesus, Annika, I didn't take you for one with the maternal instinct."

She reared herself and sprang at him. Backhanded him with the butt of the Makarov and knocked him down. "You stupid fucking..." she seethed.

Tremain touched his brow. Blood glinted on his fingertips. "Ow, that hurt."

She aimed the pistol at his head. "We have already killed one of them, the woman. We will get the others."

"What woman?"

"On Segreti's team."

Tremain groaned. "You murdered one of his people? A fed?"

"Is just the start. Maybe I kill you too."

"Go on," he sneered. "Your bosses in Moscow know about this? How you've singlehandedly derailed everything I've set up for you, because the FBI shot your stupid son? Who should have been trained to know that he should have stood down instead of assaulting federal agents?"

"I am his mother! And he was my son!"

Tremain looked at the gun and felt no fear. "Another reason I don't have kids. If you're going to kill me, Annika, do it now because I'm tired of your bullshit. Or if you want to execute the plan, listen to me. We can still get it done."

"There is no time."

"You've got all the time in the world. No one's going to be quantum-security safe for ten more years."

"Is necessary to do it now. After Ukraine we are squeezed

between NATO and China. Mother Russia will collapse if we do not negotiate terms from strength."

"You people have a mother complex." He shook his head. "Okay. Give me six months and some money, and I can make it happen. The Indians, see—"

"My orders are not six months! They are now!"

Tremain pushed the gun aside. "Annika, I think it's time you start managing expectations. We are done in this country. I've more than held up my end. Your men shot me and I'm still here. What's it going to be?"

"Segreti will come to arrest you."

"I'm not doing this again. No."

"You will obey me."

He gestured at the TV behind her. "You think he's the only agent they've got? Half his team's shot or dead."

"But he put you on TV."

"Wait a minute. No, he didn't. That's not how any of us operate."

"Who then is smearing your name across the media?"

"The reporter. Justine Jarman."

"This Segreti likes that blonde bitch."

"Maybe. I've already tried that approach."

"We will try it one more time."

"He won't buy it."

"She will."

Tremain was tired of this conversation. "Justine? I doubt that."

She smiled. The way he imagined a T-Rex would smile. "The girl is not bait. She is collateral. You are bait."

"Annika, no—"

She pulled the trigger.

Chapter 42

For Segreti, being FBI had always been about focusing on what was in front of him: evidence, a case, a target. Mission. Duty. Country, whatever that meant. Family, hot dogs at Madison Square Garden, Old Glory on her pole hanging over the porch. An excuse to shoot enemies like Gregor Pavlova, aka Volkov's son.

Yesterday he had endured. Five officials, five hundred questions, none of them flattering. Nothing about the present, just returning to the past—the scene of a crime. ADIC Church had been quiet, letting the others try to figure out if the shooting had been legit. Segreti answered in monotones and let the reports do the talking.

Church could be boisterous off duty and with a cocktail in hand; at work, she was all business, but always engaged, on top of things, vibrant. Leading. But in that stuffy meeting room, she had been withdrawn. Numbing herself. Segreti had taken this as a bad sign.

Chlebek's report probably saved him: she had written that he had acted in self-defense against the bodyguard's assault. She had rescued him from the grave. In return? He had failed her.

The committee didn't need to provide him with the reasoning of its vote, but he knew he'd been acquitted of a wrongful shooting. This wasn't the end of his problems, because Coburn Bergman's attorneys were still suing him and the Bureau. But as far as the FBI's internal process was concerned, Segreti had acted properly.

All he knew was that the vote had gone his way three to two. The Bureau preferred unanimous decisions, and there was usually a conversation among the judges to ensure a unified front. Three to two: those dissenting votes must have really wanted to punish him.

He had slunk back to his apartment and ordered Uber Eats. Cooking a meal would have been more therapeutic, but he didn't want to go down to Essex Market. Just another reminder of his behavior, his lack of self-control. Feeling dirty all over, he took a shower while he waited for the food. Toweling off, he glanced in the mirror and noticed the scar on his shoulder. He'd taken a bullet for his job. Was he still that man?

He ate his chicken chow-mein thinking about Justine, wondering if there was anything to that. He had sensed her flirting with him, testing the waters. He admitted to himself that he liked her. But did he like her because of who she was, not just because she was hot? Did he see in her drive, guts, absolute commitment—the things he thought had embodied his own approach to life—or was he just making up a fantasy of starting over? Was it teenage-level escapism? It didn't matter. The shootout at the ship boneyard had crushed whatever feelings might have been possible. She had radiated hostility. If the damsel had been distressed, Segreti had the feeling it was because of him.

The next day Segreti walked to the office. His colleagues gave him curt nods, a brief hello. He was damaged goods.

Being cleared of the shooting didn't count. Taylor and Chlebek were dead, Tremain was out there, the Russians were a threat. But it had been okay for him to kill a Russian op. Great.

He half-worked at his desk, trying to focus on Belmont's latest reports, but he really couldn't concentrate. He was awaiting orders. If there were any orders.

Then Belmont hurried over. "You seeing what's on the TV news?"

"Enlighten me."

Belmont showed him a clip on his cell phone. The anchor, in a red dress, expensive hairstyling.

Shocking allegations of treason...a former employee of the National Security Agency has been identified as passing on cyber-weapons to Russia...This man, Robert Tremain, is said to be wanted by the FBI...The cyber weapon, codenamed 'Red Fidelity', uses quantum computing to expose the entire secrets held digitally by the US governments and US corporations...related to the shootout reported yesterday, in which this FBI agent, Helen Taylor, was killed, along with two unidentified assailants...

Segreti swallowed, trying to keep calm, keep his stomach from churning up this morning's coffee.

Belmont said, "*Archer's* is still offline. She took this to *Vanity Fair*. It's on their website."

"And now it's everywhere," Segreti said, but he was thinking, *I told her no. I told her not to use Tremain's name.*

But he'd given it to her.

"What's our next move, sir?"

Segreti didn't think they had one. Tremain was either disappeared or dead. No way he was going to resurface now. And the Russians were going to turn this into a diplomatic shitshow.

His phone rang, which spared him having to answer Belmont, but Segreti knew this call was not going to bring him comfort. "Yes, ma'am?"

"My office. Now." Church hung up.

Segreti got out of his chair and put a hand on Belmont's shoulder. "You're a good agent. Stay that way."

"Sir?"

He walked to ADIC's office and closed the door behind him. Church sat at her desk. She looked like hell—hair frayed, eyes brimming with wetness. "Where did that reporter get Tremain's name?"

"From me."

"And the details about Red Fidelity?"

"She figured that out on her own."

Church swiveled her chair to look out the window at the towers of lower Manhattan. "Special Agent Taylor was a hero," she said. "A real goddamned American hero."

"Yes, she was."

"And this is how you honor that legacy?"

Segreti wanted to object, but he also wanted to agree. He looked down at his twined fingers. He wanted this moment to end, but he didn't want the future it promised.

"There's something out there that's evil," Church said. "People, forces that act only to harm. To deliver pain and suffering." He knew that. He'd found Chlebek's body. He knew all about his enemies. "That's what we're up against. Not some imagined idea of evil, but a tangible malevolence that preys on innocent people. That's who we fight. It's not just about duty. It's being prepared to make a sacrifice."

He knew about his enemies, but did he know the first thing about himself? "I know."

She stubbed a finger on her desk. "Gun and badge, phone and passkey."

He didn't argue. He put them on her desk.

"You will remain in New York for questioning and render to me any intelligence I require. Otherwise, you are suspended from active duty."

Segreti knew he could have asked about a review process, but he also knew the wheels of bureaucracy would turn. *So let them.* He walked to her door.

"Segreti, for what's it's worth…"

"Ma'am?"

"I voted against clearing you for that shooting. Yesterday I felt bad about it. Today I don't."

* * *

He took the subway to the Upper West Side and walked to Justine Jarman's apartment. He didn't know if she'd be there, didn't have access to new information anymore. He thumbed the buzzer and waited.

She wasn't home. He waited in a Dunkin' nearby and nursed a lousy coffee and kept an eye on the street.

It was late afternoon when he finally saw her. Blonde hair wrapped up tight, those dangerous cheekbones visible a mile away. She was dressed in slacks and a pert blue jacket, big handbag slung over her shoulder. She looked good. He didn't want to look at her like that, but she had a tush that he wished he could put a hand on.

Stop… you're not here for that. He'd come to seal his fate.

Segreti jogged her way, calling her name and waving. No surprises, no ambushes.

Justine was exhausted, walking on fumes. The all-nighter to finish the story had left her discombobulated. She knew the deputy editor at *Vanity Fair*. They wanted the story, agreed on a price pretty quickly. She lied when she told them she had *Archer's* blessing, given it was out of action.

The story hit like a bomb. The dailies were all over it, then local TV, then CNN and FOX. Social media had a heart attack. Paul Chow called her, seething.

"You might have asked me first," he'd said.

He was right. In her resolve to get the story out, she hadn't given him or *Archer's* a second thought. She didn't think he had supported her, but hearing his voice, echoing depression, she realized that he had paid her salary for three years even though she had been off on her undercover work most of the time, instead of producing copy. And for most of that, she had dragged Bert along with her.

"I'm sorry," was all she could say.

"You should be," Paul replied, "because you're fired."

Given the way the story was going viral, she didn't feel immediately threatened. She could get a job anywhere now. But once the story was out, she had lost all control. Her written version had begun with Bert, protecting her on North Brother Island, and ended with his death. But he vanished: in the new telling doing the rounds, there was just Tremain, NSA, dead FBI agents, Red Fidelity.

She got it. Of course that's what counted. Russians and a traitor killing US law enforcement here in New York, as part of an operation to get their stolen malware into play. Bert was just collateral damage. And Marta would think Justine had sold Bert's memory down the river, for personal glory.

She was thinking of Marta, fearing the woman's response,

when she heard someone call her name. She turned and saw Segreti trot across the street.

More trouble: if anyone had a right to feel anger toward her, it was Segreti. She'd run this dialogue through her head more than once, justifying leaking Tremain's name, but she hadn't actually expected to run into him. Or, rather, for him to show up.

She smiled. It was a nervous defensive reaction, because she didn't know what else to do.

Segreti approached her and, seeing Justine smile, felt like it was the first nice thing that had happened to him for a while; maybe the first nice thing since he took on the case.

"Agent Segreti."

Her formality caught him off guard. Like, what was he supposed to say to that? No, it's Special Agent in Charge Segreti? Except he wasn't that either, not anymore.

"It's just Ed."

She hadn't expected him to say that. So, he wasn't here to chew her out?

"Okay, Ed." She resumed her walk toward her apartment building. "Is this about the story?"

"It is."

"Don't expect me to apologize. I know I burned you, but after everything I'd been through...after losing Bert..."

"Your report got me suspended."

She stopped at her entrance. "It did?"

"Tremain's going to disappear now, thanks to you. He won't see justice." That much was true, Segreti was sure. He had made plenty of mistakes, but the Bureau had been all-in on catching the traitor.

Justine thought this over. She had known the FBI wouldn't

welcome her story, but it was the NSA that she was worried about. Red Fidelity had been their code. Tremain and Klinger had been their employees.

"Would the NSA let you get him?" she asked.

"That was my job."

She pulled an errant strand of hair back into its place. "I have my own idea of justice, Ed."

"I know. Throw light on things that should remain unseen."

"Says you."

"You think you're doing the right thing, upholding freedom of the press. But your actions have consequences, Justine."

"I know. *Archer's* fired me."

That surprised him. "They did?"

"They didn't appreciate me taking the story to a competitor. The fact that they're still blacked out by malware didn't matter."

"Karma's a bitch."

"If you think so. You want to be mad at me? Yell at me for divulging Tremain's name, embarrassing people who deserve to be embarrassed?" She gestured to the street, the city. "Go ahead, yell."

He didn't know what to say. He had come here to do the only thing he could think of, but got detoured by this conversation. The cliché of being beautiful when you're angry popped into his head, because it was true.

"I've lost good friends," he said. "I don't want to lose anyone else. I thought I'd see how you're doing."

"We're friends now?"

He shrugged. "We could be. If that's what we want."

She saw in Segreti a man. A lost man. He had saved her life. She had been stupid to take Tremain's word and go try to find him on her own. If Segreti and his people hadn't showed up, Tremain would have kidnapped her. Or worse. And Segreti hadn't done or said anything about it. A lesser man would have bragged, or tried to make her feel like she owed him something. She didn't get that feeling now. She had seen him swagger, confident in his tall, magnetic looks. He had an aura of determination. That's what had intrigued her from the outset. Yes, she found him attractive. But not the macho stuff. He was too trigger-happy, too certain of his own authority. The world was full of men like him and it wasn't better for it. But he hadn't come here to lecture her or demand something. He didn't seem to know what he wanted from her.

"I'm not sure what being your friend means, Ed."

"I'm not here to talk terms. That's what we did before, but right now? You're not a reporter and I'm not FBI. We're just two people without jobs."

She thought this over. "I don't think either one of us was thinking about our jobs."

"You're right," he said, liking her answer. "We're not in this to collect a paycheck. That's not us."

"I guess that's good," she sighed, "because neither of us is getting paid."

"But we can still do what we do."

She raised an eyebrow. "I'm freelancing. You're the one who's suspended."

"And probably about to be fired. So let me tell you, your story's missing a few details."

"Such as?"

"Tremain's handler is Annika Volkov." He'd just committed a felony. He pressed on. "She's just arrived in New York as a Russian diplomat assigned to the United Nations. She's the one behind Red Fidelity."

She thought that over. "Why are you telling me this?"

"I don't know if we'll get our hands on Tremain, but if we do, he's going to pay. Volkov, however, has got diplomatic immunity. The best we can do is get her expelled."

"You want to embarrass her?"

"And get her out of the country as fast as possible."

"With the Red Fidelity code?"

"The Russians have that one way or another. She's the only thing protecting Tremain. If there's a spotlight on her, she won't take him along. He'll be stuck on US soil, or dead."

Chapter 43

Deborah Church found her day consumed by the last thing any manager at the FBI wanted to deal with: arranging funerals for slain agents. Chlebek's would be in Milwaukee, Taylor's outside Pittsburgh. The Director of the FBI intended to speak at both. Church's office was tasked with finalizing dates at cemeteries, selecting pallbearers, sorting out travel details, and liaising with the families. Church's personal assistant could take care of most things himself, but she was determined to be hands-on. It was what the head of a field office should do.

At least she could lose herself in the minutia of schedules and ceremonies. It was better than spending too much time brooding on what had gone wrong. There'd be plenty of the turning of machinery to investigate that in due course. But meanwhile she had a field office to run, overseeing nearly two thousand Bureau employees across five offices, from the Hudson Valley to JFK International. New York boasted six Special Agents in Charge who reported to her, covering everything from investigating the mob to counterintelligence.

Make that five SACs. One was under suspension. And as far as ADIC Church was concerned, SAC Segreti wasn't coming back to work. She had her PA prepare a job description to post on the internal employment site.

Dead agents didn't change the non-stop tempo of her day, but while she was on a call with the SAC in charge of operations support, a chat message lit up her phone. Then another.

"I'll call you back," she said, hanging up to scrutinize the messages.

Oh no.

She flipped on the television in her office.

The newscaster was saying, "...identified as Annika Nikolaevna Volkov, a Russian diplomat posted to the United Nations, where she serves as its representative on the Human Rights Council...Government sources say she was the handler for Robert Tremain, the ex-NSA employee alleged to have stolen cyber-weapons and sold them to the Russian government..."

Church switched it off and picked up the phone. "Get Belmont in here. And send in those two new guys from Counterintelligence."

Now she had a diplomatic crisis to negotiate.

The two Special Agents from Counterintelligence arrived first. They stood to one side, hands clasped in front of their belts, looking serious in their dark suits and ties. Wozniak, a bulky white male with piercing blue eyes, as well as being Afghan vet, could carry himself; Simpson, tall and thin, pale as a wisp, was fresh out of Quantico.

Belmont showed up looking sharp in a blue sports coat, striped tie, gray pleated slacks, and loafers. He had always been the office's sophisticate. Segreti trusted the man, and Church respected that—but she didn't trust him now.

"You saw what just broke?" she asked him.

"Yes, ma'am, just now."

"Was it Segreti who leaked it?"

Belmont looked uncomfortable, which she expected. "I don't know."

"Who else besides you would have that information?"

Belmont glanced at the other two agents. "I don't know, ma'am."

"Well, whoever leaked classified information is disrupting our investigation of Tremain. I think it's deliberate."

Belmont said, "Permission to speak?" She nodded. "The longer Tremain is on US soil, the more likely he ends up in prison. If the Russians want to deny Volkov's a spy, she won't take Tremain with her."

"So you think this is Segreti forcing our hand?"

Belmont said, "Whatever the source, or the motive, this gives us an opportunity. If we move fast."

"I want you to bring in Segreti. You know where he is?"

Belmont adjusted his tie. "No, but I can find him."

"Start with the reporter. If you get actionable intel on Tremain, report it to me immediately, but take no action."

"Yes, ma'am."

As Belmont turned to go, Church said, "Hang on, Belmont. This is Tom Wozniak and Eric Simpson. They're with you on this."

Belmont eyed the two agents with open disgust. "Yes, ma'am," he said.

"Dismissed." She watched him go, Simpson right behind him. "Tom."

Wozniak said, "Yes, ADIC?"

"Don't let Belmont out of your sight. Simpson's new at this. I'm counting on you to get results—quietly."

* * *

Segreti watched some of the news clips. His social-media feeds were full of reactions to Justine's pieces, mostly conspiracy theories and Russian trolls. But also a few thoughtful worries about cybersecurity, privacy, and the threat of someone being able to unzip any secret kept as ones and zeroes. Bank accounts, medical files, criminal records, home addresses, credit card numbers...the drumbeat of hacks had inured ordinary people to the risks of being rendered naked. But this was a whole new level of threat. The talk shows began to spin around what technology could do. Many of them assumed the US government had some sinister desire to control the populace. A few, though, recognized this for what it was: the opening salvo in a new era of computing power that could change the world.

He stayed in the hotel room on Third Avenue that Justine had extended on her credit card. He assumed she was under surveillance so it was only a matter of time before the Bureau picked him up. But for now, he stayed in the room and watched the news cycle. Ten hours passed, then fifteen. Justine appeared on TV and on a podcast. She talked fluently about the cyber arms market, the development of computing, and the need for the government and big companies to move faster to protect the country's digital secrets. But Segreti knew all of this. She filled his little phone's screen with her triple threat of beauty, power and...grace.

Grace. He sure could use some of that.

The Bureau hadn't shown up at the hotel. Neither had Justine.

His phone buzzed, an old personal handphone that he

had dug up after handing over his Bureau device. He didn't recognize the number. That was a red flag. He answered it anyway with a "Yes?"

"I have Justine," said a woman's voice, husky and curved with an accent.

"Volkov?"

"I must leave your ruined country. Consider this my farewell gift."

"If you hurt her—"

"Fuck off with your empty threats. She's at Floyd Bennett Field. You have ninety minutes or...kaboom."

An image showed up. He clicked it. Justine, blonde hair akimbo, looking wild-eyed and confused.

As soon as he had spilled his secrets to Justine, he had returned to his apartment. He had taken a last look at the photo of his family. Then he had gone into his bedroom, pulled a lockbox from the bottom of his closet, and retrieved the Sig Sauer P365, his concealed carry, an extra 15-round magazine, and an inside-the-waistband holster. It was a micro-compact, an easy fit in his hand but with a snub of a barrel, no match for anything serious.

He'd never bothered to apply for a New York State weapon or carry permit. He had never imagined being suspended from the Bureau, of being a civilian. Add an illegal gun charge to his growing rap sheet.

Then he left the apartment for good and went to the hotel room she had let him use. He waited there, watching and feeling boredom and anxiety and anticipation. He didn't know what to make of this setup. Of what might happen when she returned—if she returned. If there was anything to this, anything at all beyond just two burnouts conspiring to get into deeper trouble.

Now, at six o'clock, he tucked the pistol's slim holster beneath the waistband of his jeans. He was wearing a gray workout T-shirt, and he put on a black windbreaker, plain navy baseball cap and his aviators, then grabbed his dark, rubber-soled shoes.

Segreti wasn't stupid, but he definitely was scared. He dialed Belmont's number from memory.

Belmont picked up on the third ring. "Belmont."

"It's me."

"Where are you?"

"Volkov called me. Says she's got Justine somewhere at Lloyd Bennet Field. Gave me an hour and a half to get there or something bad happens. Kaboom, she said. I'm down to eighty-five minutes."

"Okay. We can pick you up."

Belmont wasn't alone. That 'we' was all Segreti needed to hear. Belmont was telling him he had been tasked with bringing Segreti in.

"Call the JFK office. Tell them to get a bomb squad over there."

Belmont hung up. Segreti messaged him the photo of Justine. Belmont had done what he could do. Segreti knew everything—his freedom, his identity—was on the line. Yet he acted with the serenity of one whose own fate was meaning-less. What mattered was saving Justine. He could imagine a future with her, even it if was just adolescent wishing. Without her, though, there was nothing but a formless horizon, eternal and monochrome.

There was nothing more to do now. He was out of time. Wait, he needed a car. There was only one person he could call.

Chapter 44

Segreti spotted the Mazda make the turn onto Lexington Avenue and groaned. The top was down and Jim Fiorinetti was clearly arguing with Missy Ram in the seat beside him. Segreti waved them to the curb. Fiorinetti propped his sunglasses on his forehead. "Okay, bro, this better be good."

Segreti opened the driver's door. "I'm driving. Sissy, you go home."

"No way, man, this is my car."

"And I'm not going anywhere!" said Sissy. "What the hell is he even doing here, Jim?"

Segreti looked around, fuming and then he leaned over. "Look, I don't have time. Someone's life is in danger, and I need to get behind the wheel. I'm not asking."

Fiorinetti saw the resolve in Segreti's mien. "I'm not just giving you my car."

"I said out."

"Where Jim goes, I go," Sissy said.

Fiorinetti grinned. "I guess we can either spend ten minutes arguing this thing, or we're just coming along."

"Fine. Move."

Sissy decamped for the tight little rear seat and Fiorinetti took shotgun. Segreti didn't care about the punk, his mind was on Justine, but Sissy's presence rattled him. He'd been supposedly looking out for her. Why the hell was he now driving her into danger?

"Buckle up," he said.

"That an order?" Sissy sneered.

"Suit yourself," Segreti said, gunning the convertible into traffic at G-force speed.

"Holy shit, slow down!" she shrieked.

"Dude, you just blew a red light."

They fell silent as they scrambled to put on their seatbelts.

"You're crazy!" Sissy said.

There was no escape from New York traffic. Rich or poor, cop or criminal, anyone on four wheels had to bow to the laws of physics, which seemed to follow their own warped logic anywhere near the city.

Segreti drove hard on the accelerator and brake, fighting wars of inches, bumper to bumper, gaining little victories in one lane, trying to win back time, minute by minute.

"So where we going?" Fiorinetti asked.

"Shut up."

He took drove to Fifty-ninth Street and onto the Queensboro Bridge. The sun was setting behind them, Midtown's skyscrapers darkening into unruly tombstones. The dying sun painted Long Island City's apartment towers blood red.

Fifty-seven minutes to go.

Segreti thought he was going to throw up. Then he saw an opening and hit the accelerator.

* * *

Justine had come to in a fit of unease. Once consciousness returned, panic seized her. The blackness wasn't the blackness of sleep but of blindness. Her hands were bound behind her in a way she couldn't understand. Her sharp inhales sucked rough cloth against her face. Then there were voices. A man and a woman's, murmuring low. Not English. Russian? Now there were footsteps with the harsh flatness of walking on something like concrete. Her muscles tightened in unison, and she swallowed the instinct to scream.

Two people. One of them lifted the hood.

She was in a place of insufficient light and long interior shadows. The ceiling was lost in darkness. The man, she guessed, was the one that had smothered her with a cloth. Her head spun and her hold on the man came in and out of focus. White, dark hair, that was it. But the woman...the woman, Justine knew.

Volkov knelt before her, eye-level. They had put Justine in a chair, her hands stuck behind her, her feet on the hard floor. Volkov, this must be Volkov. So close they could kiss.

"Stupid cunt," Volkov said.

Justine didn't know what to say. Her thoughts were fragmented, her brain fumbling with the shards. "Volkov," she managed. "Russian. Spy."

"Your stunt has brought my mission to a close," Volkov said. "But it does not matter. I told my superiors that I would accept punishment for the failure of my mission. I told them I could not abide the murder of my son. They are strong Russian men. They will likely execute me, but with honor. This is something someone as frivolous as you cannot understand."

Some memories were slotting into place...

The phone call from Bobby Tremain, telling her to meet him in Central Park. Some BS about how her bombshell report had changed everything... forcing Volkov to leave the US. That he wanted to tell his side of the story. Then the sunlit park, busy on a summer day. She'd headed that way, in a hurry. Not believing Tremain, but pride coursing through her bloodstream, knowing she was making things happen. Crossing Central Park West, oblivious to the van parked by the corner. It had all happened so fast—the man, the hand around her face.

And now here.

Her stomach heaved.

"Segreti will not risk everything for Tremain," Volkov said. "For Tremain he will be cautious. He will come with the entire FBI. For you, Justine? He will come alone."

"He'll kill you," she slurred.

Volkov shook her head. "No. I am not like some stupid villain in one of your fucking Hollywood movies. I am not staying to be caught. I am going. I am—"

Justine bent over, seized by an internal command, and threw up. Like her organs were expelling their boiling, toxic life-force through her teeth. She didn't intend it, but she puked up all over Volkov.

The woman stepped back in disgust but remained unruffled. "Consider this the beginning," she said, flicking bits of Justine's vomit off her clothes.

"Unh," was all Justine could manage.

"Soon all of your guts will be everywhere in this place," Volkov said. "Some over here, some over there." To her companion, she said, "Let's go."

* * *

Tremain listened to the exchange. Then he heard Volkov's footfalls recede, echoing against the concrete and steel surroundings. He hoped what she had said about getting a bullet in the brain back in Moscow was true. The one she had lodged in his thigh—his good leg, until she had shot him—wasn't intended to be a killer blow. Just enough to incapacitate him. They could have Roofied him, like they did Justine, but that wasn't Volkov's style.

The woman was an idiot. If she was so protective of her stupid son, why let the brat in on an undercover mission?

He contemplated the disused hangar where he and Justine sat, backs to one another. A big nothing. Like the Red Fidelity deal.

Everybody could have gotten what they wanted. He'd have found a buyer who'd be running the ultimate malware through America's cloud infrastructure, unwittingly unzipping every digital file owned by the US government. Volkov would be happy and Tremain would be toasting the whole clusterfuck from a super-yacht off the coast of some neutral country with a glamorous coastline.

But no, she'd gone bananas with this motherhood jag. Tremain had never been married. He treated women like burner phones, disposing of them one after another. He'd been happy, or at least he'd gotten laid a lot and not cared. From the way Volkov had completely lost her mind, he was pretty sure parenthood was just DNA impulses. People weren't living in trees and caves anymore, were they? No, they'd evolved. Patriotism was just another fetish, some kind of Neanderthal bonding instinct that didn't mean anything. And now he'd evolved into the life he wished to live, and Volkov had gone...apeshit crazy, he supposed.

He heard the heavy sound of the hangar doors being pushed open. Then clanged shut.

Silence.

Volkov was gone.

"Well, ain't this a pickle," he said.

"Wha—who's that?"

"Relax, Justine. I'm not going to bite." He looked down at the blood seeping out of the makeshift tourniquet the Russians had tied around his thigh. They'd given him a shot of morphine to keep him quiet. He still felt pretty good, rather philosophical about this whole thing. The sheer stupidity of it was kind of funny.

"Tremain?"

"Bingo!"

"Where are we? What's happening?"

"We're in an abandoned hangar at some airfield on the ass end of Brooklyn. JFK's a mile down the road."

"She's trying to get Ed here."

"Yep."

"She's insane."

"Agree. But it won't matter. They've strapped a few grams of Semtex to the bottom of my chair. Not sure what sets it off, maybe that hangar door, or a trip wire?" He laughed. "Anyway, even someone as unhinged as Annika can work out a detonator."

He heard the muffled sound of a car engine.

"That's her, isn't it?" Justine asked.

"Probably. I think she's going straight to JFK to catch a flight home." He laughed again, because this whole thing was so gosh-darn funny. "Love to see her walk through customs covered in your puke."

"If Ed gets here, we have to warn him. Tell him not to come closer."

"Honey, there's probably enough plastic explosive to blow up this entire building. And besides, fuck that guy. He shows up? I'm going to invite him over. Water's great, Eddie, dive on in!"

Chapter 45

Segreti drove along a long chain-link fence lining darkened scrub. This was the very end of Flatbush Avenue. Ahead, it turned into Marine Parkway Bridge and the western tip of Rockaway Beach, but here he was turning in to an old airfield, now a park that was locked up at night.

"Hold on," he said to his passengers as he made a hard left into the parking lot. Headlights filled the Mazda, unforgiving, the blinding glare of pearly gates.

Sissy screamed as he pulled the car to avoid the oncoming vehicle, and then there was the punch of mass and the screaming crunch of metal. He fought to regain control of the car as lights pinwheeled in front of the windshield. The car came to a stop, his driver's side headlight punched out, the other drilling a lonely light into trees. He turned, ignoring his own wooziness. "You okay? Sissy? You okay?"

"I'm okay," she said. "Fuck."

"You?" he said, gripping Fiorinetti's shoulder.

"Man."

Segreti held Fiorinetti's chin and gently turned his head, looking for injuries. They were all shaken, but alright.

"My car, bro, what the hell have you done to my car?"

Yeah, the punk would live.

"Stay here. Don't get out." He gave Sissy a final look. "I mean it." The driver's door had taken damage and required an extra shove to open. He clambered out.

The other vehicle was a Dodge Sprinter, a dark blue van with a stunted triangle of a front, the windshield slanting down into the hood, and no windows along the sides or rear doors. It sat astride the road, its headlights lighting up the fencing between it and Flatbush Ave.

Segreti drew his gun, held it with both hands, and trotted to the van. The impact had crumpled the driver's side, but he could hear someone turning the ignition. The rear of the vehicle was in darkness, but the white of the license plate stood out and he could easily make out the Russian diplomatic insignia. He hurried around to the passenger side. He didn't knock. The door was unlocked and he jerked it open. The interior was a riot of airbags and punching limbs. A white man's face emerged from behind the airbag and looked at Segreti's gun.

"Volkov, where is she?"

The man laughed.

Segreti seized his arm and yanked him out of the seat. He ran to the driver's side. Another white man was already making his way out, hands raised, smiling as if this were very funny.

"Get back," Segreti said, gesturing with the gun. He legged up into the driver's seat and swung his gun over the sagging airbag.

"Is Russian government property," the driver said.

Segreti turned on the ceiling light. The woman in the van's empty back was wearing a boxy suit that didn't fit her. She had auburn hair pulled back in a bun and a blandly pretty face. It wasn't Volkov, but Segreti was more focused on the submachine gun in her hands.

He dived as she unloaded. Headrest stuffing and windshield glass filled the cabin like an angry snow globe. His feet hit the ground and he saw the driver pulling a gun from beneath his jacket. Segreti already had his Sig Sauer in his grip and he double-tapped the driver in the chest. He didn't stick around to check his handiwork, Then, as the rear doors of the van kicked open, he punched one shot through the door. The woman pulled the submachine gun's trigger, like an impulse, but she was shooting in the direction of the Mazda.

Segreti fired several times as he rounded on her. She swung a bloodied arm around the door and blasted in his direction. They were practically facing one another. He felt a hot punch to the arm. He took the hit and fired point blank in her face.

The surprise of being shot wasted no time turning into pain. Hot, angry pain. He looked at his arm, saw nothing but reflective glistening off his windbreaker, and jogged around to find the final Russian. Adrenaline might be keeping him going, but Segreti was happy enough to have it.

He saw the man running for the road where another Sprinter van was driving past. Segreti must have passed it on his approach to the airfield, and the lead van, sensing its companion hadn't followed, was coming back. The passenger on foot had no weapon that Segreti could see. He was waving down the incoming van. The headlights swept the scene as the van turned. Then it halted in the middle of the empty road and the rear doors opened. Segreti ran for it. The Russian passenger reached the doors and was pulled in. The rear doors shut, tires squealed as the van completed its turn, and another figure hung its head out the passenger window. Volkov, giving him the finger as the van accelerated back the way it had come.

As he ran back to the Mazda, he called Belmont. "I'm at the entrance to Floyd Bennet field. A van full of Russian diplomats opened fire on me. Two down. Volkov's in another van, dark blue Dodge, headed up Flatbush. Can you intercept?"

"Relaying that," Belmont said. "Come in now, Ed, before it's too late."

Segreti put the phone in his pocket and ran toward the Mazda. He had to dive out of the way of its one-eyed jack of a headlight. He tried to wave it to stop. Fiorinetti ignored him, jaw set, as he drove his smashed-up car onto Flatbush Avenue, Sissy in the passenger seat. She looked terrified, but unharmed. Segreti stopped for breath as he watched the Mazda turn and follow in the wake of the Russian van. Maybe it was better they were leaving. Two less lives he had to worry about.

Segreti turned to the airfield complex. The only life that mattered to him was somewhere in there.

* * *

Justine told Tremain to shut up. The guy was high—on painkillers, on resentment, on regrets, who knew. He kept babbling while she fumed that if she was about to die, the least she deserved was a little quiet.

The hangar was airless, stuffy, magnifying the summer's heat. The only thing she could see was the back of the space, too darkened and voluminous to make out any details, but she sensed a massive object just beyond the small cone of light above her. Death, the preview.

A new sound, metallic and heavy, cut through Tremain's monologue. Must be the hangar doors, somewhere behind her.

Now she saw flickers of illumination. Voices, distant echoes.

Tremain started to make explosion noises, spaced with giggles.

She wanted this to be help. Salvation. Ed, yes, she'd like it to be him coming in here, ending this nightmare. But she also knew that the arrival of the police meant the bomb Volkov promised would soon detonate. Sweat dribbled down her nose, streaked from her hair. Not from the heat.

"There's a bomb!" she called as loudly as she could.

Behind her, Tremain said, "Shh, you'll ruin the surprise."

The voices were closer now, cones of flashlight bouncing on the floor before her.

"It's them."

"One of the chairs is wired."

Figures entered the side of her sight, hands gripping pistols and flashlights.

"Stop!" she pleaded. "Don't set it off!"

"Sir," one of the shadows said, "I think I found it."

A man in a suit lowered his torso, hands on his knees, to speak to her. A handsome Black man in a neat suit. She knew him. "I need you not to move. You Justine Jarman?" he asked.

She nodded. "My hands..."

"I know," Malcolm Belmont said. "We'll cut you loose, but then you can't move. You're sitting on a trigger."

* * *

Segreti ran past the darkened Visitors Center and found himself on a cross of narrow runways. No lights had illuminated these strips for decades. The airfield was a rough square on a spit of land surrounded by water. The sky was aglow with city lights bouncing off clouds, but the ground was dark. Three sides had low-slung hangars and service buildings, but he could make out only distant outlines. The middle of the peninsula was flat scrub and a hex of landing strips, its center lost in darkness. The flanking buildings behind him seemed to be the ones still open to the public—he'd seen a sports center and signs for a marina. He was more likely to find Justine in one of the disused hangars along another edge of the airfield.

He turned right and began to run, but the fire in his left arm raged. He stopped and tucked the injured arm into his windbreaker and zipped it high, making a loose sling. He wasn't going to be able to reload his pistol. He hoped he wouldn't have more need of it, but he held it in his right hand as he headed off. The pounding of his running was like hammering nails into his forearm, but at least the jacket had it stabilized. He could feel blood oozing down his arm, pooling inside the jacket. He'd need first aid soon or he'd pass out.

As Segreti approached the southern tip of the airfield, he saw signs for Park Police and a US Marine Corps Reserve Center. He saw lights in some of the buildings. This corner of the airfield was still in use. He turned and looked at the eastern flank. Darkness amid some hulking structures. He headed there.

He reached a wide runway and saw a sign that said 'NYPD Aviation Unit' and an icon of a helicopter. Volkov had a talent for getting away with schemes under the nose of US authorities. The aviation unit looked closed and empty. Beyond were more buildings, and then Jamaica Bay and the city. He saw the lights of a giant airliner glide past, aiming for the bright lights of JFK International.

Inside one of the hangars, he saw the lights turn on. He

trotted down a lane surrounded by darkened buildings and empty parking lots, and headed towards the one that had come alive. The night turned to day and the ground shook. A jet of orange flames blew out from behind the squat hangar, and he felt its heat, even on the far side of the blast.

"Justine!" He ran to the building and found a back entrance by a narrow alley lined with giant trash bins. The door was locked. Segreti stood to one side, shot the lock, then holstered the gun and pulled the door open.

He was in a garage with a lone pickup. He ran up concrete steps to a landing, swung open the doors, faced a corridor, and rushed through it. After the blast he'd heard nothing, as if the explosion had destroyed sound itself. He grabbed a door handle and pulled back, the metal's heat surprising him. He grabbed it again and yanked the door open.

* * *

Justine couldn't believe they were going to attempt this.

The FBI agents had tried to sound neutral, as if they were explaining to her the latest regulations. There was a timer on a detonator. The Semtex would go off if she stood up, by changing the pressure on her chair, which was linked to a radio transmitter. Or it would explode in the next three minutes. Either way, it was going to go off, and the agents didn't have enough time to diffuse the bomb.

They turned on the lights of the hangar. She was facing the rear and saw a jumble of heavy equipment and a thick, heavy gray helicopter. Two lines of cables dangled from parallel tracks of railing, bright orange against the dull ceiling, and dangled behind the chopper like a giant curtain of beads.

"See that?" Belmont said, pointing up. "That's for lifting helicopters for repair. Big heavy ones, like that Chinook."

One of the agents was at a control panel in the back. The crane rolled above the Chinook. Another agent was pulling on the chains hanging from the sides of the orange rails, seeing how tautly they wound beneath the chopper's belly.

She shook her head. "No. I don't know what you're planning, but no."

"We have a hundred and fifty seconds left," Belmont said. "I'll be with you."

She heard Tremain behind her say, "And here I can just limp on out of here."

The agents scrambled to secure the chains beneath the belly of the chopper. It looked too heavy and ungainly to be plucked up.

"Thirty seconds!" one agent called.

"Get it up," Belmont ordered and an agent returned to the control panel. With a whine, the crane pulled in the chains and the Chinook wobbled off the ground. The heavy front, with its thick Perspex gunnery, tipped forward and Justine inhaled with horror as the thing lurched towards her, about to smash her to a pulp.

Belmont crouched beneath the open portal along the chopper's flank, one hand extended.

"Clear!" someone shouted.

"I don't want to die!" she said, as if it mattered.

The Chinook loomed overhead, the gray steel monster practically touching her head. She saw Belmont's extended hand. The crane halted and the chopper bobbed dangerously, practically taking her head off.

"Now, Justine!"

She grabbed his hand and jumped as the crane reversed and the Chinook retreated. He pulled her into the cabin as the hangar burst into fire and light. The chopper swayed and she screamed in free fall. The Chinook's floor itself seemed to have melted into lava.

The inferno expended itself but the chopper was alive with heat. She and Belmont groaned as the metal surface burned their skin. As the Chinook swayed, she clambered to the side door. The explosion had blown out the lights, but the hangar's roof was aflame, and she could see the dark concrete below, too far to jump.

A figure strode beneath her. Segreti's hazel eyes reflected the flames above them.

"Ed!"

He looked around and darted out of sight.

Belmont groaned, propping himself on an elbow, hair glinting from a shower of glass.

Segreti returned, carrying a ladder with one hand. She noticed his other arm was stuck inside his jacket. Another FBI agent appeared at Segreti's side and helped him get the ladder in place.

She trembled as she descended. Segreti's good arm took her in and she hugged him. He winced and she saw his gun wound. "You've been shot."

"Volkov's getting away."

She put her hands on his cheeks. "I don't care about Volkov."

He hugged her close and she held him.

The other agent helped Belmont down. Belmont was cut up and shaky but in one piece. Justine embraced him. "Thank you."

* * *

Segreti heard Belmont say, "I can't believe that worked," when he saw Tremain beyond the hangars, looking back in.

Tremain looked a bloody mess, but he was mobile. Segreti watched him hobble into the dark.

"There goes Tremain," Segreti said.

The ceiling was on fire and starting to collapse.

"We'll pick him up," Belmont said, reaching for his radio.

Segreti watched the figure disappear as flaming debris filled the hangar. He ran through the hangar, his good hand reaching behind him for the gun.

"Ed, no!" Justine shouted.

A curtain of fiery wreckage tumbled around him. Segreti reached the hangar doors and didn't look back; the others would have retreated out the back. There was no way through that now.

The flames cast a long light onto the airfield and he saw an elongated shadow running away. Segreti hurried off the hangar's apron and onto uneven scrub.

Justine and Belmont had scrambled out the hangar's back. "Stay here," Belmont had instructed her, "I need to call this in."

But she set out immediately and rounded the building, her nose filling with toxic acid as ash rained down. She was in better shape than Tremain or Ed, and her terror had torn through the wooziness of the Rohypnol. She saw Ed's silhouette moving unevenly over low-cut grass.

Justine chased them into the center of the airfield. Three airstrips converged in a six-way hex. They were far enough from the buildings along the edge that the only light was the glowering fire of the hangar behind her and the glow of the city in the clouds. A jumbo jet hurtled overhead, bound for somewhere better.

Tremain lay on his elbows in the center of the airfield.

Segreti stood over him, gun pointed at Tremain's head.

"Do it," Tremain grunted.

She pulled up just behind them, neither man acknowledging her presence on the edge of their grudge.

"Go on, Ed, pull the trigger. I sold Red Fidelity to Volkov. I watched her murder Dimitri, helped her try to kill you—three times lucky, I thought. I gave her the names of your team, helped her find Miriam Chlebek. And guess what, Ed? She's gone, man. Diplomatic immunity. Sure, that doesn't hold up for murdering a federal agent, but she'll be through customs by now, and you won't be able to lay a finger on her. So, who's that leave? Who can you take it out on? Go on, Ed, you fucking pussy. You've already broken I don't know how many laws, so what's one more? I'll tell you this much, you did one thing right. Killing Volkov's son sent her over the edge. Imagine the damage we'd have done if she hadn't lost her senses. The Russkies have Red Fidelity, but you'll never let it run anywhere near your network. I'd applaud you if you weren't such a clown—why, hello, Justine."

Segreti looked over his shoulder and she saw nothing but pain in his eyes. Fury, too, but he hadn't pulled the trigger. He hadn't told Tremain to shut up. He hadn't decided.

Justine looked at this man she thought she cared about and waited.

"Do what you're going to do," she finally said. *Do the right thing.*

She sensed she had tied her future to Segreti's decision. That he was about to show his true colors.

Segreti faced Tremain, gun steady.

"Shoot me, you goddamn coward!"

Segreti lowered the gun. "Robert Tremain, you're under citizen's arrest."

Tremain barked out laughing and rolled to his side.

Justine walked to Ed's side. She cupped his chin. He had a smile, barely noticeable. She nodded, eyes locked on his, and kissed him. It was a shy kiss, inquisitive. He gripped her and kissed her hard. Then he sagged to his knees.

Belmont and the other agents were there, pulling them apart, laying Segreti down, another cuffing Tremain, Belmont radioing for help. Justine heard sirens and saw the flicker of ambulance flashers skirt the horizon. She took Segreti's good hand as another agent wrapped a tourniquet around his shot arm, and he squeezed her fingers tight.

About the Author

Born in the US (go Phillies!), Jamie Dibs has spent a career writing in Asia and Europe. His passions for world affairs, technology, and history infuse his fiction. He and his wife currently split their time between Hong Kong and Lisbon.

He was born in the Year of the Dog.

You can connect with me on:
🌐 https://jamiedibs.com

Subscribe to my newsletter:
✉ https://jamiedibs.substack.com

Also by Jamie Dibs

Dreadful Penny

Who is Penny Lee? Half Chinese and half German, raised in the US, she has six passports of different names and nationalities, and is able to pose as the daughter of almost anyone, from Lee Kuan Yew to Robert E. Lee.

She's also an industrial spy and professional honey trap. While on assignment in Dubai, seducing a Kazakh oil tycoon, the tables are turned: now she is the one being targeted – for death, by a killer named Viktor who bears an old grievance.

She's now on the run, with a mission to protect her long-lost sister, the last link to the life she had before she became Penny Lee. Viktor has discovered her deepest secrets and knows how to inflict the worst revenge against her. But when Viktor crosses a line, Penny can run no longer.

PART 1 of the PENNY LEE series.

Bloody Paradise

Travis Mitchell lands on the Thai resort island Samui with a broken wrist, a bag of cash, and a murderous Hong Kong crime boss on his tail. His plans to lie low on the beach vanish when Trav bumps into Mazy, a yoga instructor with a taste for booze and dangerous boyfriends.

Trav is convinced he needs to save her from Gordon, a small-time London pusher developing K-Love, the world's perfect date-rape drug. But in trying, he stirs up a hornet's nest of Thai gangsters, Chinese triads, Samui cops, and a poor janitor who cleans up after the tigers in the local zoo.

While Trav wonders whether the beautiful yoga teacher is worth the risk, Mazy decides to take matters into her own unsteady hands.

Star Fall People

Immortals walk among us. Slipping into new lives, decade after decade, from Shanghai to San Francisco: Sley falls in love with a mortal; Nadia wants to bear children; Mang amasses wealth and power.

...Until technology threatens their ability to assume new identities. Mang builds a corporation that develops artificial intelligence and turns it into a weapon of mass terror, for if he is to be unmasked, then he must rule.

The world is vulnerable, still recovering from a week-long loss of electronic communication called the Darkout. With Nadia siding with Mang, Sley can't stop the coming catastrophe.

But when Mang's AI reaches sentience, it too becomes like an immortal – with its own idea of humanity's fate.

Gaijin Cowgirl

Working Tokyo nightclubs is easy money for the party-loving Val Benson – until her number-one tipper, Takahashi, a corporate titan with sinister hobbies, reveals a map to gold stolen during World War Two.

Val embarks on an action-packed treasure hunt, from the neon-drenched streets of Japan to the mountainous jungles of Thailand. Snapping at her high heels are Yakuza gangsters; bent cops; rogue CIA agents; and Val's estranged father, a philandering Congressman.

Val is joined in her quest by Suki, a hostess desperate for a new life; Simon, a British kickboxer; and Muddy McKenzie, a washed-up Australian treasure hunter. But as they close in on the gold, can she trust them?

The Blue Jungle

Gangsters kidnap Naomi Sato, a struggling journalist in L.A.

Their boss thinks Naomi knows what's happened to his daughter.

He may be right: Naomi covers the world of porn.

It's simple. Find the girl before the goons do, and Naomi gets to live – body parts intact.

But the only path to the missing starlet goes through Bobby Feathers, master of sleaze.

And to survive, Naomi has to face a worse terror: herself.

9 7989888 823674